A SHORE THING

AN OTTER BAY NOVEL

JULIE CAROBINI

DOLPHIN GATE BOOKS

A Shore Thing © 2010, 2018 by Julie Carobini
Otter Bay Novel #2

Published by Dolphin Gate Books
ISBN: 979-8807930293
Originally published by B&H Books

Julie Carobini writes novels set by the sea. *RT Book Reviews* says, "Carobini has a talent for creating characters that come alive." Julie lives in California with her family and loves all things coastal (except sharks). Pick up a free ebook here: www.juliecarobini.com/free-book/

THE OTTER BAY NOVELS: Three novels with three different heroines, all who live, laugh, and love in the quirky town of Otter Bay on California's central coast. The town may be fictional, but you'll recognize some of its landmarks. After reading *Sweet Waters*, *A Shore Thing*, and *Fade to Blue*, you'll want to pack your bags and move west!

A Shore Thing (Book 2)

Sassy and stubborn, Callie Duflay learns that beloved waterfront land in Otter Bay may soon be developed, and confronts the architect assigned to the project - much to the chagrin of her family.

Impossibly handsome architect Gage Mitchell may be an easygoing guy, but he is not about to back off the Otter Bay project - no matter how cute Callie or her pet "Moondoggy" may be.

When Callie receives threatening letters - and her pet pooch disappears - Gage and Callie find themselves on the wrong side of danger. Despite being opponents in the battle for Otter Bay, they would be perfect for each other. But will they ever figure that out?

For my children, Matthew, Angie, and Emma—You are beautiful, each in your own way

CHAPTER 1

The rope in my hand resembled a noose. "Sorry, pup, but it was all I could find."

The stray doggy with the dewdrop eyes had found me this afternoon as I jogged along the shores of Otter Bay. I slipped the makeshift leash around his skinny neck. It was almost evening now and our trot through the woods on the way to my sister's house for Sunday supper would serve as my halfhearted attempt to find this dog's owner.

Hopefully, they're long gone because, until now, I hadn't realized just how hollow my house with its reclaimed wood flooring and single occupant had begun to sound.

It wasn't supposed to be this way. By my age—and my mother's calculations—I should be living quite comfortably as a wife and mother and keeper of a house surrounded by a white picket fence. "Men aren't attracted to tomboys, Callie," my mother always said, clutching her heart and peering into the sky. She'd always been dramatic like that. Probably a leftover from her days in musical theater, an aspiration she eventually gave up to raise children.

If only *I* understood the rewards of marriage and mother-hood. We had this conversation every year.

At thirty years old, though, I understood it fine. I just never seemed to have enough time, nor decent prospects. At least not since *The One* got away three years ago, as my mother often put it. I tried never to think about that, but whenever one of my ex-boyfriend Justin's road-hog trailer trucks sped by on the high-way, advertising the biggest and best interior plant design company the West Coast had to offer . . . well, a twinge of anger attempted to coil itself around my lungs and squeeze until I could no longer breathe.

I bought my cottage with the proceeds from selling that busi-ness to him.

My family contended that my living against the grain had kept my life from progressing to the place they deemed appropri-ate. And after a day like today, maybe it was time to slow down, to figure out what Callie Duflay's life really *should* look like, to finally admit that, yes, while I often saw the world through a different set of lenses than the rest of my siblings, it didn't have to stay that way. I stepped it up, realizing that if I was late for supper again, my sister Sheila was going to be ticked.

"C'mon little guy."

In the few short hours since he wriggled his way into my unconventional life, Doggy here had already soothed a couple of newly opened wounds, starting with the one that happened this morning during my stint as weekend assistant camp director at the camp on the hill.

I had arrived early to what might have been a grim discovery: a mouse had wedged itself inside a box of colorful two-by-three cards used for the night game. These things happen when cookies from the evening snack are packed away with games.

Fortunately, the little guy still had breath to breathe. So I headed back outside, trudged up a hillside, released him from his makeshift cell, and scooted him in a direction away from camp.

He moved slowly at first as if still gasping for life and then his speed quickened as if he knew that sustenance was only one foraging session away. Although it was early spring, the air still held a chill, especially in the shady spot where my feet stood planted. Patches of frost clung to the ground.

I spied a large plastic disc half-buried in a nest of pine needles. So I positioned that pink disc at the top of the hill, folded myself inside its tight borders, and let go. Like an oversized junior camper, I scraped and slid down the embankment, picking up enough speed to skip across cool earth and flatten new growth before landing at the bottom of the hill in a laughing heap.

It never occurred to me that someone might be watching. "Looks like someone has too much time on their hands." Natalia Medina stood over me in a navy blue tailored suit, holding a clipboard and looking more like she was about to conduct a board meeting than visit camp.

I stood, wiped one hand down the side of my overalls, and reached out to the board member of Pine Ridge Camp. "Hello, Natalia." She shook my hand.

"I'm looking for Thomas. Have you seen him?" She glanced up the hill I'd just rocketed down. An amused smile tugged at her lips. "Then again, perhaps not."

"Actually, Squid—I mean *Tom*—should be out and about soon. I had to, uh . . ." I turned toward the glistening hillside not sure how a woman wearing red leather shoes would handle a mission of mercy for a mouse. "Retrieve a sand toy."

She nodded. "I see that. Well, given your age now, I suppose it's hardly easy to resist one last childhood fling." Her shoulders lifted in a shrug and she laughed, but the squeak that escaped her mouth sounded more like a scoff.

I leaned my head to one side. "Excuse me?"

Natalia patted my shoulder. "I only meant that someone with as much education and years behind you will surely be moving on from here soon." She wrinkled her nose and lowered her voice as if inviting me into her confidence. "Assistant camp director is merely a starter job, right?"

I leaned forward, my eyes fixed on hers. "I don't plan to leave anytime soon, Natalia. I *love* that this job allows me to work with kids and to be outside so much. Besides, it gives me time to volunteer for some great causes during the week." I put on a smile. "Not many people can say that."

A pause dropped like a taut bubble between us. Natalia cleared her throat and her eyes flitted around. "Perhaps you have a point." She took a step back. "Well, I won't take up any more of your valuable time. Please let Thomas know that I was here to meet with him. Ask him to call my office, would you?"

She didn't wait for my answer.

My second wound opened later that morning when "Squid," the camp's director, invited me—they call me Seabird—to join him and a gaggle of campers on a hike through the woods to the edge of Otter Bay. After he'd shared his sandwich with me, making my heart tumble in a good way, a camper named Megan approached us. "You know what I think?" she said. "I think you two are boyfriend and girlfriend!"

But Squid's answer? "Seabird here is just too old for me."

Too *old*? First Natalia, and now . . . Squid. My eyes shut at the thought of him smiling at me so winsomely before delivering the deathblow to my daydream. Whoever said that fifty had become the new thirty had gotten it backwards. My face felt crimson, even though it had been hours since Squid made his proclamation about my advanced age to little Megan. How could I have been so stupid as to believe that Squid could have any feelings for me other than the kind of friendship that happened when two people worked together? We were cohorts, and nothing else.

I continued walking toward the bay with only a stray dog as my companion. The negative tide had long gone. Only the dramatic peaks of darkened rock appeared above the tide line, and soon that would be gone too. I always came here when troubled, and besides, walking the path was one of the best ways to prep myself for the Sunday suppers that my sister Sheila hosted each week.

By the number of lingerers found resting in contemplation on stumps of fallen trees or splayed atop blankets on the tall grass, others appreciated the solitude here too.

Three men stood together near the ridge all holding notebooks in front of them. My muddled mind nearly missed their curious presence until one of them pitched a lit cigarette over the cliff.

Startled, I said, "You just flicked your cigarette into a protected marine sanctuary."

As if I were invisible, the men looked past me. So I repeated myself.

One of them, the largest of the three, hunkering in stature, took a step toward me. I tightened my grip on Doggy's leash. The man squinted, his smile pinched and mocking. "Guess someone's not doing their job then."

My blood heated. I should have continued walking, but I was in no mood to back down—not after a day like today. "You should be ashamed of yourselves."

Three looming men stood near the edge of one of the most pristine and undeveloped stretches of land here in Otter Bay and watched me, their expressions all too familiar. Patronizing. Insulting.

Except for the one who wore flip-flops, jeans, and a button-down shirt. The laid-back one watched me with a sort of curiosity.

As if taking my side, the ocean surged. All three men sidestepped the cliff's precarious edge. Sea spray landed on the camera hanging around the neck of the bald man in the middle and he cursed.

I cocked my head. "Hmm."

He shook his head and sauntered away from the pack, pointing his lens at the land, his back to the ocean and to me. The lumbering one continued to glare at me as I proceeded along the path worn by thousands of pairs of feet that came before to this magical place. More than the view captivated people here. It was also the call of the otters, sea lions, and whales that roamed along the shore, and the song of the birds—pelicans, cormorants, and murres—that migrated overhead on the Pacific Flyway. Even those children we brought from camp, the ones bemoaning their fast from everything electronic and cellular, got lost in the adventure when they arrived.

I breathed in the clean air, and attempted to shake off the annoyance that crept up my back when I noticed that burning ash being tossed into the water. Tension still gripped my shoulders. With my mind focused on the horizon, I pulled Doggy along and failed to notice the tripod laying in my path—until tripping over it. I hung onto the leash and avoided falling by landing hard against the rough surface of a pine tree, both my right elbow and my dignity shredded. Laughter spiked the air a short distance away. Closer to me, a scraping sound chewed the earth as someone dragged the tripod off the path.

The man with the flip-flops and quizzical smile stepped toward me and his eyes homed in on mine. "Don't move."

My breathing caught for a moment, but then I ignored him and pushed myself away from the tree trunk using my other arm. Droplets of dark red blood oozed from the wound on my elbow and I winced, the breeze against my raw skin gave me a sickening chill.

"Here. Let me help." The man continued to stay by my side, his arm outstretched as if I needed steadying. His buddies were less than chivalrous, their snickers still alive.

"No. Thank you." I glanced at the length of metal I tripped over, and then back at him. Doggy began to whimper. "That looks like survey equipment."

He shoved both hands into his pockets and nodded his head once. "It is."

"Why? This land isn't being developed."

He stood silent, the corner of his mouth turned upward. The furrow above his brow told me how wrong I was.

My hands found a place to steady themselves on my hips. I ignored the shooting pain in my elbow and shook my head. "Tell me you're kidding."

He shrugged. "It's not my call. Listen, you need to get that wound cleaned up. I've got a first aid kit in my truck." He pointed up the hill. "If you'll wait here I'll run up and—"

My head snapped side to side. "The Kitteridges own this property. They'd never sell it, and certainly not to someone who would put up houses on it—"

"Condos. Mixed-use, actually."

"Mixed-use? As in offices and residences? Here?"

He nodded but made no eye contact. "Largest development this county has ever seen."

His pronouncement hit me harder than my fall. June and Timothy Kitteridge opened up this property years ago as a thank-you to the community of Otter Bay. After their popular gallery, Kitt's on Display, burned to the ground, and the county's trail of red tape delayed the rebuilding of their store, the citizens of the town took it upon themselves to pitch in once the murky waters of bureaucracy had cleared.

I glanced toward the sea where a gull dipped against a cloudy sky. The Kitteridges closed their store last year, saying they were looking forward to retirement and spending more time with their only daughter, Chloe, who had moved to another state. I had ignored the rumors that told a sadder tale. The Kitteridges were broke and had no choice but to board up Kitt's for good.

A harsh voice barked from behind. "Dude. We're gonna finish up here and go get burgers. You can call the office for your survey. It's a doozy, so it might be awhile."

Heavy boots crunched against dirt as the other men left the area. I focused on the man in charge and cocked my chin. "It's not your call, huh?"

He held up two palms. "I'm just the architect. The survey will help in the design process, once the sale actually goes through, that is." His face looked as grim as I felt.

"It hasn't closed yet?"

He shook his head and then offered me his hand. "Gage, by the way. Gage Mitchell."

He had two first names. I read somewhere that people with two first names were suspect, but then again, what about Patrick Henry and John Adams? *Or Benjamin Franklin?* A sigh slipped away from me. "I'm just so surprised . . . and so sad." I glanced again at the swell of ocean water so teeming with unseen life, and then back to Gage. "I'm Callie, and you might as well know, you'll be hearing my name a lot in the coming days."

He smiled at me again. "Really? And why is that?"

I answered his smile with a frown. "Because I think I've just found a new cause."

SO MUCH FOR THE "friendly, small-town atmosphere" he'd read within the folds of Otter Bay's tourist brochure. *I've seen friendlier women at a boxing match.* Gage shook his head at the air, picturing the now-meaningless words splashed across a shiny page in a jaunty, coral-colored font.

Gage watched Callie take the hill as she'd probably done hundreds of times before, confidently and purposefully, like a doe might leap in and around forested land. She was no docile member of the deer family, though. He could tell by the way she snapped at the three strangers who had dared to finish their work in her presence, two of whom nearly doubled her in size.

Until last night when he'd lain awake fretting over the enormity of this endeavor, everything else about this project screamed "God is control." He'd acquired this job mere hours after watching his career implode, the developer wore deep pockets and stayed out of the limelight, and Gage had finally overcome the fear of launching a dream business, in a new location.

So why did his stomach churn after this chance meeting with the town grump?

He swiveled his gaze out toward the equally tumultuous sea, just beyond the rocky cliff. A fissure of doubt unsettled him. Not over his abilities as an architect—he knew he had the skills and the passion to create what his client desired. And he also believed that the community would be proud of the finished project, a sprawling and sustainable mixed-use development. Eventually.

Maybe it wasn't what she said, but the expression on her face as she questioned him. Her eyes had narrowed just so, even as her brows knit closer to one another and her lips parted, the corners weighted down. She looked wounded. His actions had somehow wounded the prettiest if not angriest woman in town.

That shouldn't have bothered him much, but unfortunately, it did.

CHAPTER 2

I left Gage Mitchell behind to ponder my seriousness about fighting his new job, and stepped up what was supposed to have been a leisurely stroll to my sister's home. My legs moved faster, my elbow stiffer and more pain-filled with each stride. Surely even my high-strung older sister would understand when I told everyone—the whole family's having supper together—that the Kitteridge property was in peril.

Something brushed against my leg, and I skittered sideways before whipping a look down to find the dog with round, sorrowful eyes, and a long, skinny body staring up at me. Our eyes connected and, quite dutifully, he sat. Oh my. I knelt and gave him my hand to sniff which he did with little emotion. With a roll of my wrist, I petted him on the noggin. "Almost forgot about you, my friend."

Those eyes implored me with questions, but I was at a loss. I swept a look around while on my knees, massaging his body, unable to spy anyone searching for a lost dog. "Where's your family, kiddo?" I stroked his naked neck, exposing the area where a collar usually sat and the fur had worn off. He lowered himself until flat on the ground. The sun had long moved past its midday point, and my sister's chastising voice grew louder inside my head.

With reluctance, I gave the doggy one last pet and stood. "Sorry, pal. I'm late, and my sister will surely give me an earful about that. She's probably right . . . sometimes I do get distracted, but I have good reason. I really do." I peeked around again. "See, my sister is busy with her husband and her kids—Brenna and Blake; you'd love them. Anyway, she doesn't understand that when a passion burns inside me, I can't turn it off. Know what I mean?" He pitched his head to one side, making me laugh. "Okay, maybe not. We'd better go."

I broke into a jog with Doggy at my side along the winding path up a hill that led to Sheila's rambling ranch-style home in the pines. For as long as I could remember my family had never taken my causes—or me for that matter—seriously. I usually chalked it up to being the baby of the family, but I knew there was more to it than that. I had tasted success with Oasis Designs, yet, in their minds, my stubbornness made me walk away from everything I'd built.

Didn't they understand the real reason I took Justin's offer to buy me out?

I neared the top, my breathing jagged, my face overheated, when my stray friend raced me toward the peak. His tongue hung from his mouth, rubbery and pink like a warm strip of taffy. I stopped and bit my lip. *How would Sheila react if I brought him along?* As I stood there, debating how a four-legged date might disrupt our family gathering, my new friend hoisted himself on his hind legs, looking much like a miniature kangaroo. He sniffed my aching elbow and gave it a swift lick. How gross. *And precious.*

With my good arm, I placed a fist on my hip. "Okay, my new friend, you're invited. Just be on your best behavior." His tail wagged in agreement and we headed up the hill, Sheila's picture-perfect home framed in the clearing.

My sister welcomed me, if you could call it that, at the door. "You're late again." The rooster on her apron glared at me, and Sheila stared over my shoulder. "What is that?"

"Oh, Sheila, you're never going to believe—"

She turned her back on me. "With you, sure I would. Don't bring that thing in, and hurry up, we've already started eating." I watched her sidle away.

In one quick bend, I scooped up the doggy—really must find him a name—slipped along the side of the house and opened up the back gate to a long and wide expanse of manicured lawn. "Here you go, mister. Behave and maybe I'll bring you some quiche or something." He gazed at me with wondrous eyes. "Okay, some red meat. I'll find you some. Promise."

I slipped in through the slider door. "Auntie Callie, you're here!" My six-year-old niece Brenna rolled from her chair and into my arms. We laughed in unison, her hug sending us both onto Sheila's pomegranate-colored Oriental rug, the one she ordered from the Front Door catalog at half price.

She buried her chubby face into my hair, and I breathed her in. "How's my girl?"

"Ggrrreat!"

Sheila's agitated voice cut through our giggles. "Brenna, get off that floor. Go wash your hands again now."

Brenna scampered off and Sheila passed by with a platter of fish. She muttered into my ear. "You should know better."

I rose, smiled, shrugged, and glanced at the rest of the family. "Hey, everybody."

A spattering of hellos filled the air like an out of sync choir. My mother smooched my cheek and my father raised his glass in my direction. My brother Jim gave me a straight-mouthed smile, much like the one he might give my never-present nephew Kirk when he asked for the car keys one too many times, and his wife Nancy tossed me a parade wave, before glancing away.

Greta, my brother Bobby's wife, gestured to me with graceful fingers, while her other hand lay quite motherly across her burgeoning belly. As the second course made its way around the table, Bobby rose to greet me. Laughter lit his eyes as he found my ear. "Can't wait to hear what you're up to now."

I stuck out my tongue, surreptitiously of course, the way I learned to do when we were kids. With just seventeen months between us, we learned to say much without many words.

"Pass the potatoes, please." Blake, my five-year-old nephew was seated next to me. He giggled. I laughed back. "What?"

He raised his chin, showing me his shiny white teeth and impish smile. "That's a tongue twister—pass the potatoes please!"

Sheila corrected him with her eyes. "Close your mouth when you're eating, Blakey."

Greta bumped me with her shoulder. "Tell me something to keep my mind off all these contractions I'm having."

I sucked in a breath and turned to face her. My eyes roamed from her belly to her eyes. "You're having contractions already?"

Greta giggled. "Don't worry. Little Higglebottom or Mollysue still has time to play in there."

She had been teasing us with name ideas for months. I laughed and released a sigh of relief.

Sheila grunted from her spot at the one end of the table. "They're Braxton-Hicks—just some false labor pains—not the real thing."

I relaxed my shoulders, but swung my gaze back to Greta. "They sound serious to me."

Sheila passed a bowl of beans to her husband, Vince, before addressing me again. "Of course they do, Callie. Lots of serious things get your attention—always have. We all know how much you love your causes."

Vince guffawed. Jim nodded while taking in another bite of fish.

I set down my fork. "Did I miss something? I thought we were talking about Greta."

Greta touched my arm as Sheila shrugged. "I had asked you to tell me what you were up to these days."

I hesitated before picking up my fork and glancing around. "Same old thing. Working at the camp on weekends, and keeping busy on projects the rest of the time." I continued to hold my fork in midair, an empty sensation growing in my gut. "Did you all hear that the Kitteridge property is being developed?"

My mother clutched her heart. "Heavens, no! They would never!"

My father grunted something unintelligible.

I shook my head. "Well, somebody's trying to." I looked to Bobby. "Do you know anything about it?"

My brother, the younger of the two, shook his head. "Yes and no. I've heard talk through one of my investors. I didn't tell him this, but I've figured for a while this would never get past the planning commission. Are you sure that it has?"

"I'm not sure of anything. All I know is that a couple of goons were surveying the property, and that an architect has already been hired. Saw them all today." My heart thudded in my chest. "If we're going to try to stop this, we'd better get on it quick."

Sheila bolted upright against her chair. "Stop this? What makes you think *you* could do anything about it? What's done is, apparently, done." She turned to Blakey. "Eat your beans."

"Well, I have to at least *try*. Surely there's something the community can do to preserve that open space. There's hardly any of it left anymore, and property bordering the sanctuary should have special consideration. Don't you think?"

Sheila's grim expression and downcast eyes offered me her usual opinion. I'd seen that expression on her face many times.

Nancy twisted to look at Jim. "I would love to buy a home on that property once it's built. That would be fabulous!"

Jim, the oldest, sat back, his arm laid casually atop Nancy's chair. "We're not in the old USSR, Callie. Private property is just that; people can do what they want in our country, whether you care for their choices or not."

My bite of potatoes lodged in my throat like mush. I downed some water. "So if you decide to raze your house and put up a mini-mart, for example, your neighbors have no input at all? Is that what you're saying?"

Jim removed his arm from its perch on Nancy's chair, and his sober face matched Sheila's. "Take it from someone who's been around awhile longer, Callie. You may have been able to convince the church to bus homeless to services, but city hall is far too big for you to take on. Let it go."

Nancy nodded in agreement.

Greta, appearing serene amidst the thickening tension in the room, leaned toward me. "Maybe they're right, sweetie. Why bother?"

My chest tightened. I'd been in this place before, and not just physically, but emotionally too. Justin used the same tone of voice the first time he tried to talk me into selling a piece of our company to a high bidder.

"We'll never do this on our own, Callie," he had pleaded. "This guy has the bucks to help us make our dreams come true."

But the investor in question had wanted a controlling interest in the company. *Our* company. He wanted to jack up prices, use suppliers with less than reputable quality, and pay our employees dirt rates. We had only just begun, so why would I agree to give everything away before we'd even had a chance to try to make it on our own?

Jim advised me to take the money and run.

Sheila urged me to listen to Justin—then marry him quick.

Even Bobby said he doubted a better offer would ever come my way.

Not taking their advice had furthered the divide between my siblings and me, at least the older two who seemed to think it was up to them to provide parental guidance since our own were so often traveling. "Traveling away our golden years," as Mom always said.

And it definitely drove a wedge between Justin and me. If I had acquiesced early on, would our story have had a different ending?

At times I still wondered.

I took in the faces of each of my family members, aware of how quickly they moved on to other conversations and topics. Why hadn't the news about the Kitteridge property bothered them as much as it bothered me? They passed platters and flung jokes with ease. After Vince delivered a punch line, my brother Jim threw back his head and launched his booming voice to the rafters while our father smiled mildly at his model son with the comedic bent.

In the backyard, my doggy companion smashed his nose against the clear French door, his breath and wet tongue leaving a mess that resembled my mood: foggy and in disarray. While my family had moved on—rather quickly even for them—I had not. I planned to call the Kitteridges first thing tomorrow. Maybe they would have a change of heart.

CHAPTER 3

*B*obby's voice sounded groggy over the phone. "It's seven in the morning, Callie."

"You used to be an insomniac."

He sighed. "That was before we got pregnant."

I laughed. "We?"

"You know what I mean—Greta's pregnant, and she's been keeping me up late with baby projects." I heard him yawn. "And now my kid sister won't let me get my beauty rest."

Thank God for Bobby. Everyone called him Bob but me. I refused to be pulled into the stodginess that so much of my family had embraced. Despite his usual tailored, nine-to-five inspired appearance in a white starched shirt coupled with dark, pressed pants, one look at Bobby and in my heart we're five and six again, huddled at the cove during low tide, trying to pry an abalone from its rocky home—before learning that was a big no-no, of course.

He grunted into the phone. "You still there? Or did you wake me for nothing?"

"I've been thinking all night about the Kitteridge property."

Bobby groaned. "You're obsessed. You know that?"

I grimaced. "What? Am I really the only one who thinks that property is worth saving? Don't you remember all the hikes we took down there? We'd be gone for hours—"

"Of course, I remember."

My left hand gestured while I talked, even though no one was around to see it. "If we don't at least try to intervene, your baby will never have the kind of childhood you and I did."

"So what do you want me to do?"

"Advise me. Help me figure out where to turn first."

"Before I've even had my coffee?" He sighed. "Don't you think you should call the Kitteridges first?"

"Of course, and I did that already. There was no answer, though. I haven't seen Timothy's old Ford pickup rambling through town in days, and I think they may have gone to visit their daughter." I tapped my pencil on the table. "You and I are both old enough to remember how they promised to leave that piece of land open for the community—that's what they've always wanted—so my guess is that they aren't aware of the buyer's plans."

Bobby sighed again. "Or maybe they are very aware of it and don't want to face the neighbors."

"You think they know?"

Bobby's low voice challenged me. "Maybe we shouldn't interfere, Callie. They might really need the cash."

My heart softened recalling the recent rumors about the Kitteridges' money troubles. "I've wondered that too, but maybe they can sell the property to someone else. Maybe the city should buy it for a park."

He scoffed. "Fat chance. Otter Bay is synonymous with 'cash-strapped' these days."

"Oh, shush. Financial hard times or not, this is one of the most beautiful spots on earth. All I'm asking is for help in collecting information."

The tone of Bobby's voice turned lighter. "That's it? Collecting info, huh? Sounds more like you're building a case."

My sigh was drenched in exasperation. "Against a project that just might ruin Otter Bay forever!"

This time Bobby's sigh blew through the receiver. "I don't know why you always fight so hard, but okay. You can start by calling the National Marine Sanctuary office. Try searching Google for the number."

I scribbled that down. "Check. What next?"

"How should I know?"

"What about your friend . . . the money guy? He seems well-connected."

"Henry? No, no. He's a private guy who prefers to stay out of the limelight. Let's keep him out of this. Besides what he told me was said in confidence—and secondhand."

"But he may—"

"He's off-limits, Callie."

I huffed. "Okay. Fine. Thanks for the advice."

"Callie?"

My mouth twisted into a pucker. "Hmm?"

"I hope you get somewhere with all this."

I thanked my brother and hung up. Although I always put two feet forward into any situation that caught my heart, my family seemed to believe this would be my undoing. I finished college in three years including summers and took mostly night classes so I could keep the days open for whatever cause came my way: working at the garden co-op, teaching school children how to grow pumpkins from seeds, volunteering in the fight to keep the library open, things like that. After graduation, there was the interior plant design business I opened with Justin . . . I turned to the computer, hoping to dig up the Sanctuary office phone number. Within seconds, the number appeared on the screen.

"National Marine Sanctuary. How may I help you?"

I cleared my throat. "I'm wondering about some property."

"We don't sell real estate, ma'am."

I squeezed my eyes shut, hoping to clear my head. Maybe Bobby was right. Certain things should not be tackled before the requisite caffeine boost. "Sorry. Listen, I've learned that property abutting a portion of the National Marine Sanctuary is being considered for a large development, and I'm wondering why this would be allowed."

The woman paused. Had I annoyed her? "I feel your frustration. I really do, but frankly, there is not much help we can offer you. We do not regulate development in the coastal zone, unless of course the structure is to be constructed over the water. Is that the case?"

"I'm not sure. All I know is that there are plans for some kind of mixed-use development—which would be great in town."

"But probably not-so-terrific along federally protected waters. I hear you."

My heart lifted. "So you might be able to help?"

"I wish we could, but you see, our jurisdiction does not extend inland beyond the mean high tide line. My guess is that you would have to work within your local jurisdictions for permitting clarifications on upland developments."

"I understand."

"Miss?"

"Yes?"

"Good luck."

My heart sank and I glanced at the Sunday paper still spread across my kitchen table. Not one mention of an impending shoreline project lay within its pages. And although a tattered welcome flag furled and snapped in the wind from its perch on the Kitteridge home, there was still no sign of the elderly couple in Otter Bay.

My mysterious doggy friend jostled my leg, and I gave him a pet while still sorting through my thoughts. It was going to take more than good luck to figure out what was really going on down by the shore.

Monday, my usual day to plow through the housework left behind by a busy life, and yet here I was, taking another trek along the bluffs at Otter Bay.

Lord, please don't let this area be fenced off from your people.

Sheila would come down hard on me for a prayer like that. She'd say, "Prayers are for important things, not the whims of your head."

What made her think my quest was a whim?

Doggy tugged at my homemade leash. His nose had been moving faster than a hungry squirrel since the moment we arrived here. "We need to find your owner, you know." I glanced around, deep translucent blue ocean water on my left and a slow rise of land to my right. There would be chances for searching out his owner later.

"Excuse me? Do you have the time?" The woman's voice sounded familiar.

I glanced back at her. "Sorry, no. Don't have a watch."

The woman shrugged. "Me neither." She stood tall and wiry and wore a floppy hat over moppish, blonde curls. Ruth. Her name was Ruth. We'd been thrown together on the library fundraising project two years back. She had an obsession with lead ink in books and had lobbied to have testing added to the library's budget.

I smiled at her. "Ruth, right? It's been a long time, but we worked together awhile back."

She returned a feeble smile. "We did?"

My smile faded. "On the library project about two years ago?"

Her mouth puckered as she squinted and began a slow nod. "Yes, uh-huh."

I swallowed the sigh that wanted to barrel out of me. Why didn't I just say I didn't have a watch and keep on moving? Even in this small community, I had somehow managed to stay invisible to so many.

Ruth popped a gloved finger into the air. "Wait. You set up a composting system over at the library and helped build a rain garden. Right?"

Vindicated. "That's me."

She grasped my hand and gave it a few quick pumps, her glove rough and scratchy against my palm. "Sorry. Didn't recognize you at first. It's been a long time."

I put one foot in front of me to keep her at bay. She's a close talker and I'd forgotten about that. "Yes. Long time."

She lifted a bloated garbage sack with her other gloved hand. "I've been picking up trash all the way from south of the cove. I usually do this on Mondays. Never seen you here before."

I shrugged. "Probably the only day of the week that I don't make it here. I'm usually cleaning up the house after working the weekend up at Pine Ridge."

"The camp?" There. That's the expression I remembered from her. Ruth's right cheek muscle stuck in a grimace, causing one eye to remain half closed. "Bet there's a lot of mess up there."

"Not really." I considered the mouse trapped in the box with days-old crumbs. "Well, maybe a little. But teaching the kids to clean up after themselves is part of the program. By the time the weekend is over they're able to handle KP like pros."

"Glad to hear it." She dropped the bag and the doggy approached her. "Who's this?"

Again, I shrugged. "Wish I knew. He followed me home yesterday."

She squatted and gave the doggy a good scrub. "He's skinny and without a collar, so that makes him yours. Adoptees are the best kind of pets in my book. And this one's already in love with you." She gave him one more pet before standing. He came back to me and sat at my heel. "Told you."

Her comment lifted my spirit and I let the leash drop to my

side. My smile widened when I thought about telling Mom how I'd finally decided to start that family.

Far behind Ruth, a lone man paced the eastern path beneath some pine trees located at the top of the incline. His head hung forward; hands clasped behind his back. He walked to the left for several paces, and then to the right, and back again.

Ruth followed my gaze. "We get all kinds out here. Maybe he's one of those labyrinth walkers, although shouldn't he be going in a circle?"

I started to laugh, but air caught in my windpipe.

Ruth watched me. "What is it? He an old flame?"

"Not exactly." I pulled my stare away from Gage and his curious behavior. "He's an architect on a mission to turn this acreage into condos and office buildings."

"Impossible. The Kitteridges—"

"—are apparently selling this property."

She planted both hands on her hips. "Nu-uh."

"Uh-huh."

"Says who? What makes you think that could ever happen? Especially here?"

As I told her what I knew, she twisted in the breeze first looking to the dramatic sea and then back at the intense architect pacing the hill.

"But the property's not actually sold yet? Is that right?"

"I believe that's true."

"So we stop it. Plain and simple."

Relief gushed through me, a warmth cascading over my shoulders. Having an ally would be a great help, especially one with time and a can-do attitude. Hopefully she'd remember me the next time we met. "It's a daunting task, but I've got some ideas."

"I'll make some calls, you make some calls, and see who we can find to make some noise about this. Can you imagine Otter Bay without this open land?"

My listlessness returned. "No, I can't. I don't know what has happened to change the Kitteridges' mind, but it must be serious." I found Ruth's eyes. "I've been hoping to speak with them directly, to see if they might work with us to come up with a solution."

"Go ahead and do it, but I'm not holding my breath. Now, let's figure this out." She peered into the sky as if it had a mighty day planner stretched across it. "Let's meet at the RAG, say, Thursday morning at nine, after the breakfast crowd goes. You in?"

I hesitated, a tightness squeezing the muscles of my chest. I loved the beachside diner located near a spattering of quaint inns north of here. But had I gathered enough information yet for a meeting? "Okay." I paused. Still unable to fully fill my lungs with air. Agreeing to meet with others on this matter some how hadn't given me the lift I expected. "I'll come."

Ruth grabbed the bag of trash and slung it over one shoulder. She took another look at Gage in the distance and curled her lip, her cheek scrunching into that familiar grimace as she tossed me a wave and continued with her volunteer work.

FROM HIS POST ON the hill, Gage stopped mid-pace. He straightened and shaded his eyes with a notebook, the other hand poised in a greeting. Even from this distance, he could see the scowl forming on her face. Callie's dog tugged at the leash wound around her hand, and she spun toward the beach, giving Gage her back.

The congenial smile he hoped to convey, faded. He followed a path down the hill toward the sea, watching her use a boulder to steady herself for the climb down the cliff. He could've gone back to his work then. Maybe he should have. Instead, he found himself stopping an awkward distance away, watching her.

She spun back around then with a force that caused him to

reel slightly before righting himself. He watched the sunlight glint of the waves of her hair as she stomped toward him, and wearing a look that told him she had something to say.

She cocked her chin. "Didn't take enough notes yesterday?"

He felt a smile glide back onto his face. "Hello, again, Callie. Beautiful day, isn't it?"

She paused. "You know, unless you're being paid by the hour, your wallet might be better off if you didn't spend so much time around here. Could be a big waste."

He shrugged, still smiling, and glanced around. He let his arms rest by his sides, one hand still grasping a yellow legal pad and a fat pencil. "I don't mind at all. I still have much to work through and besides." His eyes found hers again, and he concentrated so she wouldn't see laughter behind them. "Can't beat the view."

She gripped doggy's leash and he strained against it. "But that's exactly what you and your cronies are trying to do—beat the view."

"Actually, I'm trying to work within it." He held up his pad of notes. "That's why I'm here again now studying the site. I like to sit, and to listen . . . to get a feel for what the land is saying."

She crossed her arms, the leash still firmly in her grip. "I'll tell you what it's saying. It's saying, 'Mosey on now, there's nothing for you here.'"

He couldn't stop himself then and a guffaw blurted from him. Her eyes narrowed, the only reaction to his show of emotion. Gage cleared his throat and looked out to sea. "Have you ever watched closely where the sun falls at different times of day?"

"Sure. I guess."

"Whenever I build anything, I study the light carefully. Make sense?"

Her pursed lips twitched before answering him. "Energy efficiency is important."

"Sure it is. But there are other things to consider. For

instance, northern light produces the most even rays. That's what your typical artist studio would need. On the other hand, southern light may provide the best illumination, but it's positioned so high that it won't provide optimum heat."

She pulled the leash taut. "So it wouldn't be the best in cool climates, then."

His smile grew across his face, slowly at first, then open and wide. She tried to keep up the bravado, but he could tell by the way her mouth and eyes relaxed, that she was softening. "You're following me."

She shrugged then, refusing to make eye contact with him. "I read."

He paused. "Still upset about the plans for this property?" He knew the answer before asking the question.

She turned her head toward the ocean and he did as well, taking in its variant blues and greens. Who wouldn't be upset to lose access to something so mighty yet peaceful all at the same time? But she knew ... she *had* to know that the sea didn't belong to the people of this town, and neither did this land. Leaving it untouched as the Kitteridges had all these years was more than generous, and yet, if one could view a heart aching from disappointment, then Callie's appeared to need some medical attention.

The only kind he could offer was education. He detected a kindred spirit underneath all that animosity. If only he could explain to her his plans ...

She swallowed, clearing her voice. "I played here when I was little."

He nodded. "So it's a sentimental attachment then?"

One side of her mouth clenched, and her eyes grew hard and small again, marring her pretty face. "Something's not right," she said, finally. "I can feel it, and I'm going to do everything in my power to halt this supposed project from going forward. Maybe the Kitteridges just need to rethink it." She dropped her gaze to the ground, as if trying to shake off some distant memory.

Gage felt his brows lift—both of them—and his mouth tightened against his cheek. "What's to rethink? They're being offered a ton of money for bare land that runs to the sea. If they're like most people, they'll take the money and head out of here."

"This is where their friends are."

"They'll make friends elsewhere. Believe me, people do it all time, and with money in the bank, it'll be easy for them."

A beat of silence passed. He tried not to stare as she tamped down her frustration. He could almost read her mind: *Who is this man to suggest that the Kitteridges would turn away from their friends and their promises that easily?* But he knew the human condition could be greedy and unkind. Surely she wasn't as naive as she appeared.

Instead of acknowledging the truth in what he said, Callie toyed with the rope in her hand and challenged him with a stare. "Something you know about personally then?"

His jaw jerked upward and he shook his head slowly. "I'm not the enemy, you know."

"You just work for him."

He nodded once and stepped backward. If she wanted to feel his dismissal, then so be it. "Enjoy your walk, Callie. I don't doubt that we'll be running across each other in the near future." Even he knew that statement could not be accurate in a town so small that even stray animals run into each other.

A gull floated down on a gust of wind and landed on a rock. Callie's dog whined and tugged at his leash. Gage geared up to walk away from her then, even though he sensed that her every nerve stood at attention, as if preparing for battle.

She spoke to his back. "Once the Kitteridges return from wherever they've gone, we'll all see how wrong you are."

He sent her a wave knowing full well it looked more like a salute. A patronizing salute.

CHAPTER 4

"*S*till no one missing a dog, huh?" I lean into the receiver and swiveled my chair to take another peek at Doggy. Those soulful eyes melted me.

Aida, the harried director from the rescue shelter, assured me again that my new companion, the one with shedding hair, who begged for scraps and expanded my heart, was all mine.

After I hung up, I bent forward in my chair as the doggy scurried to my feet. "Well, boy, if you're going to live here, you're going to have to have a name." My hands dug into his fur and massaged behind his ears. "Do you prefer a regular guy name like Jack or Steve? Or how about a beachy name like the counselors at camp get?"

He leaned his head to one side, one floppy ear grazing his shoulder.

I cooed in his face. "So you're saying it's up to me, huh? All right then, I've decided. With those big round eyes of yours, you, my dear, are now *Moondoggy*." This time my head cocked to the side. "What do you think?"

In a flash his front paws landed in my lap and he leaned

against me, his tongue bouncing. I laughed. "I take that as an approval." With a sneeze, he pushed away from me and his nails clacked down the hallway.

So like a man. With a sigh I dug into my purse. Unlike the rest of the world, I didn't carry my cell phone everywhere, so I was not surprised to find three voice mails. Did I have time for this? I still had to revise the cabin assignments for this coming weekend's camp and then fax them to our cabin coordinator, Luz. The mail symbol throbbing at the top of my screen won out and I dialed.

"Hello, Callie, it's Marie from the church. I'm wondering if you'll be here on Thursday for food distribution? Since it's still somewhat chilly outside, we'd also like to give away sweaters and sweatshirts that we've collected, which means we'll need you for a longer time. Oh, I hope you'll be here. Call me."

Food distribution! I'd forgotten all about that when making plans to meet Ruth. I made a note to call Marie with my regrets.

"Callie. Meredith Smythe from the American Cancer Society. Are you available to make phone calls for us this week? We'd sure love to have you. Please return my call. Thanks."

I jotted it down.

"Hello? Oh, my. Timothy! Timothy! Turn down that racket! I can't hear myself think. Callie? Oh, for heaven's sake. This is June Kitteridge returning your call from . . . yesterday was it? Oh, dear, I've already erased the message. Anyhow, we were out of town but we're home now and . . . Timothy! I can't hear! Oh, never mind. Feel free to call me back, dear, if you need something. So long."

Faster than rolling thunder, guilt spread through me like those hot flashes Mother always went on about, burning and unforgiving, making me sweat. Could I not have waited a few days before pursuing answers about the Kitteridge property? The more I played it over in my head, the more my body began to suffocate as if wrapped in a wool blanket during a summer heat wave.

I pictured my confrontation with those survey goons from yesterday. And today I blabbed about the development rumors to Ruth—a woman who had no qualms over making Steph Hickey, our perpetually pregnant town librarian, cry. Not to mention the tutorial Gage gave me today on sustainable housing that evolved into a standoff.

Maybe all of it was for naught. Could a heartfelt chat with June Kitteridge bring about a speedy antidote for our town's affliction?

My phone buzzed in my palm, causing me to yelp. Moon-doggy came running and I hurried to pick it up from where it bounced across the hardwood then plopped onto the floor. "Hello?"

"Hello, Auntie Callie." Greta's voice sounded more like a giggle when she spoke.

My mind lurched toward another concern. "Hey G—you're not—"

"No baby yet." Greta giggled, this time for real. "Silly girl, it's still two months off. Just calling to see if you'll go paint shopping with me this afternoon."

I scooted my butt up against the wall and leaned back. Moon-doggy licked my cheek and I pushed him away, trying not to get a mouthful of dog spit. "Pregnant women shouldn't be buying paint. It's not safe. How about we go check out this cool organic cotton store that just opened in downtown SLO instead." Greta loved San Luis Obispo, a college town just south of us.

"A lot of good that'll do me if I don't have a nicely painted room to put them in." Greta's voice picked up speed. "I want to buy low VOC paint for the baby's room."

Good for you. Low Volatile Organic Compound paint will be better for everyone. "Try no-VOC, if you can. Low still has some dangerous fumes."

"This is exactly why I called you, girlfriend. See? You know all about this *green* stuff. Anyway, since I've finally decided on a color, I want to see how it looks on the walls. Bobby promised me some time this weekend. Did I tell you? I'm going with teal."

My head rested against the wall and I smiled at the ceiling. "You sure? 'Cuz no VOC paint ain't cheap."

"I'm sure. So will you go? I need you to make sure I'm getting the right stuff and the correct shade of teal."

"There's more than one shade of teal?"

Greta's giggles filled the phone. "Stop that. Laughing makes me have to tinkle. Yes, of course there's more than one shade. Think of all those trees you're always going on about. They're not all the same shade of pine green, now are they?"

"No, I guess not."

"No, they are not. So are you going to help me or is little Tsunami or Bluebella going to have to live in a plain, ol' beige room?"

I smacked my forehead and leaned my head into my hand. "Enough with the weird baby names. Okay, I'll go. What time?"

"Afternoon-ish?"

"I'll pick you up at one."

With plans for the rest of the day made, I considered whether now would be the perfect time to call the Kitteridges and ask the burning questions. Or not. The pacing began. Was this really any of my business what the Kitteridges did with their property?

Memories swept into my gut. My dad and older brothers and other men carrying lumber into Kitt's on Display while the kids from the village played hopscotch on the sidewalk out front. Mom hiking up her skirt and joining in while other mothers dropped off platters of food and pitchers of lemonade. After the last swath of golden paint had been swept across the walls and the stunning new sign had been hoisted above the entry door, we all cheered. That afternoon we caravanned to the Kitteridge's property along Otter Bay, and it was then that June and Timothy gathered us around and announced the dedication of their land to the community.

On that land I tasted the lushness of my first locally grown olallieberry.

I learned to worship God with abandon and a few off-key notes when our teen group gathered there with guitars and youthful enthusiasm.

And Steven Diletto, high-school senior who hadn't glanced at me until that last semester of school, pledged undying love for me beneath the shade of a Monterey pine—after which he left for college.

With new resolve, I picked up the phone and dialed June Kitteridge.

SUZ'S HOPEFUL FACE GREETED Gage as he stepped into his office. "Well? Is that progress I see on your notepad?"

Gage sank into his desk chair that squeaked with every shift of his body. He hid his annoyance and offered his sister a forced smile.

She leaned over his desk to peer at his notes. "Greek. I had no idea you could write in Greek. Do you speak it too, big brother?"

Suz gave way to light laughter and it nearly turned his stomach. It wasn't her laughter that bothered him—under other circumstances he would love hearing it. What worried him was the thought of telling her about the hiccup on the horizon of an otherwise straightforward and high-paying project.

Maybe straightforward wasn't the best term for this project. No matter. Gage had plans to create something that would take best advantage of the land and the light, something sustainable that people would appreciate for ages to come. Surely even his nemesis might find it in her heart to appreciate that.

Suz handed him a crumpled white bag. "Here."

Gage reached for it. "What's this?" He opened it, the aroma too inviting to ignore.

Suz plopped into the straight-backed wooden dining table chair opposite his desk. He had planned to outfit his new office with top quality furniture. It had yet to happen. He was lucky he had a few extra pieces to pilfer from his apartment. Regardless, Suz looked content and that's all that mattered. "A turkey burger. Just the way you like it, I hope. You haven't changed your taste over the past year and a half, have you?"

His nose drew in the mouth-watering smell. How long had it been since he allowed himself the pleasure of takeout? "Slathered in mustard?"

Suz nodded. "Yup."

"Roasted green chile on top?"

A playful grin brightened her face. "Sadly, two of them had to give their lives for your burger."

"Two?"

Suz rubbed the arm of her chair. "I told them it was for a starving architect so they gave me extra."

The bitter reality of that statement made him lose his appetite. He set the bag down onto his desk and looked away. His little sister didn't need to know how hard things might have to become before they turned around again.

Suz's face turned sober and she sat up. "I'm sorry." She reached across the desk. "I was just kidding, but that was over the line. Forgive me?"

How could he be angry with that face? Suz was the miracle child their mother had given birth to when Gage was already thirteen years old. He'd always felt somewhat fatherly towards her—except when she'd drag her dolls into the room his parents always referred to as his teenage cave. Never did like finding Barbie in his closet.

He mustered up the most award-winning smile he could and

glanced back at her. "Nothing to forgive. My mind's just preoccupied. Lots to think about."

"Like how you're going to spend all that cash when you get the Otter Bay project going?" She smiled in a way that let him know she was teasing. And yet, a part of her had to understand that this project had the potential to skyrocket him out of obscurity and into the realm of the much sought-after. If only . . . if only he didn't need assurances about that right now.

His sister stood. "Eat your lunch. I'm almost done setting up your filing system and then I should leave. I have an errand to do before picking up Jeremiah from preschool—I had him stay for lunch today. Okay?" She waited in the doorway, her face expectant.

He waved her on. "Of course. Go when you need to. Give Jer a hug for me and tell him I've got something to show him when I get home." She smiled at him like she always did and turned to leave. "And Suz?"

Her hand still cradled the doorknob. "Yes?"

"Thanks for the burger."

When she'd left, Gage nestled his back into his chair. He stared out the window at the colorless, cinder block wall separating his office from the building next door. Why bother putting muscle to work on something so blah? In other times, he'd look at a dull wall like that and see a blank slate with endless opportunity. Today, it held little promise at all.

The phone rang and he lunged for it. "Gage here."

"Squawk-squawk."

Gage rolled his eyes. "Hey, Marc."

"How'd you know it was me?"

"I guessed." His shoulders bobbed when he tried to stifle a laugh. "Why are you bothering me?"

"So this is how it's going to be. You've got yourself a new best friend over there in beach town. Is that it?" Marc hollered off somewhere in the distance. "Hey, Lizzie, Gage just dumped me."

He came back on the line. "She says, 'Good for you.' Sheesh. Even my woman's against me."

"Listen to that one," Gage said. "She's not called your better half for nothing." He relaxed against his chair. Nothing like an old friend's voice to ward off an overhanging cloud of doldrums. He and Marc had been friends for five years. Been through good times, like Marc's wedding, and not so good ones, like when a car accident snatched away the use of his friend's left arm.

"You got that right. Hey, you find a church yet?"

"I did. Stopped in my first weekend here. Met a few people and one of the guys invited me to a Bible study at his home."

"And since?"

He knew Gage well. "Haven't had the time."

"Not the study either?"

"Not yet. But I plan to go one of these days." He tried to thwart Marc's inquisition. "You remember that Suz and Jer are here now, right?"

"That working out good for you all?"

"Seems to be, although Suz's pretty quiet about it all. Don't want to pry, but she probably needs to talk to someone."

"Hopefully she'll meet a girlfriend, someone to do double duty and be your woman too."

"Oh, brother. No time for that, let me assure you."

"You hit your head or something? A guy always has time for women or as in my case, *woman*."

"Lizzie's in earshot, isn't she?"

"You got that right."

Gage roared, the sound tumbling through his gut. Leave it to Marc to provide him levity at just the right time. "Fine. If you must know, I met someone recently and she hates my guts."

"Oh, so you're handling her with your usual finesse, I take it."

"Nice."

Marc laughed. "Seriously, how long can she resist your charms, man?"

Gage groaned. "Please." For the next ten minutes they caught up on each other's lives and Gage felt lightness reemerge.

His friend laughed in his ear. "Okay, buddy, gotta go. Get yourself to that church, if you don't want me coming out there."

Gage nodded. "Promise."

CHAPTER 5

"So that's it, then?" Greta hung onto her belly as I drove, my shocks bouncier than I remembered. I walked nearly everywhere, but could I ask that of a mother-to-be, especially when we're about to acquire two gallons of paint?

I nodded through my unease. "I guess it is."

"You don't sound too sure. Are you sure Mrs. Kitteridge said everything was okeydokey?"

I pulled into a spot in the paint store parking lot and switched off the engine. "She did say that, but . . ."

"You think she was lying?"

I released a sigh and focused on the store's glass doors. "Not lying, no, no. She's not the type." I turned to Greta. "You know that feeling you get when you say something but even you don't believe it?"

Greta nodded. "Like when you're sick and someone says they're praying for you and you agree and nod like you know you'll get better just like that." She snapped her meticulously groomed fingers.

My head bobbed up and down. "Yes, but even you don't really believe it's going to happen. Yes, like that. I had this feeling . . .

this feeling that she had doubts even while trying to convince me that ownership of their property was still intact."

Concern veiled Greta's eyes. "Did you tell her what you were thinking?"

I gripped the steering wheel. "Not exactly, but I did get her to admit that they've toyed with finding a more permanent arrangement for the property. She said someone had approached them with promises of keeping the property open to the public."

For a moment silence sat between us. Greta, rarely the suspicious one in the family, heightened my unease another notch. "I don't really know about these things, but it sounds fishy. Maybe that's why you're feeling uncomfortable. You don't think she lied to you, exactly, but that maybe she's holding something back."

I leaned back and lifted my chin, noticing all the dust particles embedded in the ceiling liner. "Maybe." I glanced at my sis-in-law, trying to focus instead on why we'd come. "C'mon. Let's go find little Winklebottom some nice toxic-free paint for his or her bedroom."

Greta giggled all the way inside the store. And some store it was. Fisters prided themselves on not only stocking the latest in paints, lacquers, and finishes, but also a decorating studio in the back to rival any of the big box stores. A good thing too since the closest Home World was more than twenty minutes away.

I approached a wall-sized display in the back room. "So what's it going to be? Stippling, sponge painting, stenciling? Ragging? Trompe l'oeil?"

Knitted brows and a delicate frown marred Greta's normally serene expression. "Bobby would never go for all that. Don't they have regular ol', nontoxic paint that you can just put on with a roller?"

Her squinty eyes and contorted mouth made me want to laugh aloud, but wasn't it against protocol to show such emotion when you're sis-in-law was nearly ready to give birth? Wouldn't she think I was having fun at her expense? I grabbed her hand.

"Over here. Plain old no-VOC paint. And look! They actually have more than three colors now."

The lines in her face disappeared. "Well, now, phew. But, oh no. Look at all those shades. How will I ever decide?"

If it's not one thing, it's another. I plunked a thick book of sample colors onto a table and she began to browse the pages one by one. My mind clipped along with each turn of a page.

At the next table, a woman with a brunette ponytail and heavy-looking black sweater pored over a catalog as a young salesman hovered nearby. The salesman, a cherry-cheeked twenty-something wearing loose-fitting khakis and the store's signature collared shirt, hovered behind her. We might as well have been invisible.

Greta squealed when viewing a particular page. "Oh!" Her shoulders sagged. "Never mind." We continued our search.

The salesman, apparently having acquired the nerve, approached the pony-tailed woman who continued the search for perfect paint. "May I help you, miss?"

She gasped, then placed both hands onto her chest as if trying to slow her heart. The salesman's pink cheeks reddened further. "Whoa. You scare easily."

The woman's eyes appeared guarded and she didn't meet his gaze. She turned slightly away from him. "You surprised me, that's all."

This did nothing to deter him and he pulled out the chair next to her and sat. "Can I help you find something?"

She shrunk back, as if questioning exactly how long he might have been watching her. After a long pause, she relaxed her shoulders. "I'd like to repaint the living room walls but I need to find paint that's green."

He squished his features into a quizzical state.

She straightened. "You know, as in nontoxic?" She flipped her fingers through the pages of the catalog in front of her. "I think I need low-TOX or something, but I don't see a thing in here about that."

The salesman fidgeted and nodded as if he had an idea. Greta's gaze caught with mine and she lifted her forehead as if to say, "Do something." I opened my mouth but wasn't quick enough.

The man in the collared shirt bent his head closer to hers. "It's really all malarkey, you know. Paint is paint, and we've got all kinds of it. Tell you what. You focus on the color you like and I'll have several quarts of it mixed up for you to try on your walls." He lowered his voice, but not enough that we couldn't hear him. "On the house."

Translation: while the fresh-faced salesman could spot a damsel in paint-store distress, he had no idea what VOCs were, nor why so many people were on the hunt for alternatives. By the way his customer abruptly stood and grabbed her purse from the back of her chair, it was obvious that he needed help with his pickup lines.

There were no other paint stores for miles, so I turned toward the woman as she attempted to pass by the wet-behind-the-ears sales guy. "Excuse me. I think we have what you need over here." I tapped the catalog that Greta fretted over. "And it's low- or no-VOC paint that you're looking for." I caught eyes with the salesman. "Trust me, they sell several kinds here."

"Really?" She rushed over and sat down. Several unruly strands of hair had slipped from her ponytail and swung beneath her diamond-shaped chin.

I gestured toward Greta's belly. "We're trying to find the same thing for my little niece or nephew's nursery."

The woman, who had moments ago appeared watchful and restrained, gushed over Greta's impending motherhood. "Oh, I love babies. Is this your first?"

The glow emitting from Greta's countenance could have lit the room. "Yes, our first. Everybody else in the world thinks we should find out the baby's gender, but I want to be surprised. How about you? Any children?"

An almost imperceptible shadow dimmed the woman's smile. "I do." She cleared her throat and shifted toward me. "So you said you knew what kind of paint I was talking about?"

Her quick change of subject caught me daydreaming. "Y-yes. I think you meant you didn't want paint with VOCs."

Greta touched my arm. "What are those anyway?"

I scooted forward. "It means 'volatile organic compounds' and they are pollutants that evaporate into the air especially from paints and finishes. They've been around forever, but as people have become aware of how bad they can be for us, more and more companies have come up with alternatives."

The woman nodded, like this was all new. "Wow. I had no idea. I want to surprise my brother by sprucing up his living room, but I knew he'd want the most nontoxic paint I could find. He's really into all things green."

Greta laughed. "Your brother sounds just like Callie." She nodded in my direction. "She's always giving the rest of us advice on, you know, saving the world and stuff."

A sharp sigh escaped me. "Who dragged who in here today?"

Greta's serene smile, highlighted by a sliver of light shining through the side window, would make a charming painting. What's it like to be that composed all the time? In that up-and-coming motherly way of hers, she gave her complete attention to the harried young woman who shared our table. Greta pushed the catalog she'd been viewing over to her. "See if what you're looking for is in here. I'm Greta, by the way. This is my sister-in-law, Callie."

The woman gave us a closed-mouth smile and a single nod. "Thanks. I'm Suzanna. I'm sorry to cut in on you, but I have to get going soon. I appreciate this." She peered into the catalog.

Greta waved her off. "It's no problem. I'm in no big hurry

these days. My husband will have to do the painting for me anyway."

Suzanna quirked an eyebrow. "How 'yucky' are the fumes? Can a child be nearby? I've got my brother's concerns and, um, a little one's too."

I brightened. "No reason to be scared off. Despite their lack of expertise"—I jerked my head toward the doorway that our flirtatious salesman slunk through—" this store has some great choices. It's not the end of the world if you can't, but if you *can* find the no-VOC product in the color you like, you'll be best off."

Suzanna's face relaxed and she continued to thumb through the book. "Thanks so much. Not sure what I would have done without you."

Greta giggled. "Probably would have bought the wrong paint *and* had a date for Saturday night."

Suzanna slid her gaze toward the door. She turned back to me and laughed. "How can I repay you?"

Even I was surprised by the snort that escaped from me. Greta gave a "woot" at my lack of propriety. Sometimes I have to remind myself that I'm in polite company. If this were camp, I'd get an award for a snort like that.

Greta fanned herself and rocked. "So, Suzanna, have you lived in Otter Bay a long time?"

Suzanna kept her eyes on the book in front of her, and her voice took on the air of forced nonchalance. "Um, not really. But my brother has a place here, so my son and I, we're staying with him for a while."

Greta stopped. "Your brother anyone we'd know? We've been here our whole lives, and it's growing so fast, but maybe we've met him before."

Suzanna rubbed her lips together as if mulling whether or not to continue this conversation. Why was she being so secretive? She shifted her shoulders as if still weighing her decision to divulge more about her life. "I doubt you'd know him. He's new in town too. Got here a few weeks before me." Her eyes flashed at the both of us. They appeared both sad and hopeful at the same time. She breathed in and pasted on a smile. "Anyway, Gage is a good guy—the best big brother a girl could have. Really."

She might as well have doused me with ice water. How many men named Gage could possibly live in a town as small as Otter Bay? My guess? Not many. Unless of course the Gage Mitchell I'd come to dread didn't live here at all.

Greta's touch on my arm broke my wanderings. "I don't know him, but it looks like you might. Do tell."

My brow furrowed at my sister-in-law's hopeful gaze. "Do tell, what? Do I have to know everyone in this bitty town? And isn't it possible there's more than one Gage around here?" That came out sharper than I had planned, and let's face it, that theory was thin at best. Greta's mouth fell open. She looked at Suzanna, who stared back at her. I hustled to make amends. "Sorry. I've got a lot on my mind, I guess. Didn't mean to jump on you, Greta. Besides, I know you were only kidding, right?"

Greta wouldn't look at me. "Suzanna, what's your brother's last name?"

Suzanna answered her, but focused on me. "Mitchell. So you two know each other?"

I shrugged her off, hoping my slack jaw wouldn't give away my distaste for the man. It wasn't her fault he hoped to tear apart Otter Bay (and rip out my heart while doing so). Besides, this was moot considering my conversation with June this morning. Gage Mitchell's plans were all but dashed.

I forced a smile. "Not really. We've met, but I don't know him well." *Thankfully*.

The room fell quiet as Suzanna jotted down a couple of numbers from the catalog. She stood and scooted her chair backward, taking her notes with her. "I just realized the time, ladies. I'm going to come back for my paint when I have time to wait for it. Thanks again for your help. It was really good meeting you

43

both." She started to go, then stopped and spun around. "And I'll be sure and tell my brother 'hi' for you, Callie."

Greta stared me down.

I gave her a smirk. "What?"

She glanced toward the door, still looking like a painted vision with light streaming across her body. She stroked her swollen belly. "I'm not used to seeing you all fired up over a guy." She swung her face toward me, her eyes taunting me like a cat's. "That boy must've really said something feisty for you to clam up like that in front of his sister. You're usually pretty free with your opinions. Something tells me you didn't want to share this one."

I chuckled and nodded too many times in a row. "Practicing your parental psychology, I see. That's good. That's good. You'll be all practiced up once little Petunia or Oregano gets here."

"So happy you're finally coming around about my choice of names."

I stood and rolled my eyes. "Please. Can we go now?"

Greta didn't budge. "I haven't picked my color yet."

"Have Bobby bring you back. He'll help you pick the right one."

She shut the catalog and batted her eyes. "I want to know all about Gage Mitchell first."

"Not happening."

"Then I'm not going anywhere."

I fished around in my bag for the sports bottle I'd filled with water before we left this morning and plunked it on the table in front of her. "Drink this."

She snorted. "I will not. You just want my bladder to fill so I'll have to get up. You are a *naughty* young lady."

"Again with the parenting!"

"So then, who's Gage Mitchell?"

The paunchy paint salesclerk darkened the doorway. "Mr. Mitchell? He's that guy who builds all that weird eco stuff."

We slid our gazes toward the door.

He went on. "Yeah, he came in here talking about natural paints and asking if we had a green directory in the store. I think he draws up houses and such. Anyway, he wanted to talk to the manager about providing all that stuff for some big project and I said, 'Whoa! Hold it right there. We have *normal* wall coverings in this store.'"

Greta leaned her head to one side, surveying him. "So you never told your boss?"

He puffed out his chest. "Nah. Didn't need to bother him with that."

I wondered if I should bother because something told me this kid probably wouldn't be working here long anyway. Then again, why did every attempt to preserve health have to be mocked? I set my gaze on him, taking a quick look at his name tag. "Andy, is it?"

He nodded, his chest puffed out farther than a wind sail.

"Well, Andy, first off, this entire catalog . . ." I tapped the book on the table. ". . . has thousands of paints that are safer and healthier than the *normal* everyday paint you're so fond of. Not only is it better for our environment, but it's better for all of us. Did you know that VOCs can cause headaches and nausea? Why use something that can hurt you when we have better products now?"

He gave me the classic deer in headlights look, his eyes so wide that I feared his pupils would disappear into the whites. Tempted as I was to poke my forefinger into the air and shout, "Furthermore!" I bit back my voice and softened the approach. "Listen, caring for God's handiwork is a cool responsibility, and I'm sure your boss wouldn't be too thrilled to learn not only that you oppose doing so, but that you've also turned away customers with your negative attitude."

He straightened further, pulling his neck back so far that his round chin developed a second one beneath it. We watched as his cherry cheeks inflamed to the color of beets. He left the room without a word.

Greta patted the table, her laughter hushed. "That's the Callie I know and love. You go!"

I dusted my hands against one another, like making a tortilla. "Somebody has to teach the young 'uns."

Greta's cheek quirked. "I do have one question: Does Suzanna's brother happen to be the architect on the Kitteridge property?"

With a toss of my bag over one shoulder, I moved to the door and gave her an are-you-coming-or-not look. "Yeah, I think so."

"Huh." Greta continued to lounge and she stared after me. "After that little lecture you gave young Mr. Andy a minute ago, one might think you and the eco-conscious architect were actually on the same side."

Eco-friendly or not, my dear sister-in-law couldn't have been farther off base.

GAGE TOOK A LONG sip of hot coffee, conscious of the attention his precocious nephew was attracting. Suz had appeared so worn and drawn last night that he had decided not to wake her and instead to whisk Jeremiah out of the house early and feed him some breakfast. He figured something shaped like a mouse with big ears would do the trick. His sister didn't have to know that he would be using a "buy one get one free" coupon to do so.

"Well, would you look at who we have here. Aren't you a precious little thing?" Gage recognized her as Holly, the young manager of the rugged diner with a view of the sea. Word was that she helped her aunt run the Red Abalone Grill.

Jer put down the stubby crayon he'd been coloring his paper menu with and showed Holly three fingers. "I'm four."

She smiled wide at him. "You are? Wow. I was gonna say three, so you're a bigger boy than I thought." Holly pretended to assess Jeremiah, tilting her head to one side and tapping the end of her pencil on her chin. "I know you're a big guy and all, but somethin' tells me you still like your pancake to have a face on it. Am I right?"

A sheen of juice dribbled down his chin, but he lifted it toward her anyway with unashamed aplomb. "You're right!"

She tossed him a smile, then looked to Gage. "And what can I get you?"

Gage slid the coupon toward the edge of the table. "Two eggs and rye toast."

"That it? That's not enough for a man to be eatin', if you ask me." Holly grabbed up the coupon without a glance and stuck it in her apron pocket. "I'll make it three and add on a side of hash browns on the house—Jorge makes amazin' hash browns."

Gage opened his mouth to protest, but she had already spun away, all curls and bounce as she went. It didn't look like much could stop her except for perhaps an empty coffee mug to refill or meal to deliver.

He took another sip of that coffee wishing he'd asked for a refresher and watched as several women and one man gathered together near the entrance to the restaurant, each talking over the other. The man stood just outside the circle, hands in his pockets, jangling spare change.

The proprietor of the diner, an older woman with energy to match her niece's, grabbed a handful of menus and guided them all to a table in the rear. He might not have paid them much mind if it hadn't been for their loud, animated conversation, which was a sharp contrast to the previously quiet morning.

Jer hummed as he went back to his drawing. Without warning, the boy glanced at Gage catching his uncle mid-sip. "Where's my sand dollar?"

He asked as if curious, not demanding. Gage noticed little

things like that about his nephew, and each time the revelations tugged at him. "It's in the garage at home, drying on my workbench. Remember?"

Jer smacked himself on the side of the mouth. "Oh, yeah. I remember. Where'd you get it 'gain?"

Gage put his empty mug down, and without hesitation Holly showed up, filled it, and scooted away. He clenched his thumb and forefinger around the handle. "Well, I was walking on the beach, and I found it buried in the sand. Do you remember what I told you?" Jer rested both elbows on the table and plopped his face into open hands. Though Gage feared the boy's interest might soon run out, he surprised him by staring at his uncle, rapt. "It was like a miracle to find that unbroken sand dollar there so late in the day. Especially among the rocks. Sand dollars usually live in very soft sand."

"Oh." Jer focused on the Formica table before flashing his eyes upward again. "Hey, maybe a pirate put it there!"

Gage swallowed down his sip of coffee before choking on it. "A pirate?"

"Yeah, maybe he stole the money and then put it there to hide it and, oh no, I have his pirate money now!" Jer slapped his dimpled cheek with one hand.

He warmed a smile right out of Gage. "I don't think you should worry, kiddo. I think pirates have special safes to keep their coins in. Besides, what pirate would leave his money right there in the open like that?"

His little face puckered as he considered this. "Then how come no one else took it 'fore you?"

Gage studied the little boy's face. "That's a good question. I would have to say that maybe God wanted you to have it."

Jer plopped both arms across the table in front of him, and then laid his head across them. "Yeah, God wanted Jeremiah to have it."

Holly appeared with two steaming plates of breakfast, just in time to delay the inevitable fidgeting that Gage expected. "Hope you boys are hungry 'cuz these plates weigh more than a fat tuna fish caught offshore."

Jer perked at the aroma of butter melting into a pool at the base of his happy face pancake. His eyes spied the maple syrup jug in Holly's hands. She held it over his plate. "Can I pour some on it for you?"

Jer nodded dramatically, as little boys often did, his blond hair catching wafts of air with each nod. And Gage noticed that just as he dug out his first bite from the pancake's middle, the little boy had begun to hum.

CHAPTER 6

*H*e didn't notice me. Late as it was, I scooted past Gage Mitchell and he didn't see me at all. Was he all alone with that little boy?

"There you are!" Ruth stood, her eyes nearly cloaked by the wide-brimmed mesh hat she wore. "Callie, I'd like you to meet Charity, Neta, Gracie." She turned toward the other end of the table. "And Bill."

Not one of them looked familiar. Did they even live in this town? They all nodded and murmured their greetings. As usual, I felt like the splash of cold water on a fire. Why was that?

Ruth stood CEO-like at the head of the table. She gestured my way as I took a seat. "It was at my chance meeting with Callie that I learned that the Otter Bay property is now subject to development. We cannot have this, and we must exercise every option there is to stop this audacious move."

I raised my hand as if needing permission to speak. "My apologies to all of you who took the time to come out here today, but I spoke to June Kitteridge by phone this week and she assured me that the property was not for sale after all." I hoped that sounded more convincing than it felt.

Ruth's familiar mouth quirk and the accompanying half-closed eye stared me down. "Au contraire."

Did Ruth know something I didn't? Or that I suspected? I tilted my head to one side. "Oh? Have you heard something different?"

She leaned forward. "My source tells me that someone recently called the city planning department to discuss procedures for applying for permits, and not just any permits, but ones specifically for the land along the coast."

Bill looked bored. "Doesn't prove anything, since there are still a few small empty lots ripe for building."

Ruth grimaced at him as if he was a piece of garbage she'd just plucked from the shore. "It was for the Kitteridge property, acres and acres of land. My source confirmed this."

I narrowed my eyes. "Your source?"

Ruth looked down her nose at me. "A neighbor who works as a secretary—that's all I have to say on that."

Peg, the diner's owner, arrived with a pot of hot coffee and an order pad. Neta, Charity, and Bill all signaled they would like a cup. When she finished, she plopped the carafe onto the table and positioned her pen over the pad. "What'll you have this morning?"

Ruth waved her off. "Nothing other than coffee. We're having a meeting."

Peg sighed and left without another word.

I plunked my elbows onto the table and rested on my fists. "Did they actually pull permits, Ruth?"

She hauled in a breath. "No, but now's the time to act, not after someone has already spent millions acquiring property behind this community's back."

She had a point, although could I go along with this considering June's earnest discussion with me the other day? Queasiness pulsated through my stomach. And what about Gage Mitchell? Something must be up or else this topic would not keep hanging over this town like a dark cloud.

Ruth stood stick straight, her gaze floating beyond the table to the view of beach outside the window. She exhaled slowly, allowing it to shutter through her as if the thought of losing Otter Bay had begun to weaken her. No doubt she took this as seriously as I did, but did she have to be so dramatic?

Finally she spoke. "We need a leader, someone who is passionate and driven. Someone who loves Otter Bay as we all do and who has the drive to see this hideous project laid to rest once and for all."

Gracie, Neta, and Charity nodded continuously.

Ruth was moving in for the role, I could see it in her face. And why not? She was leadership material and had the fortitude to follow her gut and fight for what she believed in. I saw that in her when we fought the closure of the town library several years back. So what if she came off as annoying and tactless at times? We all had our crosses to bear.

Something starrier had replaced her familiar grimace, as if Ruth could see into the future. She dropped her gaze to all of us. "And the person I nominate is . . ." Her straightforward eyes caught me in their beams. "Callie."

Me?

The women around the table nodded in agreement, and Bill tapped a forefinger on his temple and saluted me.

Ruth put a hand to her hip. "Well? Will you step up and run with this, Callie? We'll need investigations and financing, a motto and media coverage . . ."

My head swam with the possibilities, so much that I hadn't noticed Gage approaching our table. He strolled up without an ounce of timidity. By his congenial, open smile the others would never know why he was in Otter Bay.

Ruth, however, glared at him. I'd forgotten that Ruth had seen him before. "What's he doing here?"

He startled, but only for a moment; his grinning eyes only

slightly dimmed. Holly had apparently taken a break because she was sitting at his booth with the little boy I guessed to be Suzanna's son—Gage's nephew.

Gage offered Ruth his hand. "Sorry? Have we met?"

Ruth narrowed her eyes, and now both fists had found her hips. "You're the reason we're having this gathering today."

His blue-green eyes connected with mine. I glanced away. Ruth ignored his hand, so Gage slowly pulled his arm back rather than have it dangle in midair. "I see. Since I'm new in town, perhaps I should take this as a compliment."

We caught eyes again, although I tried to avoid it. I really did.

He surveyed the table, his hands resting loosely at his sides. "I'm Gage Mitchell. Just stopped by to say hello to Callie." He paused, his smile seemingly earnest, although who knew how he managed it? "And introduce myself to all of you, of course."

Gracie glowed as if a mythical god had come to life before her. She batted her lashes and stood, holding her white fringed shawl closed with one hand while extending the other to Gage. "How do you do?"

He held her hand. A beat longer than necessary, if you asked me. "And you are?"

Gracie blushed. "Gracie Stormworty. Pleased to meet you, Mr. Mitchell."

The others weren't quite so accommodating and gave Gage an unenthusiastic nod. He planted his hands at his waist and released a satisfied sigh. "Well, I can see you're all busy on a project here, so I'll leave you alone. Nice to meet you all." He turned to me and winked. "Thanks for being so kind to my sister yesterday, Callie. I really appreciate that."

I opened my mouth but not a word managed to make it out.

Gracie still glowed like an ember. "He seems like such a nice man."

Ruth's grimace had returned. "Well, he's *not*. Someone has hired that man to do away with the pristine land down by the otter sanctuary, and I for one won't stand for it." She twisted her gaze in my direction. "I hope I haven't made a huge mistake in suggesting you lead our cause, Callie. He's one smooth character, that one. You do realize that, I hope."

She was right. A cringe worked its way through me as I considered how his presence had a way of knocking me off my game. He wanted to keep me from messing with his plans. Of course it was all an act. Right?

Ruth waited for my response. I had spent most of my life fighting for causes I believed in, but always as second fiddle. I've always been the worker bee, the volunteer justice-seeker, never the leader.

I looked from person to person, knowing this little group would need an infusion of passion if we were going to prevail. *If* this fight truly existed, I would not want the Kitteridges to be harmed in any way. I began formulating a new plan. I wondered if I possessed what it would take to see such a plan through.

I glanced across the diner to Gage's booth only to see him watching me. He had the audacity to send a wink my way. While I've never been at the helm of any of my causes, Gage Mitchell and his devastating idea—the paving over of the community's sanctuary—gave me all the courage I needed.

A smile came over me. "I accept the position. Thank you for the vote of confidence."

Ruth's half-closed eye widened until it matched the size of the other one. "Excellent. I hope you will not sleep until you've put Mr. Gage Mitchell out of business."

I glanced over her shoulder to see Gage and an adorable towheaded boy leaving the diner. It occurred to me then that this fight might have further reaching consequences than I had originally imagined.

CHAPTER 7

"One scoop in the morning, and another in the evening. He'll beg you for more, so you must stay strong, my friend." I handed the scooper to J.D. Moondoggy had chosen the boy as his favorite neighbor, so I offered him the job of taking care of my pup during the weekends while I was working at camp. Thankfully my cottage had a doggy door already installed when I bought it. "I'll be back on Sunday. Can you handle it?"

"Yup!" J.D. fetched Moondoggy's leash from the hook on my wall. "C'mon, boy."

Moondoggy pranced over, then shied away. He came forward again, slapped his two front paws on the floor, then skittered backward. It had become a regular game.

I leaned against the wall. "I was going to tell you that you didn't need to take him out yet, but I don't think he'd let you out of it now."

Like a pro, J.D. dropped to his knees and grabbed Moondoggy by the collar. With a quick twist of his wrist, he hooked up the leash and stood. "That's okay. I want to walk him before I go to school. And I'll make sure to walk him plenty all weekend too."

J.D. gave me a grin that told me he would have taken this job for a penny.

I called out to him. "I have to run to camp now. Lock up for me too, okay?"

He nodded that he would, and I watched through my screen door as Moondoggy dragged the poor kid due west. I grinned, then began my weekly checklist, making sure I had everything necessary on hand for three days at camp: hiking boots, check; toiletries, check; Bible . . . rarely get the chance to use it, but check anyway; and overnight bag with all kinds of spares, check.

Oh, wait. My phone. Always seem to be forgetting that cellular wonder. I grabbed it making sure to unplug the charger, switched it on, and tossed it in my bag. Not more than a minute later, as I was about to pull from the driveway, a bell dinged. I had voice mail.

I cut the car engine and retrieved the messages.

"Callie! You coming soon? We've got a big mess here, and I need you. We're overbooked. Help!"

Luz, from camp, sounded frantic. But didn't I already lay out everything for her in my e-mail? Next message:

"Hello?" Pause. "Hello? This is June Kitteridge. Callie? Is that you?" A shrill alarm pierced the earpiece. "Oh, for goodness sake. That's my hearing aid again. Wait a moment will you?" Long, long pause. "Hello? This is June again. I'm back. Callie, I'd like to talk to you about something if you wouldn't mind, dear. Would you call me, please?"

I stared into the morning fog. Did this have anything to do with the building permits Ruth had mentioned? My finger hovered over the keypad, but I stalled. If the camp were really overbooked as Luz said, then I was going to be inundated with decisions about who to put where. I snapped shut the phone and spoke into the air. "First thing Sunday evening, June."

The drive to camp lasted less than ten minutes. This was only the second week of the spring season. Staffers new and old trickled on-site to prep for this season's new camp theme: "Standing on the Rock." I'd seen some of the sketches but had not had enough time to see an entire run-through.

The doors to the Adventure Room had been propped open, so instead of racing by as usual, I wandered in. Because other groups used the camp during the week, program staffers had to replace banners and other props before the start of each weekend.

Squid stood in the center of the organized chaos. His arms were crossed but his stance relaxed as he observed the staffers. My usual lift at seeing him had dulled considerably. Before I was able to turn away, he offered me a wave.

My smile felt weak, unimpressive. Continuing through the auditorium-sized space I halted at the massive banners hanging high on each side of the stage, their letters large and capped. One read SAND and the other ROCK.

Carp, who hugged a ladder beneath the first banner, called out to me. "Hey, Grandma Callie!" She smiled as if truly happy to see me, but she would change her mind if she knew how much I longed to knock over her ladder.

Squid jogged over to me. "Gotta minute?"

I hesitated. "Sure."

"I'm holding a midweek meeting for all senior staff. We have some kinks to work out." His eyebrows had a funny way of twitching up and down when he felt intense about something. "You in?"

"Well, it depends." I crossed a set of files in front of my chest, not unlike a high school student with her books. "I just agreed to head an important cause in town, and we'll be meeting a couple of times this week. When did you want to have your meeting?"

He tilted his head to one side. "What cause? Something to do with animals? Or the environment?"

"In a roundabout way, I'd guess you could say that." I lowered my voice. "I'd rather not say too much about it just yet. But between us there's been talk about a development going in on the Kitteridge property, and I'm working with a group of citizens to keep that from happening."

He scratched his beard, gaping at me. "First I heard of it."

His lack of reaction unnerved me. "Like I said, there still are plenty of unresolved issues. Suffice to say that SOS—that stands for Save our Shores—is very much in the planning stages."

He dropped his hand and gave a shrug. "Well if it's God's will, you'll know it."

We're in a Christian camp, so why did his response cause me to do a double take? I glanced toward the front as staffers ran a thick strip of masking tape down the center of the stage. My eyes found Squid again. "So you wanted to meet with me midweek?"

He blinked.

"I-I meant . . . you wanted to hold a staff meeting after this weekend. Right?"

He blinked hard, then nodded. "Oh right. Yeah. So can you be here Wednesday evening around six? Tidal Wave'll be bringing pizzas."

"Fine. Sure." From the doorway Luz waved me over with urgent, hard strokes of her hand. I inhaled for strength. "Have to go." I jogged away. Facing him wasn't nearly as tough as I thought it might be, considering my ego still smarted from his proclamation of last week that I was old and tired. So maybe that's an exaggeration? By the way it affected me, he might as well have said as much.

"It's hopeless." Luz's glasses slid down her shiny nose. She perspired when things didn't go as expected.

"Nothing's hopeless." I held out my hand for her clipboard. "May I see?"

She smirked and handed it over. "Good luck. Looks like we're going to have to make kids camp out in the Adventure Room or something."

I studied the list of cabin assignments. "What about the e-mail I sent?"

Luz puffed out a sigh laced with stale coffee. She pointed at line seven. "You forgot about them."

She was right. Somehow I'd missed the church from Bakersfield. My mind hummed, searching for an answer. I ran my finger down the list. "And you've checked with each of these church groups to make sure all their campers are coming?"

She nodded.

"Well, then. We've got our work cut out for us today."

"I'M GLAD YOU CALLED." Gage leaned against the seat back of his creaky office chair. He figured the elusive developer who had hired him would be getting wind of the project's opposition soon. It wasn't, however, his job to deliver the bad news.

The gruff voice on the line was all business. "What's the status?"

Status? As in how powerful did he think that band of mostly elderly committee members could be, save Callie and that angry one? Come to think of it, there were two angry women in that bunch.

Gage decided to stick to discussing the project itself. "Still waiting on the survey, but I've been on the property several times and have developed further vision for it than represented in the schematic design we discussed. Once I receive that survey, I'll be ready to lay it out."

"What's the ETA of that?"

Gage tapped the fat tip of his pencil on a blank sheet of tracing paper. "They tell me they'll have it available by Friday."

"No mistakes on this." His client's voice was low and despite his urgent words, nearly monotone. "As soon as escrow closes, we'll want a complete set of plans into the planning commission

ASAP. I'll keep you abreast of timing. In the meantime, make sure there are plenty of green elements in the design. We don't want no trouble with this community—lots of fringe in that area of the state."

He winced. Sustainable architecture was what he did. "Don't worry, Redmond. While waiting for the survey, I've been perfecting the placement of the buildings to maximize the best light and the naturally occurring breezes. Sitting your property well is my top priority."

"Just make sure to make it green. Stick some bamboo on the floors and solar panels outside, stuff like that, and that ought to make the rubberneckers happy."

Gage bristled at the assumptions. The idea of making something sustainable should be foundational whenever possible, instead of designing something and then asking afterward, "How can I make this green?" The ideal was to understand what it meant to create something sustainable, and from there allow the design to naturally occur.

Explaining the truth of sustainable design to his client, however, would only fall on deaf ears. Gage's fingers tightened on the phone. "If this project gets off the ground, it will be compatible with the landscape and be an inspiration to the Otter Bay community."

"*If? If* this project gets off the ground?" Same gravelly voice; higher pitch. "You doubt your paycheck?"

Gage sat up and planted both of his feet back on the floor. "That's not what I meant." His fingers raked through rumpled hair. "I apologize if—"

"You've heard something, then." Redmond swore and spoke something unintelligible into the background. "If that guy thinks he's gonna pull this one from under me, he'll have more than a lawsuit to deal with. He'd better know that. Better yet, you tell 'im that if he tries to put any more doubts in your head. Got it?"

Gage's eyes shut. He tried to picture what his caller was saying, and who he was saying it about. "I'm not sure I—"

"Are we done? I've got a plane to catch."

Suz drifted in with a question in her eyes but stopped short at Gage's expression. She clutched a thick file closer to her chest and made a quick retreat to her desk.

Gage's client's question hung between them until he shrugged it away, ready to be off that phone. "I'll be in touch."

"You do that." The line went dead.

Suz peeked through the doorway. "Tough customer?"

Gage stared at the bland wall outside his window, his voice sounding far away even to his ears. "And perplexing." He forced the conversation out of his head and swung around to look at his little sister.

"Did you want to ask me something?"

She approached him, a note in her hand. "You had a call from a realtor. A Rick Knutson."

Gage shook his head. "I've seen the guy's picture on signs around town but don't know him. Did he say what he wanted?"

"Just that he had some news on a property you were working on." One of her eyebrows lifted as if a question mark held it up.

"What's the look for?"

She relaxed her face in a hurry. "Nothing. He just reminded me of, you know, a used car salesman or something. He talked real fast and called me *honey*. Who does that?"

Gage laughed. "Hey, watch it. Our father sold used cars when he was in college." He sat forward and held the note in both hands. "A real estate agent, huh?" Gage didn't bother to ask which property the caller was referring to because, unfortunately, there was only one—hopefully, the one that would lead to more work than he could handle. He looked up. "Thanks, Suz. I'll give him a call."

CHAPTER 8

"*How* did you let this happen?" Squid paced as Luz and I continued to pore over the cabin assignments spread across her desk.

I turned up both hands. "Somehow I missed a church. It happens."

He paused and gave me a sideways glance. "It happens when your head's not in the game."

I frowned. "When have you known me to make a mistake like this?"

He took several more steps, then tossed up his hands. "Sorry, Callie. You're right. Mistakes happen."

Luz grimaced. "Just don't let it happen again, right?"

We both turned to stare at her.

She waved us off. "Ah. You both seem distracted lately, like you're here but your attention's somewhere else."

Squid and I exchanged glances. He tossed a strange little smile my direction and a sigh slid between his lips. "She's right. It's the second week of camp and something's just not jelling with the program." He stared at the fake wood paneling. "Can't figure it out and it's ticking me off."

I rubbed my lips together, my eyebrows raised. "Wish I could help, but um, we've got this little problem over here."

"What's your solution?"

Luz jumped in. "Hope that someone's bus breaks down?"

I cut her a look. "Nice. No. First off, I've never known a weekend where someone didn't fail to show up. It's a fact that people get sick. We don't like it or wish it on anybody, but it happens all the time. We'll just have to wait and see."

The lines in Squid's forehead deepened. I'd never seen him so stressed. "And if everyone shows up?"

My lips continued to run together as I considered my last resort. The boys would hate it. The newfound leader in me inhaled and let it out before announcing my decision. "The game room. We take bunks out of storage and move them in there. And, of course, move the foosball tables, etcetera, out."

One corner of Squid's mouth curled upward as he nodded, while a small smile lit Luz's face.

I continued. "Thankfully the bathroom's located just outside the cabin and it's warming up a little, enough that campers won't have to traipse outside in the early morning frost to use the facilities."

Squid slapped the sides of his jeans. "Well, okay. You have a plan."

"You doubted me?"

He bowed. "My apologies to the ever-resourceful Seabird."

"Oh, brother." Luz's previously hopeful expression had degenerated into a scowl. She glanced out the dusty window. "Don't look now but it looks like an early arrival."

Squid pulled the curtain aside, and I caught a glimpse of a renovated school bus pulling up the gravel driveway. He turned to Luz. "I'll help them unpack the bus while you get to your place at check-in." Before heading out, Squid caught my eye.

I waved him on. "It'll be fine. Go."

Luz stacked the papers on her desk and slipped them into her file. "I'm right behind you, Squid." She dropped her clipboard onto the file and scooped up the entire stack just as someone knocked on the door to the office.

"Callie?"

My breath caught. Her white hair had been swept into an elegant bun, but otherwise the elderly woman looked skinny and alarmingly frail. With her back bowed as it was, her taut shoulders pointed up like two upside down *V*s. "Mrs. Kitteridge? Hello." My questions for her collided with thoughts on camp. I needed to be where all the action was as the campers arrived. Why was June Kitteridge here? And why now?

June stepped through the door just as Luz slipped out, throwing a concerned, I-need-you expression as she did.

Mrs. Kitteridge kept her gaze fixed on me. "Please, call me June."

I drew in a breath and pasted on a smile. "Sure. Have a seat." Concern etched across her face, so to alleviate that I joined her by sitting in Luz's chair. "I received your voice mail this morning. I had planned to call you first thing Sunday evening after camp."

"I'm sorry to have bothered you. Shall I go?"

"No, no. Didn't mean it that way. How can I help you, June?" Even at my age it felt odd calling Mrs. Kitteridge by her first name.

She fingered her collar and her eyes had trouble settling on one place. "You've been asking about our property along the sanctuary."

I nodded. That familiar guilt wound through my gut. Was she about to confront me about my involvement in the opposition? Or would she finally tell me what was going on?

She clasped her hands and dropped them in her lap. "I may need your help. I know we don't really know each other very well, Callie, but I've seen you walking through town many times. Oh, and your mother is lovely."

She removed a floppy bag from one shoulder and placed it on

her lap. Rifling through it, she pulled out page after page of documents and handed the array to me. As she continued to search her purse, I came across page one marked with the words, "Promissory Note."

Her face reddened and her breathing became pronounced. My mind slipped back to my CPR training. I hoped I wouldn't have to use it.

June's bag deflated and I knew she had plucked the last of the papers from it. She dropped it on the floor and looked me in both eyes. "You mustn't tell anyone about this."

The urgency in her voice, her eyes, gripped me. "Of course. What is it?"

"It's Timothy. He's . . . he's . . ." June glanced away. Pain shadowed her eyes. "He's not well these days. He tells me things, and then forgets what he told me. Sometimes he denies he ever said what I heard." She returned her gaze to me. "And I'm beginning to wonder if maybe we signed something we shouldn't have."

Dread began slithering in and around me. "What do you mean?"

She eyed the papers in my hand. "We needed money to help our daughter start a business after her husband lost his job. It was some time ago. I wanted to go to the bank and take out a small loan, but Timothy wouldn't hear of it. He'd met a man who offered to loan us money against our home . . ."

"And?"

Regret saturated her voice. "We've been making the payments faithfully. I never thought . . . never knew . . ."

"What didn't you know?"

She covered her mouth for a moment. "There's a balloon payment due very soon, and we do not have the money to pay it."

Luz tapped on the window, her stressed-out expression burning through the flimsy curtain. I ignored her.

"Oh, June." I tried not to allow shock to permeate my voice. "Are you saying that you're about to lose your house?"

Her palm flipped upward along with one pointy shoulder. "I think so. I don't know."

My mind raced. "Have you talked with your daughter?"

She waved both palms in front of her. "Oh, no. Her husband spent most of the money we gave her, and then left her and our grandchildren. She couldn't handle this if she knew."

Silence fell like a dark night between us. What did I know about this type of thing? "Have you looked into refinancing?"

She deflated more. "Timothy gets angry when I bring it up. He says we borrowed too much for that. What are we going to do?"

I reached out to still her shaking hand, its skin loose and thin. "Why did you come to see me, June?"

She pulled her chin upward until our eyes met. "Forgive me for making assumptions, but I've always observed you to be the justice seeker of this community."

I shrunk back a little.

Those eyes were hopeful and searching now. "You may not think of yourself in that way—it's not as if your name's in the paper all the time—but I've seen you working behind the scenes on so many different causes. And that's what I want, someone who is behind the scenes helping me figure this out."

Would this be the wrong time to tell her I signed on to lead up SOS? I rubbed my lips together, trying to figure out my role in all of this. "Listen, June, my brother Jim is an attorney. He doesn't normally handle this sort of thing . . ." I didn't mention that never once had he been willing to help me with any of my causes. "But if you wouldn't mind me sharing this information with him, then maybe he could advise you on what you can do."

"Timothy hates lawyers."

"I'll make sure not to mention that to Jim."

Her head had dropped forward as if from shame, then she peered up at me. "And you're sure he won't tell anyone else?"

I nearly held my breath. "I'll make him promise."

The resolve on her face pricked my heart. "Then I would be very grateful. Very grateful, indeed."

"GAGE MITCHELL FOR RICK Knutson. I'll hold." Suz set a second cup of coffee in front of him while he waited on the phone. The acid was bad for his stomach, but he could not do without the caffeine.

"Rick here."

He jolted forward and set his long arms on his desk. "Gage Mitchell, returning your call."

"Ah, Mr. Mitchell, the architect." Knutson's voice barreled on. "Good to finally meet you. How are you, sir?"

Gage rolled his eyes to the ceiling. What was this guy trying to sell? "Fine. What can I do for you?"

"Not into preliminaries. I appreciate that. Let's see now, oh right, I called you about the Kitteridge property, didn't I?"

Gage stayed quiet and pictured Rick Knutson's blindingly white teeth on all those realty signs.

Knutson cleared his throat, and after he did, his voice sounded deeper than when he had begun. "My client asked that I pass along the news to you that everything is on schedule to take over the property within thirty days."

Gage's forehead bunched. "Take over?"

"Acquire." He cleared his throat again. "What I meant was *acquire*. Now, I'll need you to get this information to your client ASAP. The planning commission has been breathing down my neck on this one."

"You're telling me the city government is actually asking for these plans?" Gage had never heard anything so ludicrous. Planning departments were notoriously slow about issuing permits. He'd known many architects who'd crossed the line with personal gratuities just to light a fire under the process.

Knutson's voice rose again, fired up. "I'm telling you that this project is hot. No one's been able to touch this property for years and the community is itching to see something state-of-the-art built there. You, my man, will be a hero."

He doubted that. His own aspirations for growing his own independent and eco-conscious firm aside, communities weren't usually gracious about prime property going to development. Case in point: Callie and her pals.

Gage leaned back against his squeaky chair and cringed. "I appreciate the information, Mr. Knutson." He couldn't imagine why the realtor had called him in the first place. "But I'm still waiting on the survey so we're only in the schematic design process at this point. Once the survey is complete, we can move into design development and begin taking bids from contractors. It will be awhile until the drawings will be ready to submit to the city planner's office."

"Huh."

Gage's eyebrows both shot up. "Is there a problem?"

"Well, it's nothing really." Knutson's voice oozed with arrogance. "Except that I'd heard you were the best and, frankly, I'm beginning to wonder now. Surely you understand the high cost of delays."

Who did this guy think he was kidding? Realtors, or at least *this* realtor, had no idea of all the hoops necessary to create plans that would pass muster with fickle planning departments. A dart of pain pierced his right temple. Gage wasn't sure if this guy was a mole or just stupid. Then again, this was the second time today he'd been told to get on something ASAP, and did he want to bite the single hand responsible for feeding him and his family? The answer to that tumbled through him like bricks.

Gage drew in an even breath, taking his time to respond. "Certainly I am aware that delays mean money, Mr. Knutson. Be assured that my company will do everything in its power to provide the best design in a timely fashion."

Knutson's voice rose again. "Now we're talking."

Gage fixated on that blank wall outside his window. "If there's nothing else, I'll sign off."

"I'll be in touch."

Gage hung up the phone, sensing that Rick Knutson most certainly would keep in touch and more than he cared to imagine. The idea of future phone calls from that guy turned his stomach—almost as much as groveling.

CHAPTER 9

"*S*leep on *my* side!"

"No, sleep over here by us!"

Who knew that the church group I had to split up would decide to send only one female counselor? Half of their girls had to move into the game room for the weekend, and without an extra counselor, I had been elected—drafted—into duty.

It meant: Tight quarters.

Schlepping outside to use the restroom.

Little to no sleep.

"Night, girls!" I smoothed my sleeping bag on the creaky bunk in the middle of the room amidst a choir of groans. "There." The mattress sagged and the coils squealed when I slid into it. As the girls settled into their spots for the night, I lay awake awhile, contemplating this hectic day and how tempting a night in my own soft bed sounded. I whispered a prayer of thanks that J.D. had checked in on Moondoggy tonight, and began to shut my eyes.

In the dim glow of a night-light, a girl named Angel hung over the top of her bunk and stared at me upside down. Her long hair dangled like a privacy screen between me and one side of the room.

"Psst."

I peered at her with one eye, hoping to convince her I was already half-asleep. I'd been waiting for most of the day to contemplate the ramifications of June Kitteridge's surprise visit from this morning and didn't want another distraction.

She wiggled. "Are you sand or rock?"

I pulled my chin out from under the flap of my sleeping bag. "That sounds like a silly question to me."

"Really?" She flopped her arms over the rail, and I feared she would tumble out of the bed and onto the hard floor. "'Cuz that's what they asked us at camp meeting tonight."

Great, of course it was. I should have been aware her question was related to the camp's theme. Could they see my cheeks burning in the dark?

Another face appeared in the near darkness, this one small and round with a voice to match. Her name was Bailey. Apparently she and Angel had decided to double up above me. "Anthony got on the sandy side because he likes the beach."

I relaxed against my thin pillow, embarrassment averted. "He sounds like a man after my own heart."

A chorus of "ooohs" sprang up from inside the cabin.

Angel kept talking. "At the meeting tonight, they told us to choose sides. We went to the *rock* side, but it was kind of silly, I think."

Another voice, this one from Taylor, carried from the bed beyond the foot of mine. "Yeah, who cares if you want to sit on rocks or on sand? I didn't get it."

Some counselors relish times like this with their campers. Joy buoys their voices the next morning after they've had the opportunity to discuss deep, theological things with kids late into the night. Others find discussions like these terrifying. "Hmm, really?" I contemplated which camp I fell into. "Well, I missed all that tonight. Why don't you tell me about it?"

"I will, I will." Angel hopped down from her bunk, shuddering the cabin walls as she did. I slid my legs behind me as she plunked herself into my bunk. Two other sleepy girls dragged themselves over, probably unable to sleep with all this excitement. They sat on the floor in their pajamas.

"Okay." Angel showed no sign of the sleepiness that came with responsibility. "First we sang this song 'I Am the Light of the World' a bazillion times."

"I liked it." Bailey continued to peer at me from above. Angel gave her a daggered look. "I did too. I was just sayin' that we sang it like a hundred times. So anyway, after that we talked about the devil."

Bailey shut her eyes and recoiled as if she'd been given peas for dinner. "I didn't like that part."

Another voice piped up. "I thought that was cool."

Angel sighed and started again. "Squid . . ."

Another chorus of "ooohs" went into the air. Angel gave me a knowing glance. "They all think he's cute, and I just think that's dumb." She shook her head. "So anyway, Squid talked about how sometimes we think things that aren't right because it's the serpent's job—he's the devil—to lie to us. If we follow those lies, we're listening to the wrong guy!"

Bailey nodded. "So we have to listen to God. Is that what Squid was saying?"

By now Taylor had slipped out of bed and joined the circle around mine. "I think so, but we're just kids. How would we know how to do that?"

Squid's words from this morning sprang into my consciousness. *If it's God's will, you'll know it, Callie.* I weighed his statement in my thoughts. What earth-shattering bits of wisdom could I impart to these fertile little souls sitting before me? At that moment, my respect for camp counselors everywhere grew tenfold.

I pulled in a silent, deep breath. "You know, it says in the Bible that the angels of little ones can always see God the Father's face. Somehow I think it might actually be easier for you guys to listen to God."

Angel's mouth sprung open. "What? So you don't hear God anymore?"

I sat up and bonked my head on the bunk above me.

"Oh-oh." Bailey's mane of upside down hair swished from side to side. "Maybe God was saying you should watch your head, but you weren't listening."

All signs of sleepiness had vanished. Amazing how a smack on the head could bring about a spate of unleashed giggling from a cabin full of ten- and eleven-year-old girls. I massaged my crown. "Actually, I didn't mean it like that. I do believe wholeheartedly in listening to God." *That a girl, skirt the issue.*

Angel wasn't buying it. "But do you *hear* him anymore?"

For the first moment since I arrived in the midst of this active cabin, all went quiet. They didn't want my interpretation of Squid's message, but my personal story. I had always advised counselors to be transparent with their campers, and yet I'd been too preoccupied to do that with mine.

Something in my brain fumbled. Should I be honest here, and tell Angel just how busy my life had become? Or will she recognize that for the cop-out it was?

"I'll be honest with you girls. Yes, I've heard God before, but lately, not as much as I'd like to."

"Really? You've heard him? Out loud?"

"Not really out loud—although I'm open to that, Angel—but I have heard him in here." I placed a hand over my heart. "He has a way of letting me know when I'm on the right track."

Angel snorted. "And when you're about to crash into another train." She rolled over on the floor with her own laughter.

Taylor's voice took on a worried pitch. "What if we can't

figure it out? What if we go through this whole weekend and none of it makes any sense to us? What then?"

By now, I'd sat up, albeit in a crouched position. "Oh, Taylor, don't worry. And I mean *don't*. There's a question in the Bible that goes something like, 'Who by worrying can add a single hour to his life?' I want you to have fun this weekend. Laugh a bunch, and eat a ton, and soak up the lessons. You *will* learn something new —I've no doubt about that. But you can't force it, okay? Let God do what God's gonna do."

Angel screwed up her face. "'Gonna?' What kind of grammar is that?"

"Did you understand what I said?"

"Yeah."

"Well, then, my grammar did its job. Now, go to sleep. I love you all."

For the second time that night, the cabin wound down with "goodnights" all around. Bare feet padded about as the girls climbed onto beds that needed oiling, their voices twittering their myriad thoughts in hushed tones.

Bailey's voice floated above me. "Night, Callie." It took several twisting squeaks for her and Angel to settle down, but by the time they did, so had everyone else.

In the dark I contemplated what I could do for June, and for our community, and even more pressing at the moment, for the young girls in my care over the next couple of days.

CHAPTER 10

"*J*n my professional opinion, the Kitteridges are about to be financially devastated." My brother Jim stared down his nose at me, the hard line of his bifocals as unyielding as the opinion he had just delivered.

Still, I wasn't ready to give up. "Isn't there due process or something?"

He slapped the pages onto his desk. "Sure, maybe if they had borrowed from a bank or a reputable mortgage company. But they didn't do so, Callie. They took out a loan from a private lender—a sharp one." He drummed his fingers on the stack. "I will say this, whoever advised them to sign off on this kind of loan ought to have his license revoked."

I crossed my arms as I stood there in Jim's office. After the weekend I'd had, it took all the strength I could rally to call on my ultra-important sibling this rather hazy Monday morning. Especially when I'd missed the family's regular Sunday gathering. "What are their options?"

He grimaced. "If the balloon payment is not paid by the due date, the private party can file a lawsuit the next day. This contract allows for the lender to take possession in the event of nonpayment." He sat in his high-backed chair, looking lawyerly and quite definite. "Theoretically, a default judgment could be entered within 45–60 days and they could be evicted."

"It's that ironclad?"

"Appears so."

I uncrossed my arms and ran my fingers along the grain of Jim's desk, my voice losing steam. "Is there anything they can do?"

"Yeah, they could sell the land bordering their house—the same property you seem to think you have a vested interest in—and that will provide them with enough to pay off their loan. Brilliant stipulation—wish I'd thought of it."

"You can't be serious. That lender took advantage of the Kitteridges and you know it."

Jim shrugged. "Happens all the time. People shouldn't sign agreements they do not understand."

"And there's nothing else that you, my smart attorney brother, can suggest for them to do?"

"Yeah, they could come up with the money within the next six weeks in order to be safe." Jim threw both hands up and gave me his signature "See-it-my-way" expression. He did that whenever he had decided that a particular conversation was nearing its end. "Listen, Callie, you can't help them on this one. They were foolish in signing this."

I shook my head. "An old couple's home is at stake, Jim. We have to come up with a way to help them."

"Says who?" Jim let out an obvious sigh, the kind that told me that even if he could help, he wouldn't. It wasn't worth his time. "Callie, this is the same song and dance we've traded since you were a kid. Stop trying to save the world. It can't be done."

I crossed my arms again and cradled my elbows. "I'd like to think that it could."

Jim stood. He leaned both fists on his desk until his body stretched across its surface, causing me to take a backward step.

"I wasn't going to be the bad guy and point this out, but weren't you the one who came tearing into Sunday supper last week ready to take the Kitteridges down?"

"I was just stunned by what those goons had said and how they treated me." I lowered my head until all I could see was the plush, ebony carpet at my feet. "I-I really hadn't had a chance to think of the Kitteridges' part in all of it at that point."

"Even though, technically, it was their property you were so bent out of shape over." He was bullying me. I could tell by the tone of his voice and I hated it. Why, after so many years, did I let him get away with that?

I lifted my head until our eyes met, which meant that I had to rise to my toes and crane my neck. "So what you're saying is that this is too tough for you to handle."

Now I'd done it. If skin could look warm, his had begun to sizzle. His silence roared through the office, taunting me to apologize. Instead I stood there. And waited.

His smile returned, the same patronizing smile I had seen as a child every time I asked to go along with him and his friends to a movie, or an ice cream. Even a trip to the grocery store would have been nice. Jim's normal skin tone had returned, and he lowered himself into his wide-armed chair. "My suggestion to you is to save all your money from your camp job and hope it's enough for a down payment."

"Down payment?"

He tossed the stack of Kitteridge documents to the edge of his desk. "Yeah, for a nice ocean-view loft at Otter Bay."

GAGE PERCHED UPON A rock, his arms wrapped around his shins, one hand gripping his other wrist, as he stared into the far-reaching expanse of watery jade from the edge of Otter Bay. Moments like this, when the air and water kept reasonably still, reminded him of his childhood, a time when he'd run his dog Luke down a path through pine and scrub until they'd come to the edge of the lake. Lake Forever may have had a glorified name, but it was merely an oversized pond.

Still, he liked to go there and let Luke tear around wild while he rested on a rock and contemplated the ripples on the water. Much like he was doing now. Only this time the water reached farther than his eyes could see, and the ripples crested every once in awhile when the wind decided to blow.

The irony of his growing fondness for this spot, which was slated for development under his direction, was not lost on him. If only he had the resources to buy this plot himself, he would build something respectful and harmonious with the land—and then leave the rest wide open. For what, he didn't know. Squirrels to skitter about? Otters to coast by without worry over debris dropping off high-rises built by overzealous developers hungry for the profit margin that came with density?

Or maybe . . . a family?

Not now. He couldn't entertain such a proposition, because for one his sister and nephew depended on him for survival. Neither he nor they had planned on that fact, nor the more sobering reality of Suz's husband—Jer's father—landing in jail. He still couldn't believe the guy had done what he'd done.

Gage blew out a sigh with force. Truthfully, though, his sister's bad fortune had little, if any, effect on his immediate plans because Gage had not cared deeply for a woman in a long, long time. He glanced around. After being unceremoniously tossed from his last job, Gage could have settled anywhere. He had long since passed his exams and become registered in California. As a single guy with no one but himself to worry about, he had built up some savings and had determined to start his own company in a coastal community. So he landed here in Otter Bay. Who was he kidding? The lure of a mammoth-sized job awaiting him had everything to do with that. Still, he could not shake the sense that a larger force was at work.

A woman appeared before Gage, her shapely figure casting a shadow over him. "Praying?"

He blinked. After daring to wander back to this spot, Gage might have expected to hear Callie's voice, but somehow he hadn't, and now here she stood at the top of the rickety steps, glaring at him.

He shrugged a shoulder. "Maybe."

The gritty look on her face faltered. "So how does that work exactly?"

"Prayer, you mean?"

"What I mean is I'm praying one way . . ." She glanced around before making eye contact with him again. ". . . and my guess is you're praying the exact opposite."

Gage chuckled and unfolded his legs, allowing his feet to land on the ground. He rested against the rock he'd been sitting on and kept her gaze. "He's a big God, Callie. I'm sure he can handle it."

It happened again. Something faltered in her expression. Did she have a problem with God? Or the fact that Gage was not the godless enemy she had made him out to be? Or maybe she spotted a speck of chive stuck to his teeth.

"We're going to fight this all the way, you know."

"I understand. Quite a gang you gathered together for the fight, by the way." That wasn't called for and he knew it, but such a pain she was! He couldn't find it within himself to avoid frustrating her if only a little. He gripped the cold, rough surface of the rock beneath his fingers. What did she mean they were going to fight this all the way? How far did she think that pretty face would get her and the geriatric crew she'd recruited for her cause?

She stared at him as if stunned, and for the briefest instant, he felt another stab of remorse over his flippant comment. But then her eyes narrowed at him and if she had access to a kitchen drawer, he thought she might stab him on the spot. Such beauty, wasted on an angry woman.

Her intense stare bore into his. "First you carelessly make your presence known before all avenues for saving this property have been explored, and then you foolishly mock the people of this community." She shook her head slowly, deliberately, as if he were a child. "You are making this easier for me than I had given you credit for."

Ouch. He swallowed, trying not to show how bitter his pride tasted sliding down his throat. "Glad I could help." His voice sounded weak and insincere, even to his own ears.

"How altruistic of you."

"Okay, give." Gage adjusted his body against the boulder before flashing two open palms in an attempt to end the stalemate. "I don't care to fight with you, because as I've said before, I'm only here to do my job. Maybe if you'd give this thing a chance, you would see just how well the design for this project will complement your community."

Callie's laughter exploded in a wave of snorts, and Gage waited for her to blush and apologize for the unladylike outburst. She didn't flinch. Instead she took a step, halted, and looked him up and down from his sneakers to the tousled-hair tip of his head, as if daring him to cross her. Her chest rose and fell. Had her animosity tired her? "You go on thinking that, Mr. Mitchell. Just go on thinking it." She pushed past him, and as she did her face lingered uncomfortably close to his. "Enjoy the view."

He fought the urge to seize her arm. "Wait. What did you mean when you said you were exploring avenues to save this property? My understanding is that it has already been sold and is ready to change hands. Pretty straightforward—unless you have knowledge to the contrary." He paused, watchful. "Do you?"

She opened her mouth but it hung there, wordlessly. Her eyes flitted about as if unable to find a solid place to land. When she licked her lips, Gage looked away. He could hear the pattern of her breathing before she finally spoke. "Really, Mr. Mitchell, how silly do you think I am? Give away my strategy to the enemy?" He thought he heard her smirk. "Come on now and give a girl more credit than that."

CHAPTER 11

hat was close. After the disappointing visit to my brother Jim's office—a cliché if I ever heard one—it pained me to run into Gage Mitchell at the Kitteridge property. I had strolled the beach to regroup and planned on climbing the hill on my way home. I was unprepared to see him there, of all places. I tried, but he needled his way under my skin. What's worse—I almost gave away June's secret. After she begged me to keep the information to myself, I nearly threw it into the architect's face as proof that all was not right with this deal.

For the first time since Friday, I could see that keeping this secret presented a challenge.

I disliked admitting this, even to myself, but there were moments when I noticed glimpses of something pleasing about Gage. When I reached the top of the stairs, he didn't notice me at first and I studied him briefly, noting a wistful, almost longing expression on his face. It felt familiar to me. Could he have been having second thoughts?

Our eyes met and good sense rematerialized within me. In his gaze I saw a flash of appreciation and it turned me cold. Worse, he talked of God, then followed that by mocking the townspeople.

I trudged up the hill toward home, shaking my head with each step. Instead of Gage being the person that, for one irrational instant, I considered someone to confide in, I realized he may be playing me.

"There she is—Madam President." Ruth stood to the right of the well-worn path, a sagging trash sack over one shoulder, her other hand formed in a salute.

My head jerked. "Didn't see you there."

"That's all right. You got your head in the details I'm sure. Wanna give me a heads-up on what you'll be reporting tomorrow night?"

I swallowed hard. The memory of June's desperation clenched at my heart. "Worked all weekend, but I do have an idea I'd like to run with."

Ruth's face went on alert and she leaned in.

I inhaled and thought out my words. "But let's wait until we're all together. I've got to get home to take my dog for a walk—been a busy day, you know?"

The hand that had been raised in a salute moved to Ruth's hip. "Sure. All right." She raised her chin until her eyes were visible beneath the rim of her hat. "Been thinking about those Kitteridges lately. Have you talked to them yet? Must've been given some offer to go back on their word like that."

"Oh, I don't know. Things happen and people change their minds sometimes."

"So you haven't talked to them."

Why did I get the feeling that, in Ruth's mind, my leadership was in name only? "Actually I have. Like I said, I've got an idea, so I'll see you at the RAG, okay?"

Carp, from camp, pulled up next to us on a mountain bike, her back tire kicking up dust as she went into a skid. "Hey Seabird! Thought maybe I'd see you around."

Ruth cocked her head.

I smiled at the counselor, momentarily forgetting how much she likes to tease me about my age, then turned to Ruth. "Seabird is my camp name—it makes it more fun for the kids to call us by nicknames. And this is Carp. She's one of our weekend counselors." I gestured toward Ruth. "Carp, I'd like you to meet Ruth."

Ruth nodded. "Nice to meet you. Is that Carp for the town of Carpinteria down near Santa Barbara? Or for the fish?"

Carp giggled. "The fish, definitely. I've never been that far south."

Ruth puckered. "Haven't seen you riding around here before. You new in town?"

Carp straddled her bike, and let her hands drape down the front of her handlebars. "I go to college down in SLO but decided to stay around today to check out the town more." She flicked a look my way. "You're my inspiration, Seabird."

"Really?" My eyes widened. "Why?"

"Well, at first I was gonna drive down to my dorm last night, then drive back up here today. But then I started thinking about how you always talk about saving fuel and how you walk everywhere." She shrugged. "Seemed like a waste of gas to do all that driving around, so I stuck this bike into the trunk of my car on Friday and just spent another night at camp." She patted her bike. "You really can see a whole lot more when you're not stuck in a car."

I clapped my hands. "Cool. I love hearing that. You picked a perfect day weather-wise too."

"I'll say." Carp's gaze led to the horizon. "I'm usually so busy with the kidoodles at camp that I don't have the chance to just *be* out here on the bluffs. It's mesmerizing."

A sly smile creased Ruth's face and she slid a look my way. She was in recruiting mode, I could feel it. So I stepped to the plate—and changed the subject. "I've got a doggy that needs some love, so I'll leave you here to soak up the beauty. By the way, on

Wednesday I am going to meet with Squid and a few others on the board. If you have any comments for me to take back, I'd—"

"I do! Some of the kids, well, they don't seem to be understanding the message as well as they should. The counselors have been doing a good job of filling in the gaps, but I don't know. I just think we need to make the presentation more clear." As soon as the words tumbled from her mouth, Carp waved both hands in front of herself, as if wanting to take them back. "I didn't mean that Squid or anybody was doing a bad job or anything."

I touched her shoulder. "I'm sure you didn't. If it helps, Squid's been reworking the presentation and looking for reviews and suggestions. Like you said, I had some great discussions with my kids over the weekend and that could go a long way."

Carp's face lit up. "Oh, that's right. You got a chance to play counselor. Fun, huh?"

"Oh, sure. No sleep, freezing toilet seat—yeah, that was cool." I laughed. "Seriously, though, the girls were so ready to grow. I'd forgotten how precious it was to see their transformation."

Ruth fidgeted. It appeared that she was looking for her escape so I addressed her. "I'll see you tomorrow night, Ruth."

She nodded, her hat flapping up and down. "That's right. And I'll be expecting a full report." She turned to Carp. "And good meeting you, missy. Just be careful you don't ride that bike of yours too close to the edge. There's some erosion going on that could be dangerous."

Carp hopped onto her bike. "Aw, thanks. That was sweet of you to warn me." We watched as she waved goodbye and coasted downhill.

"Warn her, my foot." Ruth muttered loud enough for me to hear as I hiked up the hill. "I'm just hoping not to see any more damage caused by careless humans."

I brushed aside Ruth's thoughtless comment and focused instead on my brief conversation with Carp. She was right. Something was missing in the weekend presentation. Still, as

Gage said, our God is a big God and I had no doubt that he would fill in the gaps for our campers.

My feet froze in place. Did I just agree with something Gage said?

GAGE TYPED IN HIS voicemail code, hoping he didn't have to hear his client's gruff voice right now, issuing him commands. Hearing Marc's voice on the line, however, wasn't much easier.

"Dude, Lizzy wanted me to call you . . . you know, just to check on your status Are you settling in? Found a church? Things like that. Put me . . . I mean, help me put my wife out of her misery here, 'kay?" Marc lowered his voice to a conspiratorial tone. "You know how she worries about you."

Gage squeezed his eyes shut, drew in a breath through his nose, and stretched his shoulders toward his ears. He gave his head a tight shake. What did he ever do to deserve such a friend?

Gage dropped his face into his hands and muttered to himself. "Hypocrite." He felt his cheeks flush at the single word spoken into the air. Of course, he wasn't referring to Marc. Never! Instead, he spoke the word about himself.

Gage leaned back against his squeaky chair, his head a tangle of heavy emotion. He recalled the way he let Callie Duflay believe that he prayed on a regular basis. He knew better. Worse, God did too. He sighed, not the feathery exhalation of someone who's been inconvenienced, but the kind of wretched sigh that escapes from lungs held taut from discontent with oneself.

This move to Otter Bay had not solved all his problems. On the contrary, everywhere it seemed, he found land mines ready to explode. His phone rang again, but he immediately switched off the sound, not caring to see who was on the other end. Instead, he kept his head bowed, and began, "Dear God . . ."

CHAPTER 12

"Here, put this on." Greta handed a white face mask to me and snapped the elastic band.

I hopped backward. "Why do I have to wear one? I'm not pregnant."

My sister-in-law dug one elegant fist into her now ample hip and hung the mask from the fingers of her free hand. "Because if I'm going to look like an alien, then so are you."

I sighed. Pregnancy-brain affected us all. I secured the mask around my mouth and immediately felt remorse for having eaten so much garlic with dinner last night. "Where to?" My voice sounded muffled.

Greta motioned for me to follow her down the hall to a room with tall windows and partially painted walls. Bobby rolled color onto the previously dull surface while wearing ear buds and humming "I Heard It Through the Grapevine." He couldn't hear me cackling behind him.

Greta smacked his rump to get his attention, and I turned away from the marital display. *Please.*

Bobby pulled one bud from his ear. "Hey, Callie. What do you think?" He waved the saturated paint roller around his head.

"I think you should keep your day job."

He stuck out his tongue then leaned and gave me a swift smacker on the cheek. "You're in good spirits today I see. Nice mask."

I blew him a raspberry and quickly regretted it. With one hand, I pulled the thing off and handed it to Greta. She wagged a shaming mommy finger at me, but I only laughed. "So you really did go with teal." I paused and looked around. "You know, it really looks good."

Greta perked, her eyes smiling. "Really?"

I gave her an appraising nod. "Really, *really* pretty."

"You mean handsome." Bobby's paint roller froze midair.

I clasped my hands. "You're having a boy?"

Greta shook her head and led Bobby back to painting. "No. We don't know. He's just worried that if we do, this room will look too pretty."

I sent him a mock glare. "You're not into that whole pink for girls and blue for boys thing, are you little brother?"

He looked to Greta, then at me, as if this were a trick question. "No comment."

Greta laughed. "You two are so weird. Speaking of boys, I wanted to tell you that I gave out your number yesterday."

Bobby quipped. "Nice segue."

His wife slapped his shoulder, then grabbed me by the elbow. "Remember that girl we met? Suzanna? She was in the paint store yesterday at the same time we were, and we got to talking, and well . . . she asked for your phone number."

Bobby stopped but didn't look at us. "You'd better explain that, G."

She gave her head a tiny shake. "For her brother. The one who's the architect. Remember him?"

"Tell me you're kidding." I pulled away from her. "Why would you do that?"

"Well, she asked about you and thought you were so nice to

help her. She said you saved her a trip to another paint store! Anyway, she thinks her brother is lonely and that he needs a friend and thought that since you two are so much alike that you'd be a good match."

Had pregnancy caused Greta to lose all sense? "You do remember who Gage Mitchell is, right? The architect who wants to desecrate the Kitteridge property?"

Greta smoothed back a curl. "Are you angry? It's just, I don't know. The more she told me about her brother—how cute he is, and 'green' he is—I just thought you might be able to get past your differences and at least show him around Otter Bay a little. He's new around here. Did you know that?"

Bobby stood in silence. He was like a cat. Maybe if he froze in place, I wouldn't see him. But oh, I saw him all right. "And where were you when I was being set up with the enemy? Huh?"

"*No me recuerdo.*"

"Right. Don't pull that high school Spanish on me. You *do* remember, mister. Thanks a lot for watching my back."

He dropped the paint roller into a pan, shrugged, and opened both palms. "You expect me to get in Greta's way when she's doing God's work?"

I threw my head back and scoffed. "Don't bring God into this!"

Greta gave her stomach several *there-there* pats. Her face had begun turning a darker shade. "I'm sorry I upset you, Callie. It just felt like a divine appointment to me. What were the chances of running into Suzanna at the same store two times in a row? I haven't gone to a paint store in years, then all of a sudden I'm in there twice and meet a woman whose brother speaks your language. He's single and you're single so . . ."

"So you figured you'd meddle." I unfolded my arms and glanced away once I became aware that tears were forming in Greta's eyes. "Listen, forget it. It was a nice thought, but be assured, Gage Mitchell would never call me, especially for anything personal. You can take that to the bank."

"Why?" Greta wasn't giving up. "Wait. Have you and he had more encounters?"

My pause swelled like Greta's belly. Silence hung for an uncomfortable beat. "Let's just say that I'm moving forward with a plan that will send him back to where he came from, and he's not too thrilled with me." I scoffed. "He even had the audacity to make fun of my group's efforts."

Bobby stepped up. Splatters of teal covered his shoes, pants, and fingers. "What's going on with that, by the way? Henry stopped by yesterday and when I casually mentioned your concern, he seemed to think the whole project was a done deal."

"How does he know?" The statement bothered me. "Does he have some inside information?"

Bobby shrugged. "Don't think so. But as you probably know, he's got a lot of friends on the new council, and from what he's heard, they're already poised to fast-track the project once the plans are completed."

Plans. Gage's plans. "Fast-track? Tell me more."

"Basically that means that once all the legalities are taken care of, development plans will be moved to the front of the stack for consideration, and if everything's in order, they'll get the stamp of approval more quickly than usual."

"But why? What's the hurry?"

Bobby picked up the roller again, dipped it in the paint, and rolled off the excess. "I really don't know, Callie. It was just a casual conversation. Henry was in to discuss my plans to expand the storage center, and Tim Kitteridge happened to be leaving after a visit to his unit. I didn't mention anything about it to him. Anyway, one thing led to another and suddenly Henry and I were talking about the Kitteridge property."

"So if I were to do a little snooping at the planning department—"

"Don't you dare. I need Henry's support to expand my business so don't let on that I've mentioned any of this to you. Wouldn't want him to think I can't be trusted with confidences."

My forehead scrunched. "So he said all this to you in confidence?"

"No, nothing like that." He stopped and sighed. "We were just shooting the breeze, but it would still look bad if he knew I was repeating our conversations."

Greta touched Bobby's arm. "Okay, you two. Either of you want a soda? All this shop talk is making me thirsty."

I turned to her. "Actually, you really should be off your feet and as far away from wet paint as possible."

"It's that healthy paint!"

"But still." I hugged her to me. "Come on, I'll go with you to the kitchen."

We left the room, but my mind lingered on the fresh news that SOS would have to work quickly to stave off the plans for the Kitteridge property.

IT WAS EITHER A double espresso or this. A severe jolt of caffeine might have been the easier route, but coffee in the evening could have an adverse effect, one that might keep him up all night and put him back on the exhaustion treadmill. So he shed his jeans, pulled on a pair of shorts, and hit the ground running.

Maybe not *running*, but he was jogging all right. The stress of the past few months had put too much time between him and exercise, and to avoid injury he'd have to start slow.

He wound through the village, over the bridge, and past the inn-dotted road that abutted the beach. A couple and their two daughters sat at a window-side table at the Red Abalone Grill eating ice cream and something panged in his chest. Suz and Jer should be living that life. Instead, they had run away from their home and the stigma that came from living with a drug-addicted, incarcerated husband and father.

He pressed on, allowing the rhythm of his cadence to lull his mind away from the intricate knot that had formed in that impossible-to-reach space between the shoulder blades of his back. He hauled in a lung-filling breath. Seagulls sailed overhead, as did the occasional mallard, and even a formation of pelicans on their afternoon snack hunt. Although he felt a slight pull running down his calves, his breathing stayed even, and not surprisingly Gage felt stronger than when he had begun.

With his second wind providing the needed energy, he charged up a brief rise in the road so enthralled with the land-scape that it had not occurred to him that once he crested that hill, he would be at the south end of the Kitteridge property. And there it was—the all-encompassing view, the rock he rested on, the man-made stairs down to the shore—all there. Not to mention, the memory of his verbal sparring with Callie yesterday.

Why did this woman he barely knew get to him so easily? His head dropped forward and he squeezed his eyes shut willing away anything that would hinder his workout.

Too late. He slowed to a pathetic jog and figured that at this point, he might as well consider it a brisk walk. He blew air from his lungs and glanced around. As the sun made its descent, so did the distraction of sound and memory. The sea had calmed, the scent from woody scrub surrounded him, and crickets had begun their night music early.

For once Gage wanted to walk this land without thinking about hindrances, to run across the expanse and consider the possibilities. True, in order to do that, he would also have to push away the snapshot in his head of preliminary drawings that showed just how thorough and far-reaching the coverage of this land would ultimately be. Still he dreamt. Progress was not evil in itself. If only he could find a way to be the bridge between the community and those who had hired him.

Heavy breathing galloped up from behind, and he spun around. A tan-colored dog with bright eyes greeted him, his pink tongue dangling out the side of his mouth. "Hey, boy. What are you doing out here all by yourself?" Gage squatted and petted the dog with one hand while grabbing his collar with the other. He fingered a makeshift tag. "Moondoggy, eh? Maybe your owner's not as hard-nosed as she acts." He rubbed Moondoggy's head and neck. "It's quite a mouthful but I like it."

Holding onto his collar, Gage craned his neck, searching for Callie. All he spotted was an elderly man in a plaid shirt and jeans hiked up to his waist. Concern furrowed his brow. He turned back and cupped Moondoggy's face, expecting to give him some reassurance before setting out to find the dog's home, only Moondoggy sprung from his grip like a kangaroo in the outback.

"Wait!" He forgot about the gentle strain in his calves and tore off after the dog. If it were his animal roaming the town by itself, he hoped someone would do the same for him. At least he told himself that's why he was doing this.

At the top of the hill, not far from where he'd met Callie and her new pet for the first time, Moondoggy halted like he had spotted a slab of raw beef hanging from a pine branch. Gage slowed not wanting to spook the dog again. The animal watched as Gage slowly ascended through a thick bed of dry pine needles. Then, just as he was about to take two final steps to reach the top, Moondoggy darted off again, this time back down the hill and in the direction of town.

Score: Moondoggy the mouse = one; Gage the cat = zero.

"Shoot." Gage rested his hands on his knees while gulping air and watching the dog romp along until he was a far-flung speck on the land. He moved his hands to his waist, took a few deep breaths, then hobbled back down the hill. He was not surprised to discover Moondoggy waiting for him at the edge of the property as if to say, "Just so you understand, I'm the one in charge around here."

Moondoggy stood on his hind legs and slapped his paws on Gage's midsection, scraping his long front nails down his shirt. He eyed the dog. "So you think I'm going to pet you now? After all that?" He reached out then and gave the dog a begrudging rub of his noggin. "Yes, well, let's get you home."

He didn't recognize the street name, so Gage had no choice but to follow the little guy home. Sure, he could've called Callie—his sister had given him her number for who knows what reason—but why give her fair warning of his arrival? He had her dog, and that meant he had leverage. She would have to put away her arrows and play nice.

A pang of something—guilt at the thought of watching her squirm—coiled through him.

He had barely reached the house when he heard, "Moondoggy!"

His remorse intensified when he saw her red-rimmed eyes. Callie dropped to her knees and threw her body over the pup with the wagging tail and happy jowls and hugged him. Gage stood there, trying not to look like a dork as he listened to her sniffling.

She looked up at him while still clinging to the dog. "Where was he?"

"Found him over at the Kitteridge property wanting to play. Tried catching him but he was too fast."

Her eyes showed relief. "Well, then, thanks for staying with him until he made it home."

Gage glanced at the cottage behind her. Simple structure with lime plaster exterior, frameless windows, and a meandering path of blue solar lanterns. "This your place?"

"It is."

A small plot of cannas, asters, and lilies flourished in tended soil set away from the home's foundation. A neatly formed berm surrounded the floral display. "You're into rain gardening, I see. Impressive."

A guarded look in her eyes returned. "It's not that hard."

"Some might disagree with you."

"They'd be wrong."

Of course, because everyone who has an opinion other than yours is wrong. He cleared his throat, opening his mouth to speak, but she beat him to it.

"Thanks again for bringing Moondoggy home. I don't know what I would have done—"

"Don't mention it, and I should be thanking you. He gave me the workout of my life." Gage laughed and something lifted in his heart when he saw a smile shaping Callie's lips. She had a natural beauty and might have been the first woman he'd ever met who didn't run to put on lipstick before heading outdoors. He wondered if her skin had ever seen a puff of powder or whatever it was that women used daily.

She stood and hoisted Moondoggy into her arms unbothered by the dog's weight and gangly limbs. "I've got a thing to get to. So, I'll see you, I guess." She batted thick eyelashes at him. Did she do that on purpose? He watched Callie climb the stairs of her porch, dash another look his way, then disappear inside.

Maybe, in another time, their friendship might have grown and flourished like that rain garden behind them. A beat passed as he stood on the path outside. When had he become so sappy?

CHAPTER 13

"You're late!" Ruth met me at the door of the RAG, a clipboard in her arms.

I blinked back tears. "Couldn't be helped. Moon-doggy got out and I couldn't leave until he was safe at home again." I didn't mention that my knight was the known enemy, nor that his presence at my home had caused me to reel almost as much as my dog's disappearance.

"Not to worry. I filled everybody in on the name of our group and got them all to give me their current contact info." She tapped her clipboard. "They are all ready to do what must be done."

My eyes hovered over her clipboard. Many of those I'd invited via e-mail had come. "Good. You can take notes."

Quickly it became apparent that we had doubled in size. Familiar faces of our community sat around not one table, but two, some chatting amiably, others sending waves of heat with their frowns. The scene accelerated my pulse. Was I ready for this?

Ruth pulled at the sleeve of one of the newcomers until he

hauled himself from his chair. "Eliot, I'd like you to meet the leader of our group, Callie Duflay."

He was young and sprightly, with black hair spiked at the crown, and he wore wire-rimmed glasses in an apparent attempt to age him because he could not have been more than eighteen or nineteen years old. He slipped his pen and notepad into his left hand and reached out to shake my right. "Eliot Hawl, with the press, ma'am."

"The press?" And had he just called me ma'am?

"SLO Press, covering county news. Hope you don't mind if I sit in?" He puffed out his chest. "I will have questions."

Media coverage. I had toyed with getting the papers involved eventually, but so soon? My mouth went dry like cotton and I tried to pull my thoughts together, the thoughts that had scattered about the neighborhood during my search for Moondoggy this evening. It didn't help that when I called June this morning, she cried and begged me not to share their predicament with anyone else. She calmed way down when I presented her with my plan.

Now, it was time to convince everyone else.

You're a leader, Callie, not a follower. My mother's words propelled me forward. I shook Eliot's hand. "Pleasure to meet you. Glad you could join us today."

When he and Ruth had taken their seats, I motioned for Holly. "Would you leave us a couple of coffee pots with more cream and sugar?"

The waitress with the unruly ringlets and bright smile nodded. "Will do."

I glanced about the table, making eye contact and trying to remember everyone's names. "Thank you all for coming. I see more have joined our cause, and that's great."

Eliot's hand darted up. "Are you aware that the Kitteridge project is on fast-track status with the planning department?"

Stunned. *The kid's done his homework.* If I answered him in the affirmative, I'd probably have to tell him how I knew. I kept my expression calm. "I will take questions after the meeting. Now, getting back to—"

"Once I heard what those Kitteridges were up to, I had to come!" A woman with a sharp nose and angry eyes crossed her arms in a huff.

A man across from her dumped the last of the sugar into his coffee then stirred it so roughly some of it splashed onto his place mat. "Selling to developers after all this time. I'll tell you what—that Tim better watch his step at my feed store!"

Things were flying out of hand. Somehow I needed to grab hold of the string. "Friends, please, wait. Let's not get too upset with June and Tim." I paused and pressed my lips together. "Sometimes things happen for a reason."

There. Diplomacy. Didn't have a whole lot of experience with it, but I was trying.

"So you're defending them?" Oscar, one of our local fishermen, spoke up. "We've got to be respectful of that area, Callie. The otters are coming back, but what's going to happen to them once the area begins to erode from overbuilding?" He shook his head, rattling the wire hooks hanging from his hat. "I can tell you that the quality of fish around here has already gone down from all the pollution that comes from dirty runoff. It's bad, Callie, really bad."

He was right. Yet somehow we had to strike a balance here. How in the world could I get them all to see?

Steph, our town librarian, raised her hand. "Callie, I sympathize with the Kitteridges. I thought they would never shut down their store, but when they did and the rumors about their money problems surfaced, well, I became very worried for them."

Ruth cocked an eyebrow. "What sort of money problems? That ol' dog Tim do some risky investments or something?"

I shoved my flexed palms toward the crowd. "Listen. Rather than speculate on all that . . ." Rumors had been flying for months about the Kitteridge's financial health, but it was not my place to give the specifics. I inhaled through my nose and put on a happy face. "I suggest we try something amazing and unchartered for this area. Please, hear me out."

Ruth stood and began shushing everyone, repeatedly flapping her right hand downward. Eliot crouched and snapped a picture of me from an unflattering angle. Holly breezed in to set coffee pots within arm's reach.

As the crowd grew quiet, my heart swelled with excitement. If we pulled this off, we might just have a win-win situation at our feet. I drew in a confident breath. "Okay, everyone, here's what I propose."

"WHAT IS IT?" Suz stood alongside Gage as he peered at an oversized document on his drawing board in the morning light.

"It's the survey I've been waiting for."

She bent over the document. "You, big brother, must be really smart because this thing looks like hieroglyphics to me. What are all the swirls and numbers about?"

Gage smoothed back the curled page. "They're all necessary parts of the survey, Suz. Actually, this one is actually more like a map showing natural and man-made features of the project site. It also provides exact height in feet above sea level. So what we have before us is a topographical map that encompasses all the open property at the Kitteridge property."

She eyed him. "So this will help you get going on your plan, then."

"Right." Gage studied the survey while making mental notes for later. "It will help me lay out drainage patterns and slopes and vegetation, things like that. Then I'll use it as an underlay beneath my own site plan."

"So exciting, isn't it?"

Gage looked away from his work and met his sister's gaze. Although in the midst of personal troubles, she didn't show it. She seemed downright happy to be carried along for the ride on this project. "You're right, it is. Some people like to drive around showing off the properties that they've built; and while I don't have a problem with that, per se, I'd say that this is the thrilling part for me."

"The journey."

He swallowed, noticing a tinge of sorrow pass across her face before her smile returned. "Yeah, the journey."

Suz straightened and smoothed away the crease in her skirt. "Then get to it."

After she left, he reached for his coffee mug only to realize it had been drained. No matter. A hot-off-the-press survey gave more of an adrenaline boost than caffeine did anyway.

"I forgot to bring these in earlier." Suz dropped a couple of local newspapers on Gage's desk. She also had a coffee pot with her and filled his empty mug.

"Bless you."

She laughed. A headline caught his attention and wiped the smile off his face.

SAVE OUR SHORES:
SOS GROUP AIMS TO OUST UNWELCOME DEVELOPMENT

Gage ignored his coffee as he opted for the morning news instead.

Callie Duflay, president of Save Our Shores, has a message for waterfront developers: You're not welcome in these parts. The riveting blonde and her mighty band of angry residents met last night at the Red Abalone Grill. Aside from drinking enough coffee to finance a third-world nation, their mission was simple

—fight a project planned for the popular open land known as the Kitteridge property.

Gage set the paper down. The article's cheese factor aside, this was bad news on any day. He glanced at the survey on his desk. Especially today. His eyes followed the text to the bottom of the page, then he obeyed the directions and turned to page four.

Speaking on the condition of anonymity, an aide to one of the town council members had this warning for SOS, "It would behoove Miss Duflay to stay out of the way of progress. The council is comprised of upstanding citizens within our own community, and I assure you, they all have the best interests of Otter Bay at heart."

Yes, sure, that would make her run away, cowering. He read on, noting the brief profile written about Callie and highlighting her many humanitarian efforts. Apparently she even sponsored children in other countries. He grunted and skipped to the last paragraph.

Only time will tell if SOS will heed such advice. As of now, the group is moving forward with a plan to buy the property from under the developers. They are about to embark on an aggressive fund-raising campaign, one that will help them achieve their goal of making the Kitteridge property open to the community—forever.

Gage crumpled the newsprint with one hand. This must have been the "thing" she had to get to last night. She hadn't let on either. No, not a word about her plans to him—even after he saved her dog from certain danger. He reached for the warm coffee and took a bitter sip. Maybe if he had not chased that animal home, she would not have made it to her little gathering in the first place.

"What's got you?" Suz wore concern on her face. "Two minutes ago you were like a giddy eight-year-old, but now your upper lip is all twisted up."

"Bad news about the Kitteridge property."

"What? Already? You were just telling me . . ."

He pressed his thumbs to his temples and raked his fingers through his hair noting how much he needed a haircut. He motioned to the newspaper. "That woman you met at the paint store—Callie—remember her? She's heading up some group that's trying to thwart the project."

Suz's forehead crinkled. "Let me see that." She smoothed the paper and her eyes tracked the article. Gage tried to interject a comment, but each time she would stop him with a flick of her forefinger and a "shush." She made it to the end, inhaled, then handed the paper back. "I don't know much, but if there's one thing I do understand it's that people are broke and you can't squeeze money out of a dried up turnip. I think she's bluffing. There's no way this small town can come up with that kind of money that fast. Take it from one who knows, money's hard to get and even harder to raise from others."

He glanced at her sister. She wore her life lessons with fierceness, and for once in a long while he recognized her for the strong woman she had become. "So I should just forget about it, then? Is that your advice?"

She shrugged. "Of course not. When this thing crumbles, Callie's going to need some broad shoulders to lean on, and you'll be there."

"You can't be serious."

"I absolutely am. Dead-on serious, big brother."

He sputtered. He had no idea if he'd ever be able to say two words to the woman after this, let alone be a source of support. "That woman is a thorn in my side, or haven't you noticed?"

Suz laughed. "She keeps you alert. That's good."

"Or exposes my need for a tetanus shot!" He tossed the paper into the waste can.

His sister sighed. "Don't you get it? You need to get that girl on *your* side. Listen to her concerns, open the communication between you two, and when things fall apart, she won't see you as the enemy anymore."

"Oh, really. She'll just see me as the great guy that I am." He smirked, followed by a sigh. "And why would I even want to do this, Suz? Why should I care?"

Suz's gaze slid downward. "I missed out on the perfect guy, Gage. All because I was afraid of a little work. Good relationships take work, but I wanted things easy. Seth asked me to move across the country with him as he searched out a new life." She wrinkled her nose, pausing. "But I wanted to stick around with my friends and keep hanging out on Saturday nights. I wanted all the trinkets that money could buy, but I didn't want to wait around for Seth to find the perfect job and to build up his savings. So I let him go." Tears spiked her lashes. "When Len showed up and said all the right things—bought all the right things—I made a hasty, shallow decision and married him. And you know what's funny?"

He couldn't imagine.

"I ended up moving all the way across country anyway." The smile on her face didn't reach her eyes. "Isn't that a riot?"

Gage reached for her hand. "You've got Jer."

Suz sniffed and wiped away a tear with the back of her hand. "That's right. God's way of reminding me there is always a silver lining." Her eyes connected with Gage's. "I can't say if Callie's the one for you, Gage. But I do know that you've run into her more than once lately, and every time you do you come back looking like some lost puppy."

"You been spying on me?"

"It's a small town." She nudged him before slowly making her way to the office door. "So why don't you give her a call?"

Gage sat in the silence, thinking on the advice Suz had offered. It sounded crazy, ludicrous.

He picked up the phone and dialed.

CHAPTER 14

"Greetings, Madam President!" Tidal Wave plopped a soggy triangle of pizza onto a flimsy plate and pushed it toward me.

Starved, I picked up the plate. Grease slid across my palm. "Really, TW, you can just call me President Callie."

"Hee, hee." Tidal Wave's chin bounced when he laughed, forcing evening stubble through the folds. "Saw your picture in the paper."

I nodded. Those were the same words Gage used when he surprised me with a phone call today. I had no idea just how many people in town kept up with the local news. By the number of times I'd been stopped on my walks, you'd think it was everyone. "That was me. Could've been a better angle, don't you agree?"

He blushed and kept his focus on slicing the monstrous pizza before him. "I cut it out and put it on my fridge."

I punched his solid shoulder. "Oh, you did not!"

He looked at me stunned, eyes wide, unsmiling mouth. My gut felt hollow. Did Tidal Wave have a little crush? A pause, and then he roared, a garble of laughter falling from him. "Just having some fun with you."

His was no longer the only red face in the room. I directed the most even look into his eyes; the most serious tone into my voice that I could muster. "I'll have a second piece."

His eyebrows shot up and he hesitated and bit his lip before quickly scooping up another drippy slice and plopping it onto my plate. "Yes, ma'am."

He didn't see the sly smile on my face as I walked away and headed to Squid and a gathering of board members at a nearby table.

"Hello, Callie." Natalia had shed her woman-in-the-board-room look for more casual low heels, capris, and a button-down blouse. "I've been reading about you. You have been a busy lady."

My mind hesitated. Did I need more opposition in my life? True she appeared welcoming, but then again, Gage sounded congenial on the phone today too. Suspicion rose in me then, and it reared itself again now. While I wished to find another table, I relented and took a seat across from Natalia. "It's been a whirl-wind already. So far, there's been positive support in the community."

"But will that support translate into dollars?"

"I'm hopeful that it will. One of our SOS team members set up that Web page mentioned in the article, and already several thousand dollars in pledges have come in."

"Impressive!" She tasted a bite of the salad in front of her, obviously brought in from the outside, and then set down her fork before turning to Squid. "Maybe Callie should become part of our fund-raising team here at camp. We could use someone with fund-raising knowledge on future campaigns."

Squid downed a cola and shrugged. He glanced my way. "Yeah. Maybe."

I smiled. If she wanted to pump me up in front of Squid, I wouldn't stand in her way. "Thanks for the boost of confidence,

Natalia. Right now is not the best time, but I would certainly love to share all I learn with the camp board. This place means a lot to me."

"Thank you, Callie. I can see that."

That was probably the most civil, uncomplicated conversation that Natalia and I have ever had. One newspaper article and, like others in the community, Natalia seems to have developed an appreciation for my contributions. Squid, however, seemed more contemplative than usual.

Natalia wiped her fingers with a napkin. "Would you like to start the meeting, Thomas? Everyone appears to be here now."

Squid rose from the table. The faint lines at his eyes appeared deeper than usual. "Evening, everyone. Thanks for stopping by tonight. As you know I've been mulling over ways to make our weekend camps more viable for the kids. But before I get to that, we've got some quick business to discuss."

Squid seemed preoccupied tonight. His eyes flitted about rather than conveying the directness that those of us who worked with him were used to seeing. He cleared his throat. "Camp's busier than ever. We get calls every day with new registrations, but unfortunately we've had to turn away some great people."

Luz piped up. "Not always."

I slouched in my chair. *Really, Luz? Must my blunder of last weekend be brought up now? In front of both board and staff?*

"There have been few exceptions." Squid's mouth lay flat. "The board and I have been discussing the possibility of building more cabins. The problem is we use every square inch of our outdoor space already, plus we'd need to raise funds before we could even begin."

Natalia smiled, giving me a nod. You'd think this would make me feel honored and maybe even important. Instead, the idea of tackling anything larger than what I've already proposed to SOS boggled me.

Ted, one of the board members, held up a bent forefinger. "I have an idea, Tom. What about two-story cabins? More kids, yet we keep the same footprint."

Natalia leaned back in her chair, arms folded. "Too costly. That and we would probably have the fire chief after us all season. Also, I think there may even be a rule against younger children sleeping on the second floor."

Luz grimaced, elbow on table, and chin in hand. "So if we don't have just the right mix of kids, we could still find ourselves with too many campers and not enough beds. Great."

Squid fidgeted with his beard. I couldn't recall seeing him do that before. He rolled his shoulders back from their slumped position and raised his hand. "Maybe we're getting ahead of ourselves, eh? All of this is food for thought at the moment. We obviously can't do anything about this right away, but we will be looking thoroughly at all ideas. If anyone comes up with the miracle solution, you can call me or Natalia." He clasped his hands. "Moving on."

For the next five minutes or so Squid proceeded to work through a boring checklist of maintenance items that needed fixing. Normally Squid ran meetings the way he ran a night camp gathering for two hundred kids. He'd spiral footballs into the crowd and tell some groan-worthy jokes then follow up by using his megaphone for effect. Tonight, however, my former crush was off his game.

My mind wandered. Maybe I only imagined Squid's perplexing state. The past day and a half carried with it the low of nearly losing my dog (and having to humble myself, tear-stained cheeks and all, before Gage), and the incredible high from the huge community support for the Kitteridge property acquisition, complete with a media plug and name recognition. Not to mention that rather confusing phone call from Gage.

"I realize that we're on opposite sides of the court, Callie," he had told me. "But I'm not going to try to convince you to stop your fight. If you ever have any questions about my plans for this project, you just ask. Will you do that?"

I didn't know whether to pitch my phone across the room or present him with a lengthy list of questions, the answers of which would give me ammunition to up the fight. Could I do that to another person? Take what they freely gave and then turn it against them? Or maybe that was exactly what Gage Mitchell surmised: that my conscience would not allow me to use someone that way.

He was a crafty one, all right.

Squid stroked his beard again and the motion yanked me back into the meeting. He had made it to the bottom of his list and I couldn't recall a thing that had been on it. I set aside my plate and focused on him.

"Getting back to our campers, there's always the danger that their experience with us will be the high." He gestured to the airspace above him. "But we're not about mountaintop experiences that have nowhere to go but down. Are you tracking with me here?"

The room fell silent. Squid dropped his gaze to the floor, his eyes shut. When he lifted his head, his eyes were sharp, focused. "It's about giving them an experience that is so real, so vibrant, that they'll go home changed. Different. My hope is that people around them will want to know what they've been up to. Not what camp they attended, not the name of their counselor, but what happened *inside* them that has changed them for the better."

He spoke with deliberateness and passion. "At the same time, I don't want the message to get so convoluted that they can't even begin to live it. Does that make sense?"

I spoke out in the quiet room. "I think so. You want them to understand the essence of faith."

Squid cast his attention toward me. "And that is?"

As a person of faith, I knew this one by heart. "To serve God, of course. To live for him."

Squid watched me. "Exactly. Yet how can they do that if they don't understand how to hear his voice?" He stared at me for a beat longer than felt comfortable. Had he heard my middle-of-the-night confession to the girls in my cabin? I had admitted to them my struggles, yet had not spent one minute sorting them out for myself.

Ted cleared his throat and raised a finger again, offering his own take on what direction he thought the message could go, and I sat back, trying to rein in my buzzing thoughts. One thing I knew, I had better think of a way to work faith into my plans.

GAGE CRACKED HIS NECK. First the left side, then the right. He winced and rolled his shoulders, but it did nothing for him other than accentuate his fatigue. With a few clicks, he shut down his computer and waited for it to power down.

Suz had asked him to work late tonight, fixated on painting his entire living room. She had planned to put Jeremiah to bed early, then finish up what she'd started earlier in the day. He shut his eyes, remembering the first week she and Jer had spent with him. She had found some leftover paint in his shed, paint he had used in his former house and didn't want to part with. While he was away at work one day, she painted his bathroom a rich shade of Chocolate Loam.

Initially, he reacted with a tinge of shock and a lot of apprehension. He had his own ideas of what he would like to do with his home once he had the time—and the resources. But Suz's eye for design and the meticulousness of her work won him over. Vaguely he remembered their mother saying Suz had artistic ability, but for all he knew at the time, it was nothing more than motherly bragging. He knew better now.

Although he had the utmost confidence in his sister's skill and designer eye, he was tired. Gage hoped she had all the time she needed to accomplish her goal for the day. He yawned, picked up his office phone, and dialed home.

Suz answered on the fourth ring. "Hey."

He sat back against his chair. "How's the painting coming along?"

"I'm in the homestretch." Her voice was breathless, as if rolling paint onto walls as she spoke. "Because of all that sun we get, the first coat dried enough for me to add another."

He shoved two soft pencils into his desk drawer and slid it shut. "Great. Can't wait to see your handiwork."

"Oh, but don't come home yet. I have a surprise and don't want you to see it until I'm finished. Okay?"

He stifled a sigh, and stretched his forehead in an attempt to hold his eyes open. "Well . . ."

"Stop at the RAG and have something to eat. I bet you haven't eaten all evening." She paused. "I'm right, aren't I?"

He chuckled. "You're such a mom."

"Of course I am. Why are you laughing?"

"Not laughing at you. It's just new to me, that's all." He glanced at the clock on his credenza and grimaced. "I guess I could use some dinner."

"Great! Chew slowly and I'll try to have this done and the place all cleaned up before you get home. See you."

She clicked off. He grabbed his coat and slipped out the door, the rumbling in his stomach holding at bay his other pressing need—to crawl into bed. When he arrived at the RAG, much of the patronage consisted of teenagers gazing at each other and the occasional, solitary diner. The hostess, Mimi, doubled as a waitress. She led him to a table against the window and took his drink order. Coffee. Black. Decaf.

She delivered it in seconds along with a kind smile. "You're in late tonight."

He smiled up at her. "Hunger knows no schedule."

She cackled. Mimi looked to be in her late forties. She leaned against the booth opposite him. "I've seen you here several times. New in Otter Bay?"

He sipped the coffee and nodded. "I am. Gage Mitchell. Glad to formally meet you, Mimi."

"Same here. Most everyone comes in here if they're in this town any length of time. I've been working for old Peg since my oldest was in diapers."

"Really? How many children?"

"Four. All of them girls. I love 'em to death, but all those hormones in one house gets more than I can handle sometimes. Work is a blessing."

He threw his head back, grateful for a hearty laugh. "I guess so."

Mimi glanced across the diner as a bell jingled announcing another diner had entered the place. She smacked him on the rotator cuff. "Now don't be getting the wrong idea about women from me. You fellas need us just as much as we need you!"

She laughed and Gage followed suit. He gave her an "I hear you" nod as she motioned with a flapping hand for someone to join them. Apparently his table was the designated gathering spot for the evening.

He held the mug in his hands and glanced over his shoulder. Callie approached. For someone who had sounded strained and suspicious during their five-minute phone call this morning, she sure had a nice smile on her face. Then he understood. She had no idea who sat in the booth next to where Mimi stood.

"There's the girl of the hour," Mimi called out and turning her back to him. "I heard you were in the paper this morning, Callie."

"Yes, yes. Lot's going on."

"Well, now, I haven't had a moment to read it myself, but it sure seems like a big project to handle." Mimi rocked side to side when she talked, the bow of her apron rustling against his booth. "Are you sure this is what you want to do?"

Discomfort crept through him. He felt like he was eavesdropping even though the women stood not two feet from him on the other side of Mimi.

Callie spoke. "I'm doing this for all of us."

"Oh!" Mimi jumped to one side, exposing his presence. "Where are my manners? Callie, this is Gage Mitchell. He's new in town. And Gage—"

He didn't bother putting out a hand, but offered a friendly smile, albeit somewhat forced. "We've met. Hello, Callie."

Mimi bubbled. "How nice that you two know each other, what with him being new in town and you being a lifelong resident." She reached over the table behind Gage and snatched a menu from the two teens who seemed to have eyes only for each other. "Here's another menu. I supposed you'd like to sit together."

He had decided to help Callie out, one last time. "No, I don't—"

Callie plucked the menu from Mimi's hand. "Sure. That would be fine. Thanks, Mimi."

Mimi spun away still chattering. "I'll come right on back with a hot pot. It'll be just a second or two."

Callie slid into the seat across from Gage, a blend of tired and pretty all rolled into one exasperating woman. He continued to cradle his mug, searching for something to add to the phone conversation that went nowhere this morning.

He needn't have bothered because Callie had a lot on her mind.

"I don't know what that phone call was all about this morning, or what kind of tricks you have up your sleeve, Mr. Mitchell, but I'm not leaving here until we understand each other. Completely."

He took one last, slow sip, set down his mug, and realized his appetite had vanished.

CHAPTER 15

*G*age needed to understand that I was no damsel in distress. Nor was I naive. On the contrary, I wondered just how much he knew about the Kitteridge's dire predicament and how that knowledge might be driving his own actions. Of course, I couldn't ask, because that would be betraying June's confidence. While his phone call from this morning may have caused me to wobble momentarily, I had been ruminating about it all day, and my suspicions had mushroomed.

Now as we sat with this table as a dividing line between us, I hoped to see on his face what I could not hear over the phone: his hidden agenda.

He set his coffee down and clasped his hands on the table. "As far as I'm concerned, my meaning was completely clear. But if you did not understand it, then I apologize for that."

I ignored his sarcasm. "People don't just call up their enemies and offer to help them. Did you really think I'd fall for that?" I stopped him with a raised palm. "Wait. Let me answer that. No. I would not."

Although his lips remained in a flat line, it looked like he was hiding a smile. Faint crow's-feet appeared.

I watched him through narrowed eyes. "Did you have something to add?"

He shook his head, but the smile in his eyes remained.

I gripped the table and slid from the booth. "This is a waste of time. You're just laughing about this."

"You've got me wrong. Completely." All trace of the smile vanished. Gage hung his head and moved it side to side, exposing waves of sun-streaked hair. With his tanned skin and untamed locks, Gage could pass for a surfer, if surfers wore Dockers and collars, that is. He raised his head. "I would never laugh at you."

I glanced away, suddenly fascinated with the classic yellow and red bottles at the far edge of our table. My heart pounded and I wanted to send it to bed without its supper. This made no sense. *He* made no sense.

His eyes captured mine and didn't waver. A golden shadow framed his lips and trailed down his chin. "Let's just lay it out on the line here, Callie. Can we do that?"

He sounded sincere. My mouth had gone dry. Annoyingly dry. But I managed to croak out, "Sure." I slid back into the booth.

Gage unhooked his hands and stroked the speckled design of the Formica tabletop with his fingertips. "I feel for you and for this community. Like you, I've begun to appreciate the land in question. I've spent time on it, watched the sea life, felt the bones of it, if you will." He sighed and lifted his head. Those eyes again. "It's a magnificent place."

My shoulders relaxed. "So you understand."

"To a point." Gage sat up straighter. "I've got a new business to run and this is, quite frankly, our first big project."

My forehead lifted. "You're a new architect?"

Gage shook his head. "No, not at all. I've worked under some of the best. I've learned what I like, and what I don't care for in this business, and this is one of the reasons I chose to open my own firm." He continued to stroke his fingers across the table surface. "I'm a big believer in divine appointments. Something tells me you feel that way too."

I hesitated. That seemed rather forward, even for him. "I do."

"That's exactly how I felt when this project fell into my lap. I have wanted to open my own eco-firm for months, but just needed a push or maybe more like a harsh shove." A closed mouth smile lit up his face, those eyes. He clasped his hands again. "I wasn't even sure where to settle. That's one reason why, when this opportunity arose, I embraced it."

"Why are you telling me all this?"

"Because I can see that you are a reasonable person. You know what it's like to pursue things that are meaningful to you. That newspaper article sure listed a lot of them. For instance, all those children you support . . . did the reporter get that number right?"

I stifled a sigh. Supporting children through Compassion International was a pet cause, but Eliot surprised me when he asked how many and I blurted out the truth: five kids. Even most of my family didn't know about them. "He did, but I shouldn't have admitted that to him. It isn't right to put myself on a pedestal. Anyone would—"

"Do the same thing? Hardly. No, I'd say that shelling out enough to feed and educate five children each month is not something ordinary people do."

"The Von Trapps did it—and then some."

Silence, followed by a burst of laughter, flowed from Gage. "You got me there." He continued to laugh. "Good one."

As his laughter dissipated, Mimi showed up with an expectant look on her face. I fidgeted with the menu, even though I knew everything listed on it. "Just a cup of your chicken soup tonight."

Her brows, painted a shade too light, rose and pulled together. "Well, I hope you're not feeling sick." She laid the oily back of her hand to my forehead. "Nope, you're cool as a cuke. And for you, Gage?"

He handed the menu to Mimi without looking at it. "Turkey burger, medium rare, mustard only, and a green chili on top."

"Some gal just ordered the same thing not more than a couple of days ago. Must be a trend." She stuffed her notepad into a pocket and jetted to the next table.

Gage peered at me, a remnant of his laughter still warming his face. "Comfort food all around then, eh?"

"Yes, but not in a good way." I sighed. "Just came back in from a meeting at camp where I work. Collected enough grease from the pizza to fuel my car."

"Hmm. Not good."

Silence draped itself over us. And over me, fatigue, the kind that sneaks up on you after adrenaline courses through the body, much like a rushing river does along a mountainous pass, carving new grooves into the earth until it sputters dry. Without thinking, I shut my eyes and dropped my head forward to stretch my neck then rolled my chin all the way around. My eyes popped open to find Gage watching me. "Sorry."

He waved away my apology. "I'm with you. If Suz hadn't decorated my house with drop cloths and ordered me to stay away, I too would be asleep by now." He held up his coffee mug and winked at Mimi who zipped over with a hot pot. He took a fresh sip. "But then again, I can't complain. I intimated this before, but I received more confirmation that this move was the right one when just after I arrived, my sis and nephew showed up needing a home."

"May I ask? When we met, Suzanna seemed, I don't know, distracted maybe? Like she had a lot on her mind but didn't want to share it. Just a sense I got."

"You're right. Things have been rough for her and Jer. I probably should let her be the one to tell you about it; you were the first person in town to reach out to her. Despite our differences, that meant a lot, Callie. A whole lot."

"Thanks." His compliment threw me again. Second time today

that Gage Mitchell had something surprising to say to me. My stomach churned. Was it hunger for real food, or an emotional stew of conflict brewing in my gut?

"All I'm trying to say here is that I believe God led me here to this job so I could provide the home that my sister and nephew need. I have no doubt in my mind about that. So I'm sorry if you thought I had some kind of trick up my sleeve." He smiled at me while folding his arms onto the table and leaning toward me. "But being hated just isn't on my to-do list. If truth be told, the only trick I could be accused of was trying to help you see that I'm not the ogre you think I am."

"And that maybe when I figured that out, I'd drop the SOS project?"

He shrugged. "Guess that was naiveté on my part, wasn't it?"

His face held a more rueful look now, although his eyes glimmered. Part of me wanted this whole thing to go away, but it wouldn't, so neither would I. There was too much at stake for the Kitteridges, the community, even for myself. I shrugged. "Sorry."

Mimi served me a steaming cup of soup and packet of crackers, and slid Gage's burger concoction in front of him. "Water?"

We both nodded.

"Right up." She scampered to the kitchen.

Gage picked up a fry. "My offer still stands. Even though you may reject me, I'd still like to give you an insider's glimpse into what I have in mind for the property."

I swallowed a spoonful of soup. It tasted bland. "I'm not rejecting you, just your work."

He raised an eyebrow.

I put down my spoon. "Don't get all artiste on me. I know all about the reject-my-art-and-you-wound-me theory."

He bit into his burger, then wiped his mouth with a napkin. "So you don't buy it?"

I shrugged, two palms up. "Whatever floats your boat."

"My sister might challenge you on that. She's the true artist in our family, and I'm only beginning to see how much art means to her."

"Yes. That's right, the painting."

"Not just any painting, but freehand art, applied directly to my walls. She made the bathroom a masterpiece in one day with a giant sunburst. Knocked my socks off."

I smiled. "Really."

"Well, no, not *really*, but it surprised me. She and I have a lot of years between us—"

"I've noticed."

Gage dropped his burger onto his plate and sat back, eyeing me. "Oh have you now? How subtle of you to say so."

Nimbly, I took another sip of soup, the second helping better than the first. "Anyone who knows me understands how little I care about age. That was my attempt at humor, but I apparently need work on delivery."

"Not necessarily. That Von Trapp line was good."

I glanced at the ceiling before looking back at Gage, unable to hide the glint that had formed in my eyes. "This is true."

Laughter erupted at our table as Mimi appeared with two glasses of ice water with slices of lemon floating on top. "Dang, I missed the joke." She winked at me. "Now see what breaking bread together can do for relationships?"

She sped off and I allowed the afterglow of laughter to keep my spirit buoyed. I tried not to think about how the fight ahead might affect the friendship with Gage that, despite my every attempt to avoid, continued to bud. Instead, I searched my mind for some common ground—other than the obvious.

A lightbulb switched on inside my head. "Do you think Suzanna might be interested in doing some painting for me . . . as a job?"

Gage's right eyebrow arched and he paused, as if considering the idea. "I think she would love that."

I pulled my gaze away from that highly-arched brow of his.

"All this talk about painting has made me long for some fresh color in my cottage, but I just don't have the time to tackle that. I'd love it if she would consider working for me." I didn't tell him that depending on how she did there could result in more work for her at the camp. "Let me give you my number—"

"She has it."

"Oh. Right."

A moment passed and Gage raised his glass. "To finally finding something we can agree on."

I raised my own glass and clinked it with his. "Here, here. To common ground."

ELVIS HAD NOTHING ON him, for as Gage drove the windy road to his quaint home near the shore, the lyrics of "All Shook Up" assailed his mind until he wished he could push a button and force the voice in his head to be silent. His daily thoughts about Callie and her righteous anger and cause-fighting spirit had turned tonight into something altogether new and fresh. Frightening, even.

Part of him welcomed the change. He wasn't immune to the hope that someday he might find a relationship worth sacrificing everything for, a woman whose body and heart would replace his round-the-clock consumption of work with a passion of another kind. Lack of enthusiasm from either side of the equation, however, would kill a bond in its infancy.

This is what shook him to his middle. Gage fought the stirrings within himself, almost wishing them away. He realized that it would do no good to allow himself to fan the flames of ardor only to have them doused by a gully-washer of a rainstorm. And yet desire had sprung up from some dormant place, and at the moment he was doing nothing to bat it away.

The front porch light welcomed Gage as he turned into the drive. Although the front bedroom was dark, a glow shone from the living room, a sign that Suz's artistic ambition had yet to wane for the night. Youth. Sometimes he felt much older than his thirty-five years. At the same time, some of Suz's zest for life had found its way beneath his skin and pumped the equivalent of fresh oxygen into his veins. Worries that may have buried a more cynical man had failed to throw him into despair.

Before he could slip his key into the lock, Suz flung the door wide open. "Hey, you're home!"

"I am."

Her hair ribbon had failed in its duties because uncombed strands sprung up every which way. And while an apron may have saved her clothing, finger-width smudges of paint swept across her cheeks, chin, and nose. Her almond eyes peeked from beneath unruly bangs reminding him of Jeremiah after a day at preschool.

She halted and tilted her head to one side. "What's up with you?"

Gage shut the door behind him. "Nothing much. Tired, but that's all."

"Right." She squinted at him. "You have a goofy look on your face. You got a secret?"

Astute question. If keeping feelings tucked away where they could not do damage meant he had a secret, then he supposed he would have to lie. "C'mon. Show me why you kicked me out of my own house."

She surveyed him warily but relented and lifted one lovely hand into the air à la Vanna White. "You like?"

His gaze riveted to the room. The giant sunburst that Suz had painted on his bathroom wall had surprised him. If she had told him about it ahead of time, he might have discouraged her and guided her toward a more masculine image. When he saw it, however, he was awed and glad he had not said a thing beforehand.

Now? Similar thoughts ran through his head. "Wow. This is beyond what I imagined."

"You like it, then?"

"Beyond words."

Suz had managed to transform his white living room into a warm, elegant sanctuary. The walls no longer appeared flat but uneven, textured, and layered with rich tones. "I've seen this technique before, but . . ." He turned to her. "How did you learn to do this? It looks like plaster but it's—"

"Paint! I know. It's a Tuscan technique, or at least a method that makes it *look* Italian." She took a breath; her smile dimmed slightly. "Probably the only other good thing to come out of my marriage."

"It's stunning. And the trompe l'oeil?"

"That I learned on six months' worth of Saturdays at the rec center. I'm glad you like it because I hadn't time to sketch it out before putting it up there."

"Freehand?"

"Of course."

He shook his head, smiling. "Thanks for all the effort. It's classic and beautiful." He paused. "You know, you could make money doing this."

"What? This?"

He laughed. "Of course you could. It would probably be a lot more fun for you than hanging around my dull office all day." He didn't have to tell her that her income would skyrocket with a career change. *Any* career change. Until the Kitteridge project got completely off the ground and he began finding smaller in-between jobs, money would be tight.

"But don't you need me?"

Her face sent him back in time. She still could pout like the very little sister. "I'll always need you, kid, but I'll make do."

She thought a moment. "Then I'd like to try. If you really don't mind."

"Actually, I'm glad you said so. I mentioned your work to Callie, as a matter-of-fact, and she expressed interest in hiring you." He deliberately worked to make his voice sound even and nonchalant.

Suz's eyes popped open wide. "You ran into her tonight! You did. I can tell."

He slipped one hand into his pocket and glanced around the room, as if continuing to admire his sister's handiwork. "Yes, she happened to stop by the diner tonight and we talked." Gage turned his focus on Suz. "About you."

She blew a raspberry. "Right. You want me to believe that I was the main topic of conversation between the two best looking, single people in town. I'm not daft."

He threw his head back, laughter barreling from him. "You are too much."

She poked his shoulder with a paint-encrusted finger. "And you, my brother, are in denial."

He gave her a mock glare. "Are you interested in the job or not?"

"I'm more interested in that look on your face every time you run into her." She paused and when he did not react, she let out a sigh that threatened to awaken Jeremiah. "All right, yes. I'm interested. Guess I should give her a call, unless of course, you'd like to make it for me?"

He tried not to laugh at the sneaky grin lighting up her face. He rolled his eyes. She made him feel young with this high school style banter.

She slapped him on the upper arm. "Fine. I'll call."

Much like a teenage boy with his heart hung out for a wrenching, Gage's spirit lifted at the thought of his sister working closely with Callie. Strangely, it threatened to plunge at the very same thought.

CHAPTER 16

"Why don't you ever answer your phone?" My sister Sheila's voice in my ear at half past eleven at night startled me. "I've been calling all evening!"

"I'm here now." I tossed my keys onto the table and slid into a chair as Moondoggy danced around me like a starved animal. "What did you want to talk to me about?"

"I saw the article, Callie. *Everyone* saw it. Well, I would have seen it if I had the luxury of time in the morning—like certain people."

Pow. Punch number one.

She continued. "I didn't need to read it anyway. That article was all *anyone* wanted to talk about. I could not shop or bank or pick up children without someone, somewhere stopping me to discuss the SOS campaign."

I bent to pet Moondoggy and he nudged my face with his wet snout. I returned the favor with a quick back-of-the-ears massage while balancing the phone between my own ear and right shoulder. "I'm so glad to hear that. We need all the support we can to make this happen."

"You're serious."

"Of course. Did you expect anything less?" I said this knowing she probably did. Sheila always seemed to have an opinion about how I spent my time. She never got past the fact that I had moved beyond baby-of-the-family status into full-fledged adulthood.

"Callie, this isn't a bake sale to raise money for kids in Africa; this is a war you are embarking on. People with money and a lust for developing prime land do not lay down their weapons at the first sign of retaliation. They turn up the heat."

"Who cares?" Moondoggy sat, so I flipped through the stack of mail on my kitchen table.

"And have you thought at all about how dragging the family name through the mud will affect our parents and your siblings?"

Pow. Punch number two.

It was always about her or them. My sister had been annoyed with me since I was two and refused to allow her to dress me in chiffon. Oil and water. That's how we'd always been. She broke in to my meanderings. "I don't think you're even listening to me."

"On the contrary, I heard everything you said and I'm disregarding it." I gave Moondoggy one more long stroke of my hand along his back, thankful for the friendly face that greeted me at the end of the day. "Sheila, you are the only soul in this town who seems to have a problem with me and/ or this project." I stuffed down the vague memory of Squid's skepticism. "Even the architect and I have talked and he's not standing in our way."

Sheila snickered. "Well, of course not, Callie. He's no dummy. He knows you don't stand a chance of winning against his client, so why would he want to burn a bridge? There's no doubt I'm right about that, and if you tell me he's single and handsome, then I'll *know* I'm right."

Pow. Punch number three. Only this one hurt. It may have even done some damage. I watched as Moondoggy scampered away. The adrenaline that gave me the boost to drive home withered and disappeared. She was right, of course. Gage and I may have called a truce, his sister Suz may freshen up these walls and paint me something fabulous, but in the end, my new architect friend hoped—probably even prayed—that I would fail.

"Can I ask you a question, Sheila?"

"You may."

"When all these people you talk about—the ones who approached you on the street about the newspaper article—when they mentioned my work with SOS, well . . ."

"Spit it out."

"Did they sound unhappy? Were they upset about the community raising funds to buy the property?"

Silence.

"Sheila? Did I lose you?"

"No. I'm still here." She sighed and in my mind's eye her mouth and eyes were closed and she was breathing deeply through her nose. "If truth be told, they were surprised and excited. Every one of them."

"Well good. I'm glad to hear that." My eyes shut. "Sheila, I know you and I haven't always agreed on environmental things, but I want you to know that I understand what I'm doing. It's just so hard for me to worship God with one eye and watch while every last bit of his creation is destroyed with the other. Know what I mean?"

"Fair enough, I suppose." Sheila's voice lost its edge. I knew she felt the same, even if she didn't have it at her mind's forefront. "Let me ask you something, Callie."

"Go for it."

"Why in the world, if you have been sponsoring all those children, did you not share that with the rest of the family?"

And then I knew—the real reason for my sister's late night call. Should I tell Sheila that I had hidden certain things in my life in order to protect myself from the opinions of my older siblings? And what if she learned that Bobby and Greta knew about my children in faraway lands? I had not set out to hurt her.

"Listen, Sheila, it just never came up. Come to think of it,

Brenna and Blakey have seen their pictures when they've played in my bedroom. Hadn't they mentioned it?"

She let loose an exasperated, motherly sigh. "They are children. Of course they didn't mention it. I'm just disappointed that I had to read such important aspects of my little sister's life on the front page of the newspaper."

I frowned. "You mean the paper you didn't have a chance to read today?"

"Don't be so literal. You know what I mean."

She meant I'd snared her in a white lie and she hated that. In the long pause, I wondered what it might be like to have a big sister to share things with. Although if I tried harder . . . "Listen, Sheila—"

"It's late. Get some sleep, dear. I read that a cold snap might be blowing in this weekend, probably the last one before summer, and with all you are involved in, you will need your beauty sleep."

"Sure. Thanks. Kiss the kids for me."

We clicked off for the night and I couldn't have been more grateful.

CHAPTER 17

*T*he flurry of interviews and phone calls and canvassing had made me more tired than a camp counselor after a night hike with a hundred ten- and eleven-year-old boys. Still, with several large sponsors pledging their support—including the possibility of a large contribution from the Otter Bay Banking Association—I could smell success on the horizon.

It was Friday morning and my other duty called, the one that helped me pay my mortgage. If Moondoggy hadn't poked his nose beneath my comforter, I would have slept clear through the sunlight and my alarm and everything.

At the first sign of my eyelids lifting, Moondoggy whined and chased his tail. In dog language, I interpreted this to mean he wanted breakfast.

"C'mon. Let's eat." I padded to the kitchen, slower than usual. Why my dog would not interpret my body language and hush up was beyond me. "Okay, I'm moving." I poured kibble into his dish and gave him fresh water, but he had disappeared.

I peered around the corner. "Moondoggy?"

He whined and stood nose to door at the front of the house.

I cinched my robe tighter. "What is it?"

He didn't budge so I cracked open the door. No one there. No cat or errant bird. No one, yet when I tried to shut the door, Moondoggy threw himself against it. "Oh brother. Wait." I gave him the command we'd practiced and he stopped short so I could slip onto the porch and investigate further.

There. A white envelope stood out among the green of my rain garden. The moist air licked my bare legs as I hurried to retrieve it. Unlike the foliage dressed in dew after a foggy night, the envelope felt dry to the touch. I glanced around, but saw no one.

Back inside Moondoggy continued to act agitated. "You are one perceptive pup." My words did nothing to calm him or my own growing unease. It took some effort, but I finally coerced him to settle down and eat by hand-feeding him. He developed a one-track mind for his breakfast after that so I sunk into my couch, tore open the envelope, and read the note inside:

Leave the land alone, lady.

I turned it over. Blank. That's it? Leave the land alone? My eyes narrowed. Or what? The sparsely worded note was in pencil, written as if done hastily in a moving car. I tossed it aside and watched it flutter to the wood floor.

Coward. I figured there might be some opposition to my idea to raise funds to buy the Kitteridge property, especially from the developer with plans to denigrate the land, but perhaps I had given him too much credit. I figured that at some point I might receive a phone call or an unannounced visit to the next SOS meeting.

But this? A threatening note left in my rain garden?

My cell rang, jarring the eventful morning. I touched my chest where my heart resided, neglecting to check the number on the screen. "Hello?"

"Callie? It's Steph Hickey, from the library. Great news!"

Blood raced through my body. "Hi, Steph." I steadied my breathing. "What's your news?"

"The Friends of the Library have decided to hold a book sale the weekend after next and here's the news: all proceeds will go into the fund to save the Kitteridge property! Isn't that wonderful?"

A shaky smile found its way to my face. "That is good news, Steph. It truly is."

"And already, a man from the valley stopped in and donated a very nice collection of books to sell."

I nodded, my thoughts in a jumble. "That's great. Really great."

"I couldn't wait to tell you. Remember, the rest of the prayer team and I'll be praying! Enjoy your day, Callie. Ta-ta." She clicked off.

What might a good book sale bring in? Seventy-five, maybe eighty dollars at best? I wagged my head. I had been fielding these types of calls for the past two days, thankful that so many had gotten behind the cause. Local businesses such as The Italian Bakery, Mott's Shoes & Pearls, and Simka's Shop on Alabaster Lane had all pledged significant amounts. Just last evening, only a day after my impromptu dinner with Gage, I learned that Holly over at the Red Abalone Grill had named an all-organic, dolphin-safe salad after me: the SOS Callie.

With a huff, I retrieved the unwelcome note from the floor and stuffed it into the pocket of my robe. Moondoggy laid at my feet and I brushed his fur. I felt my eyes flash. "I refuse to be scared off by a coward, Moondoggy."

My companion only quirked his head, but somehow, I knew he understood.

"WHAT ARE YOU SCARED of?"

Suz paced in front of Gage's desk. "What if she doesn't like my painting?"

"Callie?" He leaned back in his chair, wincing slightly at the squeak. He stretched out his arms, threaded his fingers together, and cradled his neck into his open palms. "She'll love your work."

"How do you know that?"

"Because she appreciates art, and what you do qualifies. Trust me on this, okay?"

She slowed her pacing. "I'm meeting with her this week and Tori will be babysitting Jer."

"Tori Jamison?"

"You know any other Tori's?" She grimaced, flashing her eyes at him. "Sorry to be short. I'm just nervous. Yes, Tori Jamison. Her mom works at the preschool—I think I mentioned that, right?"

He chewed his lip as he thought. "And I read that her father's one of the new council members too. Busy family."

"She's a nice girl and Jer likes her, so she'll be helping me out here and there."

He released his hands, plopping them on the desk in front of him and leaning forward. "Good. If I can, I'll stop in and check on them."

Suz stopped pacing, her face filled with relief. She propped both hands on his desk. "Really? Thank you, Gage. I appreciate it."

"Go on now." He winked at her. "I've got work to do."

She hesitated, her brow knit by new concern. "You're moving forward on the Kitteridge property, aren't you?"

He nodded once. "Yes. We're in the design development stage and I'm ready to draw it up."

"Is that hard?"

"Well, I wouldn't call it hard, per se, but it is time consuming." He turned the computer screen so she could see. "This is when all those drawings you've seen me working on are fed into the computer, and we'll be able to see how far-fetched my plans might be. By the way, they won't be."

"You sound pretty confident."

He turned the computer back around and shrugged. "Never let them see you sweat."

"I see. So then what? You give it to the builder?"

"Almost, but not quite. After my client approves these plans—there's usually quite a bit of back and forth in that phase—I'll need to plot it all out to the highest degree of accuracy."

She stepped back, casually crossing her arms. "Sounds intense."

He nodded his agreement. "That it is. I probably won't be much fun in the coming days, but I will help you as much as I can."

"Do you run anymore? Swim?"

He pursed his lips. "That was random."

"With all this work you're going to need some kind of outlet to de-stress. I remember when we were kids, you would run for miles or swim at the park pool. Don't you do those things anymore?"

"Rarely. Well, I do run when I can." He thought back on the recent day when he found Callie's dog. It took deliberate strength to keep from smiling over the memory. He shoved it away. "I haven't been swimming in at least a year. Might drown if I tried now."

"Maybe you can get back into it by teaching Jer like you taught me."

"That's right, I did. Wow. How did you remember that?"

"I may have been little but I remember a lot, like what a great teacher you were—unless a bikini strolled by. You left me hanging on the side more times than I count!"

"Categorically untrue." He laughed.

She tapped her chin with a fingernail and peered at the ceiling. "Maybe I ought to rethink this idea of you teaching Jeremiah. Especially with that Callie around."

His smile faded and he rocked forward, dropping his eyes to the work on his computer screen. "No worries there."

"Why not?"

He exhaled a groan. "Don't you have work to do?"

She forced a laugh into the awkward moment. "C'mon. I'm just teasing you, though I really am serious about you finding a way to let off some of that stress. You will try, right?"

Her face held the fear that both of them knew. Their mother died from a heart attack at fifty and that fact lived somewhere behind their quest for healthy foods and protectiveness of each other. Still, Suz didn't need to keep meddling in his love life, now did she?

The phone rang and he reached for it but not before acknowledging his sister. "I will try. Promise. I have to get this." He put the phone to his ear. "Gage Mitchell."

"What do you know about this SOS group?" Redmond. His client cranked his gruffness up a notch.

He took a breath. "I know they're a serious group of locals who are opposed to development on the Kitteridge land."

"There's nothing they can do about it."

He thought about Callie and her plans, knowing Redmond was probably correct. "My understanding is that they are trying to raise enough money from the community to buy the property from the Kitteridges themselves. I agree that theirs is a tough hill to climb."

"You got that right." He swore. Twice. "This project's been moving as it should from day one. Ain't no little band of yokels going to stop it."

"Any chance of their fight slowing us down?"

"Not if I can help it."

"May I ask how far along escrow is? If they were to be able to raise enough money—"

"They won't. And don't worry about the other logistics—I've got that covered. You just get those drawings done and fast. Where are you on those plans? We have to be ready to pounce ASAP. We don't want that group to think they'll have any chance to win this fight."

Gage swallowed. "I should have something to you by the end of the week."

"Good. Do that. I'll be in touch."

They hung up and Gage fought off a swirl in his gut. Why did he sense that, despite his words to the contrary, Redmond was more worried than he let on?

CHAPTER 18

*T*welve cell phone messages. Twenty-eight e-mail messages. And a driver sped up to greet me at a stop sign on my way home from camp. After the long, hot weekend I'd just endured with two hundred kids and a laundry list of duties that left me caked with dirt and longing for a cool bath, the last thing I felt compelled to do was attend Sunday supper at Sheila's house.

After missing last week, however, I saw no way out of it. I scanned all messages, answered two of them, grabbed a shower, and headed outside. The cool breeze brought on by a descending sun wrapped around me like a soft shawl, and I embraced every minute of my walk opting to leave the cell phone at home rather than endure its penchant for interruption.

Daffodils and tulips dotted the yard around Sheila's sprawling home, but that pretty packaging did little to help me forget my sister's late night phone call. Why did I let her bother me? My parents would be here after their latest trip, and I had not seen Brenna and Blakey since our last Sunday supper together. Reasons enough to chin up.

The door swung open at my touch and I stepped inside. As

usual, the rest of the family had arrived before me and noshed on appetizers around Sheila's massive kitchen island. Thankfully that meant Bobby and Greta were here, my allies in the often-strained world of my sister's home.

As the aroma of fresh baked food made my stomach tumble. My mother kissed my cheek. "Callie, my famous daughter! I've heard all about it. My you look . . ." She knit her brow. "Do you ever eat, my child? Come, come, and have some of Sheila's feast."

"Hi, Mom." I glanced at my father who sat in a chair drinking a beer. "Hey, Dad." I gave him a peck on the cheek, his smooth-shaven skin cool to the touch. He smiled in his bland but congenial way, but said nothing.

My mother wore a scarf around her head, its colors reminiscent of an Impressionist painting. Her matching skirt swished as she moved. "Darling, we had the most fabulous time in Carmel. We visited every gallery and bakery in town and your father, the romantic devil, coerced me to walk for miles along the beach. You do know the sand is like powdered sugar, don't you?"

My father gave a guarded shake of his head, letting on that my mother, as usual, was exaggerating. In all likelihood, their walk was not much more than several yards.

"Well, you look very rested, Mom." I waved at the rest of the clan and threw my arms around Greta's neck, although it was getting tougher to do. "How's our baby today?"

Greta glanced down at her belly. "Weatherbee or Fruitashia has been keeping me up all night."

I laughed and searched out Bobby. "Keeping you up too, then?" I asked him.

He gave me a weak smile that disappeared quickly. His gaze flitted away.

Sheila swung through the kitchen, a stack of folded cloth napkins in her arms. She spied me. "Good, Callie, you're here. Take these and put them around the table."

If I weren't so startled that my usually punctual sister had yet to lay out her formal table, I might have been put off by her order. Since my hunger had been replaced by an awkward, sinking feeling in the hollow of my stomach, I was grateful for the opportunity to step away from the family, if only for a few moments.

Blakey stumbled into the room and scampered into a chair. Brenna followed close behind, tiny hands on equally miniscule hips. Her eyebrows furrowed. "We have a bone to pick with you, Auntie Callie."

I stopped. "Oh, really? What have I done?"

Blakey tipped his chin up. "Where you been, Auntie Callie? We never see you anymore."

I continued with my table setting duties. "Well, I've been working and volunteering for all sorts of things."

Blakey pumped his legs beneath him, causing him to rock on his mother's good dining room chair. "Like what?"

"Yeah, what? Mother says you're making a lot of people really angry." Brenna's face, which made me chuckle when I first saw it, turned darker. I saw her future and my heart twisted.

"She said that? Well, honey, I don't think anyone is all that angry with me. Did your mother say she was?"

"She said *other* people." Her tone sounded too sharp for a six-year-old.

I bent to face her. "You might as well learn now that you can't control what other people think about you. My philosophy is to do what I think is right and *que sera sera!*"

"K what?" Brenna's face had gone from sinister to cute and confused. That was the girl I knew.

Blakey laughed. "I think she has a friend named Sara!"

Sheila marched in and set a stack of her best china onto the buffet adjacent to her table. "Blake and Brenna, you both go get washed. Hurry." She pulled a hinged, wooden box from beneath the buffet and set it on the table. "Here's the silverware."

She left without making eye contact. I stood wondering if I

should bother setting a place for myself as the kitchen ought to be much warmer. I didn't have time to ponder this as the rest of the family trickled in and took their seats: Jim, Nancy, Vince, Mom and Dad, Greta and Bobby. Brenna and Blakey stomped to their places with Sheila pulling up the rear. The usual chatter came along with them all, but I neither jumped into the conversation nor sensed I was invited to do so.

Still I sat and joined hands with my family. After Vince said grace, Mom began to regale us with detailed descriptions of every morsel of gourmet food that she and Dad had tasted. ". . . and the lamb, braised with mint jelly, was superb . . ."

I spooned several in-season strawberries onto my plate and kept watch on Bobby, waiting to catch his eye. He and I used to pick wild strawberries behind an old lean-to shed by the camp. We never washed them and the telltale sign of red berry juice splotching our skin got us into trouble every time.

He hadn't looked at me since the meal began.

Vince spoke from the head of the table. "Maybe you ought to ask Callie." He motioned toward me with the tip of his knife.

Startled, I glanced around. "Sorry? What did I miss?"

My mother's hands froze in the air as she awaited my response. "I was just telling everyone that Carmel is filled with celebrities of all sorts, bit actors and politicians, we saw many of them." She turned and touched my father's wrist. "Didn't we, darling?"

My father nodded and touched the hand Mom had laid on his wrist.

"And I was wondering aloud what it must be like for those whose names are in the press to enjoy a breezy walk through downtown Carmel." She turned to Vince. "Are you saying that our Callie is becoming a celebrity in town?"

His shoulders rose and fell as he sliced a hunk of roast pork on his plate. "Some might think so. In a relatively short amount of time she has managed to whip up some of the town's folk into a frenzy. Listen to this, yesterday one of my clients wanted to talk more about Callie and her tenacity than his insurance policy. The guy wanted your number too, but Sheila wouldn't let me give it to him." He smiled and pushed a bite of pork into his mouth.

"Really!" Her mother clapped her hands and held them, her mouth agape.

I gasped and looked to Bobby for support. He just chewed his meal, giving me an occasional glance. "Is everything all right over there, Bobby?"

Greta patted his arm. "Poor man. Works all week, then paints all weekend."

I leaned my head to one side. "So you're tired?"

Bobby kept chewing, his eyes glaring, angry, like we were kids and I'd just eaten all the strawberries without offering him one. He swallowed his bite. "Something like that."

Jim coughed. "So, Bob, how's business?"

Bobby dropped his silverware onto Sheila's good china, its rattle sharp and reverberating.

Greta jerked. "What's wrong, honey?"

My brother glanced sideways at her, then back at me. "You couldn't just leave this one alone. Had to get involved and shake up the whole town."

I touched my fingers to my chest. "I don't understand. I thought you supported the fight for the Kitteridge property."

He rolled his eyes. "Yeah, sure, make a little noise. Get them to lower the density of their plans or dedicate a portion of it for parkland, but out-and-out purchase the property? Do you know how much money has already been invested?"

"No. Do *you?*"

The family peacemaker looked like a bull ready to charge. "I know you've been getting a lot of props lately, Callie. Some people do love what you are doing, but there are a whole lot of others out there affected by this campaign of yours. Have you thought this all out?"

"Who? You mean the developer? The architect? Future buyers of all those condos?" I glanced at Nancy who lowered her eyes.

He shook his head. "You are a brilliant woman, but you just don't understand business. Think about all the businesses in town that would benefit from a project like that." He pointed at Vince. "You could insure all those new residents."

I waved my hands. "Okay, so let me get this straight. My evil scheme to protect the Kitteridge property along the marine sanctuary from development is prohibiting local businesses from flourishing. Have I got that right?"

Greta's face paled. "I think he just means that this has happened so fast, Callie. We don't really understand all the consequences of your plan." She turned to Bobby. "Isn't that right, sweetie?"

I shook my head. "Something happened, Bobby. What is it?"

Greta's face registered surprise. She looked to me then her husband.

Sheila passed a tray of muffins. "I think I speak for all of us when I say that we've had enough of this subject for one evening. Oh, to have a Sunday supper without controversy." She fanned herself and I half expected Sheila to fall into a Gone-with-the-Wind type swoon.

Bobby crouched forward. "I'll tell you what it is, you know my chief investor, Henry? Remember him? He called this morning after reading yet another news story about the unstoppable Callie Duflay and told me quite bluntly that if SOS succeeds, he might not have a good reason to invest in phase two of my storage facility."

Greta gasped. "What? Why?"

He twisted his face toward her. "Because if our community refuses to grow, then he sees no need to continue adding storage space in town."

My shoulders drooped. "That's ridiculous and you know it,

Bobby. You are already bursting at the seams without this development. Can't he see that?"

Bobby wouldn't meet my gaze. "Who am I to challenge his reasoning? The guy makes his living investing in other people's dreams. If he thinks losing this development will have a negative impact on business, then I take notice."

My mother's strained chuckle disrupted the thickness hanging in the room. "My Callie." She fingered the string of polished red beads hanging around her neck. "You've been a mighty busy girl. All this in just two weeks?"

Sheila licked her napkin and ran it over Blakey's face. "All this talk about how this will affect local businesses brings up something I've been meaning to ask, Callie." She turned toward me, while smoothing out her napkin and dropping it into her lap. "Have you considered how this will affect the Kitteridges?"

Jim and I exchanged a glance. Careful here. It would be too easy to betray June's confidence right now. One word of the Kitteridges' troubles, however, and this conversation would be over. The sliced potatoes on my plate were getting cold, but I nibbled on them anyway, taking my time to answer. I placed my fork back onto the plate. "June and I have spoken." I felt Jim's stare. "And they are more than willing to entertain a sale to the community should we be able to raise the money." In time.

Sheila shifted her eyebrows. "Well. Then they are generous people. You are lucky." She threw up her hands and reached into a drawer beneath the buffet table behind her. "I almost forgot. One of the parents from Blakey's kindergarten class asked me to give you this." She held out an envelope. "It's a donation to SOS, but don't expect it to be for too much. They drive an old van."

I accepted the envelope from her, still aware of Bobby's palpable anger. The last thing I wanted was for his business to suffer. "Thanks."

Our mother clapped her hands. "What say we all have a toast, hmm? Go on everybody, raise your glasses." She surveyed all of us. "Now, here's to adventure—for all of us."

"Here, here." Laughter burst forth. Water glasses clanked. Cheeriness, however, eluded me until Brenna and Blakey slid from their chairs and surrounded mine. While the rest of the family started up new conversations while continuing to dine, I swiveled to get a better look at my young niece and nephew.

Blakey sat on his heels and whispered up at me. "You should take us for ice cream sometime."

Brenna nodded, her voice also a whisper. "Yeah. You should. You have been very busy lately, Auntie Callie."

I smiled. "I have, haven't I?" I brushed her bangs away from her eyelashes.

She leaned in until I could smell her pure, childlike breath. "My mom wants me to cut them but I think I should make my own decision about that. Don't you?"

I sucked in my breath, trying not to laugh. "Well your mama has your best interest in mind. Still, I think you are smart to tell her how you feel."

Brenna's large eyes implored mine, her voice still a whisper. "I won't tell her you said so 'cuz that might make her mad."

I pressed my lips together. "Fine. How about I take you for ice cream after school tomorrow?"

Blakey bobbed his head and threw a fist into the air. "Yes!"

Aside from my parents whose job it was to love me, it was nice to know I still had a few fans left in this family.

CHAPTER 19

*H*olly, rocketing by with a tray full of food, nearly ran me over as I ducked for cover after entering the RAG.

"Hey there, sorry!" she called over her shoulder.

I waved her off and righted myself. My mind had been a whirl from early this morning when I stepped outside to water my rain garden and I remembered the note I'd found over the weekend. It irked me that my brain continued to give the incident second thoughts.

In the back of the restaurant, the core leadership group of SOS had gathered to discuss the latest updates and news regarding the Kitteridge property. I hurried toward them when a voice snagged me from one of the side tables. "Callie!"

"Squid?"

He tapped a finger on his forehead, saluting me. I raised my hand in a wave and then noticed a wispy blonde sitting next to him. Her silken white hair split at her shoulders. "This is Peyton."

She waved four fingers at me.

"Hi." I cocked my head at Squid. "Thought you had already headed back to SLO for the week."

He shook his head, probably hoping I didn't notice the almost imperceptible look he sent Peyton. "I had some things to take care of up here. How about you? What brings you to this fine dining establishment?"

I glanced to the back. "A meeting with the SOS group."

His eyes lit with recognition. "Ah. Well, don't let us stop you, then." His eyes lingered a beat longer. "See you Friday?"

I smiled and shrugged. "Guess we will. Nice meeting you, Peyton."

She waved the same four fingers at me again, and I tried not to think about how young and skinny and, well, *young* she appeared.

The core group of SOS sat in the back sampling pastries and sipping coffee. I poured myself a cup and addressed them. "Thanks everyone for meeting here today. Great to see you all. I'm going to run down our list of officers and if you have something to share with the group, now would be a great time. Okay, let's start with PR. Ruth?"

Ruth stood, clipboard in her hands. Even inside, she wore her signature floppy hat. "Heavens, it has been a busy week." She turned to me. "Plan to get even busier."

The group laughed.

She continued. "Now, Eliot, with the paper, will be running a regular feature on the progress of SOS. I've given him all of your contact information as he'll be wanting to get quotes from you all. And for heaven's sake, try to make yourselves sound intelligent. No 'uhs' or 'ums' or long-winded speeches that mean nothing—you're not politicians! Think: sound bite."

Gracie raised her hand. "I don't think I understand what that is."

"It's a snippet of a statement, Gracie." Ruth sighed and looked to me. "You're an expert now. You explain it."

I sat up straight, contemplating how to put this in simple terms. "A sound bite is usually just a few words or one sentence.

The words have to be important so that newscasters and writers will replay or rewrite them over and over again."

Gracie nodded her hands folded in front of her. "Something pithy, then?"

I held back a smile. "Yes. Pithy. That's good."

"Moving on." Ruth looked at Bill. "You. How's the word of mouth going with the geezers down at the donut shop?"

"Good. Good." He bit into a peach Danish, chasing it down with a swig of coffee.

"All right then. Neta, did you get the latest report from the bank?"

"That I did! And you're going to be thrilled, just tickled." She groped around for her notebook while we waited. After retrieving it, Neta stood in silence.

"Well?" Ruth's eye had closed halfway. "Get on with it."

Neta jerked. "Oh. Sorry." She examined her notes, adjusting her reading glasses. "As of this morning, we have received $29,382.00 in pledges."

We all burst into applause. My mouth popped open. "Wow. Really? That's . . . it's fantastic. How much of that money has been received, roughly?"

Neta peered through her glasses again at the scrawling on her notepad. "Says here the bank has received a grand total of $1,200.50." She looked up. "Do you want me to read it again?"

I swallowed and shook my head. "No, but I think we'd all better impress upon people that there is a deadline. We must have cash in hand for the Kitteridges to be able to accept our offer."

"Phew, oh Callie, you're still here." Steph blew in, her cheeks flushed, her belly threatening to birth twins. "I gotta sit."

"Absolutely. Take my chair." I helped her into it. "What made you come all the way down here?"

She gaped at me. "Don't you remember? I said I'd be the head of the prayer team."

"Of course. Yes. I knew that."

"Just came by to tell y'all that we've got you covered."

Ruth bent forward. "Covered? What do you mean 'covered'?"

Steph blew out a few Lamaze-style breaths. "Covered in prayer. My team of women meets twice a week to pray about all our needs. We should meet every day—everybody seems to have so many needs. Anyway, we've been meeting and praying and listening to God and I don't know, just felt like I should be here."

Ruth batted at the gnat that crisscrossed in front of her face. "Can't imagine why."

I placed a hand on Steph's shoulder. "Thanks for coming. I'm grateful." I scanned the group. "Well, I don't know about you, but I've got much to do. I'll be working with our Webmaster this afternoon to set up ways to get the word out to the community. So if you won't mind, I'd better—"

"Wait!" Ruth held her clipboard out like a stop sign. "I forgot to mention that you're being interviewed today on the news."

"Today? What time?"

She glanced at her notes. "Down in SLO at 3:30. You'll be on around four. Meant to tell you but with you running late again and all the things I've been doing, I forgot. Here." She handed me a sheet of paper. "Here are the directions. Wear something dark and solid, so you look professional."

Television. Probably the best way to get out the message about our campaign, but I'd never been on camera; never even been in a crowd scene during a televised event. Would it be cowardly to admit how the thought of being interviewed on camera made my knees quiver?

It would and I knew it, so I glanced at Ruth. "Good job, PR Lady. I'm all over it."

Thing was, I had no idea what that entailed.

HUNGER HAD DETERRED GAGE from inputting even one more piece of data into the Computer-Aided Design software on his computer. He pulled into his drive, grateful he lived close enough to dash home and eat a late lunch or really an early dinner, still able to return to the office for another long night.

A sleek, black car, far less practical than his truck, sat in his drive.

He called in through his front door. "Hello?"

"Hi, Mr. Mitchell."

The babysitter. He had been so focused on the intensity of his work that Gage had forgotten that Suz would still be at Callie's, and Jer's babysitter would be here with him. He scooped up Jer as he ran down the hall. "Hey, buddy. This your new sitter?"

Jer bobbed his head. "She's funny."

Gage leaned against the wall while Jer bounced in his arms. "Is that right? Nice to see you again, Tori. I just stopped in to grab a bite to take back to the office with me."

"That's fine. We're just playing. Wanna go get one of your toys, Jeremiah?" She plucked Jer from his arms and scampered with him down the hallway.

Since Suz and Jer moved in, the refrigerator held more surprises than it had with just a bachelor in residence. Leftovers made the world go 'round, he always thought, probably because their mother loved to cook. That and she sold Tupperware for a time, so something could always be found burped and sealed within the many-sized containers they owned. From all the dated terra-cotta hued plastic inside their fridge, Suz had acquired much of their mother's collection.

He set an iron skillet atop the gas burner and began warming his lunch: turkey stroganoff over egg noodles. As the kitchen began to swirl with the aroma, Gage's stomach protested the long wait. He switched on the television in the living room to pass the time.

Commercials on every channel. He increased the volume and turned to check on lunch. Jeremiah's heavy steps clomped down the hall and followed him into the kitchen. His nephew clambered onto a chair. "Whatcha eatin'?"

"Your mother's stroganoff. You hungry?"

Jer pumped his head forward and back. Tori wandered in and laughed. "You eat a lot!" She looked at Gage, her eyes agog. "I already gave him a big lunch and an even bigger bowl of ice cream. And he's still hungry?"

Gage's smile grew deeper. "He's a growing boy!"

A voice wafted from the television. "Our visitor today is a young woman who is making quite a splash in her community and quite quickly, I might add."

Gage glanced at Tori. "Would you mind going and shutting off the TV? I've changed my mind about watching it."

"No prob."

The stroganoff sizzled and Gage dished up two bowls of different sizes. He called to Tori, "Would you like something to eat?"

She didn't answer so he peered through the doorway, into the living room. The young girl stared at the screen. With her hair pulled back into that ponytail, he could see the stern grit of her teeth, the furrow laced above her brow. "Tori?"

Both hands had found her hips. "This girl's got a lot of nerve."

Curious, Gage blew on Jer's food then set it in front of him. He carried his own steaming bowl with him to join Tori in front of the television. "Who is she . . . oh."

Callie sat opposite the reporter looking composed, confident, and . . . stunning.

Tori stayed focused on the screen. "My dad says she's a spoiled brat who gets whatever she wants. He says she's trying to steal some old peoples' land."

He couldn't take his eyes off Callie's face. "Why would your dad say that?"

She flicked him a backward glance and he tore his gaze from

the screen. "My dad's on the town council. He knows all about this stuff. He says if she doesn't back off, there could be trouble."

"For who? For the old folks?"

She shrugged. "Don't know. But if I were votin' age, I'd make trouble for her. Listen to the way she sits there and acts like she's doin' what everybody wants."

Newscaster: "Tell us about your cause."

Callie: "Great. Thank you. Okay, well, SOS—Save Our Shores —is a grassroots effort to save the beloved open land on the bluffs in Otter Bay. We are citizens who believe in the benefits of land being available to the community. This particular area is right next to the national marine sanctuary."

Newscaster: "And your group is concerned for the animals in that sanctuary?"

Callie: "Yes, we are. That area is particularly popular with otters, and as you are probably aware, otters were nearly extinct not too many years ago."

"See? She's just some earth-lover with an agenda."

He nearly choked on a noodle. How many teenagers talked like that? He abhorred hearing Callie's reputation defamed, especially from someone so obviously guided by a parent's opinion. Yet he knew that news coverage like this couldn't be good for his project. He still held out hope that SOS would fail, of course, but didn't like the idea that the group's fight might also present an indefinite delay for the project.

"Just *wait* until my dad hears about this."

Gage swallowed another bite. "Is your father's interest in this cause related to his work with the town council?"

"Yeah, I think so. All I know is they were all getting ready for some big project when—whoosh—in comes this lady and her harebrained ideas."

Again, how many teen girls use words like *harebrained*? "I see. And your father would be aware of this because, around here, the town council and planning commission are made up of mostly the same folks."

She wrinkled her forehead and paused, as if thinking. "Yeah, that's right. I think so."

Newscaster: "How is your cause progressing?"

Callie: "We're doing well. I learned today that pledges are pouring in from businesses and individuals alike."

Newscaster: "Congratulations are in order then!" She laughed and flipped her hair, peering into the camera. "Quite a feat in a short space of time. Before you go, Callie, why don't you tell our viewers how they can help?"

Callie: "Sure! You can find more information about us by visiting this station's Web site. SOS is fighting for the community, for our visitors, and for the otter population swimming in those waters—but we can't do it without your help! I urge you to make your donation quickly to Save Our Shores."

Tori used the remote to turn off the television. "Grrr." She used a sassy, mocking tone. "SOS is fighting for the community, for our visitors, and for the otter population swimming in those waters. C'mon, Jeremiah, let's go find something fun to play with."

Jer slid from his seat and, leaving his bowl half full, ran into the living room. "Yeah!"

Gage finished his bowl of pasta and headed back into the kitchen to wash up. Callie had poise and presence on that screen, and if it weren't for this project between them, he might have picked up the phone to tell her so. He rinsed his and Jer's bowls and shook off the excess water. As it was, if he was going to be able to stay focused on the job at hand, he had to forget about Callie and SOS for the time being.

It didn't help, however, that Jeremiah's teenage babysitter could so readily recall Callie's carefully crafted sound bite.

CHAPTER 20

*J*une's gratitude-filled voice poured through the receiver. "Callie, I phoned to tell you how beautifully you handled that television interview, dear. Is it true? Are there really that many pledges coming in?"

Pledges, yes. Actual money? Not so much. I'd pulled my car to the side of the road to use my cell phone because I couldn't remember where I had stashed my ear buds. "Yes, June, pledges are definitely coming in. And hopefully, my interview today will spur people on to really get involved." *How's that for a positive attitude?*

"Wonderful!"

I pressed my lips together, thinking. "You know, June, I'm wondering if you have thought any more about going public about your predicament with the loan." I scratched my head and glanced in my rearview mirror as trucks and cars sped by me. "I just think that if people knew what you were up against—"

"Then they would feel sorry for us."

I swallowed before speaking. "It's nothing to be ashamed of, June. Your story is one people can relate to because, well . . . who couldn't have made a better money decision at one time or another?"

"You don't understand. Timothy has been getting worse. He walks that shoreline every day, like he's saying goodbye, but every time I bring up the subject, he won't hear of it. He doesn't want our private business splattered all over the newspaper." Her voice shook. "Says it'll kill him—and I don't want to be the one to put that man into his grave."

"I understand."

"He's confused. I'm confused. Sometimes I think I should not have bothered you. We can just turn over the house and take the money for the other property, then go and live a modest life with our daughter and grandchildren." Her voice still sounded shaky. "Wouldn't be so bad."

I clenched a fist. Traffic whizzed by rocking the car. "Not like this. I'm sure your daughter and the kids would love to be closer to you, but not like this. Let's not give up hope, okay? My voice mail is filled with messages I've yet to listen to, so something tells me the interview today had a great impact. Don't lose heart."

"Thank you, dear. I will try not to."

For the first time in hours I allowed myself a minute to think. My head found the seat rest and I nestled into it, closing my eyes to shut out the day's worth of noise and decisions. My phone buzzed.

"It's Ruth." She hollered into the phone like she too was parked on the side of a busy speedway somewhere. "You were somethin' on that telly, I don't mind pointing out to you."

"Thanks. Not too corny?"

"Nah, but who would care anyway? A little corn could do some good. Our Web guy says the site's been lighting up with pledges brighter than Times Square."

"Really?" My shoulders dropped. "Fantastic."

"Hold on. I haven't told you the half of it. It looks like we got ourselves a little clandestine meeting going on with the town council. My source tells me the developer of this property is in a snit about SOS. I hear they're trying to get some kind of go-ahead approval before the fact. Can you beat that?"

Unbelievable. I pressed a fist to my forehead. "That doesn't smell legal to me. Doesn't that violate the Brown Act?" Then again, Ruth had been known to befriend "sources" who might better be described as elderly women with nothing but time to watch the world through the split in their drapes.

"Any chance Kitteridge might have signed over the whole place right from under us?"

"Not a chance. I just . . . well . . . June promised me that as long as we come up with the money in advance of her deadline, the property will be sold to the community. And I believe her."

Ruth sniffed in my ear. "What deadline?"

My breath caught. "The uh, you know, date before the developer planned to buy the property. You know, before the community got involved. I've talked about it."

She huffed. "Maybe. Here's what I think: June Kitteridge could tell those people to go jump in the ocean if she wanted to, but she would never do it. That woman doesn't have the backbone of a flea. Now Tim, he could get rid of those people. Deadline . . . phshee. He oughta tell them to stick that deadline where—"

"Where and when is the meeting tonight?"

Ruth harrumphed. "Well, technically it's not a *meeting* because there are laws against that. It's just a *gathering* of friends, supposedly. Friends, who just so happen to be wanting to buy the Kitteridge property, at the home of a town council member, who just *happens* to be one of those in power to approve or disprove the project. So anyway, this non-meeting will be up at the Jamison house. Know where it is?"

I scoured my mind. Jamison. New council member. Teenage

daughter. Pleasant-looking wife. This piece of information contained facts. "I can picture the family, but not where they live. He's new on the council, right? Are they up on Sutter's Way?"

"Yes, he's a new council member, which isn't saying much since most of 'em are new. And wrong about the house—they used to live there but now they moved to one of those sprawling places at the top of the hill on Cascade. Can see the whole ocean from up there."

"I see."

"So what do you think, Ms. President? You think we oughta crash their party, make 'em invite the public in to their little shindig?"

Ruth smelled blood. Her voice quivered in a low growl sort of way. No doubt she'd like nothing more than for me to lead our band of revolutionaries through the pines and across the Jamison's gleaming marble floors that led to a sanctuary of sorts for all kinds of underhanded business dealings. Maybe she was right. Nip secret activities in the bud before they can gather the steam necessary to blow away their competition.

Then again, wouldn't it be better to observe a malfeasance in the making firsthand? To allow questionable activities to play right into the hands of the enemy? Or had I been reading too many suspense novels?

I pulled in a breath and allowed it to flow out again. *Be the leader, Callie.* "Let them have their meeting, Ruth. Right now, I need you to follow up on the PR that you've so brilliantly choreographed already. Why don't you have the Web guy pull a clip of my interview today and upload it to YouTube." *Good, Callie, good.* "Let's beat them by creating an impenetrable campaign of goodwill, one that will endear our cause to the community we represent."

She chortled. "I've taught you well. Very good then. I'll trust your judgment on this one. I only hope we won't be sorry."

We clicked off the line and I glanced into the growing line of traffic. Nothing but brake lights as far as my eyes could see. I released a heavy sigh. Ruth needn't have worried. If it were at all possible, I would not allow this ill-timed meeting to go on without the benefit of evidence.

I only hoped that traffic would clear soon enough for me to make it home to Otter Bay—and up the winding hillside to the group that gathered on Cascade Court.

BACK IN HIS OFFICE, Gage rubbed the heaviness from his eyes. They stung, which usually meant he had worn his contact lenses far longer than he should. He'd planned to remove them when he slipped home for his late lunch and replace them with glasses, but became distracted by Callie's undeniably alluring presence on his flat screen TV. That and the way she so confidently answered the reporter's questions while staying fully intent on burying his career.

His office phone jarred him with its ring. "Gage Mitchell."

"Gage, my man. Rick Knutson here."

Gage glanced at the clock on his desk. Its digits glowed red, much like his eyes. "Yes, Rick." He had no patience for the nettlesome realtor's games tonight.

"You're working late. I'm impressed. What say you shut it down for the night and come join the boss for a nightcap and some good old-fashioned conversation?"

He had to be kidding. Was he beckoning me? And at who's behest? Redmond's? "Thanks for the invitation. Maybe some other time."

"Whoa-whoa-whoa. C'mon, man. Take a break. No one can work all day and still be a prince." The man's voice oozed like butter through the phone. Nauseating.

Gage scraped his fingers over his scalp. "I really do not have the time—"

"Better make the time for this. Wasn't easy setting up this soiree tonight. Your boss'll be there along with various towns-people who have clout around here, if you get my drift." Rick snarled. "And if we're going to crush this merry band of revolutionaries trying to carve us out of jobs, we need to make sure we're all on the same page. Capiche?"

The cloak and dagger routine was getting old. If this meeting was that important, why hadn't Redmond phoned him himself? No sooner had this thought come to mind when a new e-mail popped onto the screen.

Rick sounded impatient. "So we'll see you at the Jamison house, then."

Gage clicked on the bold-faced message calling from his inbox. It was from Redmond, inviting him for drinks and conversation tonight on Cascade Court. He clicked "delete" and, reluctantly, gave Rick the answer he wanted to hear.

Twenty minutes later Gage made the drive up the hill toward the Jamison home, still kicking himself for not removing his contacts. The mixture of moist air and approaching headlights blurred his vision, causing him to squint. He had hoped to be home by now, tucking Jeremiah in for Suz and hearing about her day working on Callie's cottage. The kinds of things he'd be doing once his business took off—hopefully with a wife and child of his own.

No time for that. The custom homes perched on this undulating land were visions, the kind that pulled him out of the bed in the mornings. High-end, well-designed beauties, all of them. He checked the address highlighted on the curb with the one he'd memorized.

This was the one. The driveway was filled with expensive cars, sleek and dark, but polished so well that they glowed in the moon's light. He parked his truck on the street and weaved his way up the drive, recognizing Tori's car parked at the front.

Only a glimmer of artificial light seeped from the front windows and no noise whatsoever greeted him besides the cricket serenade drifting from an adjacent field. He took the first step up the wide, molded porch and stopped. His tired eyes picked up a movement to his right. Gage stood a minute, frozen, wondering if he was about to be accosted by a wild animal and if so, why he hadn't already hightailed it to the front door.

He took the second step and heard a sneeze. A human one. One dainty, human sneeze. His eyes had absorbed enough of the darkness now that he could more easily make out his surroundings. Someone ducked and ran behind a stand of trees.

Curious, he stepped away from the house and onto plush, wet grass. He followed a shallow rustling, winding his way around to the side of the property that lay unshielded by fence or wall. Instead, a newly planted stand of pines struggled to create a barrier between the home and curiosity seekers. And through that flimsy stand of baby pines, he saw a familiar figure crouched beneath a window.

"Callie?" He tried to force laughter and the tinge of shock from his voice.

She whipped him an annoyed look, her face illuminated enough by the partial moon for Gage to see the scowl forming in her eyes. She impatiently waved him over, one slender finger pressed against her lips.

Gage approached, bit back a smile, and squatted in the dirt, close enough to draw in her scent. The effect, a longing that tugged, startled him. "What are we doing here?" He didn't bother to keep the tease from his voice.

"Ssh!" Callie's fingers clung to a window ledge, keeping her from settling onto the cold ground. Seeing her there, holding onto that ledge, made him want to wrap his arms around her and allow her body to ease against his. He shook away the image.

A spike of laughter from inside the house jarred the silence between them. Gage moved his mouth closer to Callie's ear, a strand of her hair tickling his nose. "We toasted to common ground the last time we were together. Had no idea you were being so literal."

A soft groan slipped from her lips. Male voices churned together on the other side of the glass, volume turned up. Callie put a hand up to stop Gage from saying another word, only when she did her fingertips brushed his cheek, sending a heated ripple through him. Quickly she pulled her hand away.

As she did, a million thoughts surged inside Gage's head. He didn't care that his knees would soon begin to ache from his weight, nor that moist earth was oozing its way into the patterned crevices of his shoes, only that he and Callie were inexplicably alone, arms and hands brushing against each other, the mingle of fresh pine and her perfume buoying his senses.

As quickly as they had risen, the voices on the other side of the window died down, signaling that the party had moved deeper inside the house. Gage realized that he didn't care one iota that he wasn't inside that place, sucking down martinis and slapping backs over the next best project to hit Otter Bay. Sure as that crescent moon shined above them, he knew he would rather be in this precarious predicament than anywhere else.

Callie shifted and let out a sharp breath. She turned her face to meet his gaze and glared at him, her voice a hiss. "I knew it! So much for our truce! You're on the side of the enemy, I get it, but do you have to participate in something so . . . so . . ."

Her eyes glowed, burning him. "So . . . what?" He put the brakes on his voice, keeping it low, trying to keep the emotion out of it. He tried interjecting some levity. "You're upset that I didn't ask you to join me? Is that what this is? Would you have said yes if I had?"

Her face curled in disgust. "Join you for *what?* An old boy's club meeting? Come. On."

She turned her head toward the window, stretching herself just enough to peek through a sliver of an opening between two shutter slats. Her blonde hair spiraled down her back and it took all of his fading strength to keep from brushing it with his fingertips.

A sigh fumed out of Callie as she turned and slid down the home's outer brick wall, her shoes sinking into the dirt. "They're gone." Her eyes flashed at his. "Seriously, what are you doing here, Gage? Spying?"

He huffed out a sigh of his own, perplexed. "I could ask you the same thing, now, couldn't I?"

She crossed her arms and looked away. A glower tipped the ends of her mouth. "What do you think?"

He raised both eyebrows, willing himself to keep his fingers from smoothing out the downward curve of her lips. He steadied himself with one hand against the earth and took a moment to gather air back into his lungs. "Well, I think . . . I think . . ." He raised his chin and found her gaze locked on him, her breathing visible, her chest rising and falling in rhythm. Was she having as much difficulty resisting him as he was her?

He wouldn't wait to find out.

Gage's free hand found her chin and he held it gently between his thumb and forefinger. She gave no resistance to his touch. "I came here because I was invited." He controlled his breathing against a jagged heartbeat. "But strange as this may sound, especially after what we both represent, I would rather be hiding in the dirt with you."

A flicker softened her mouth and the girl who always had some retort on her tongue, said nothing. Instead she watched him with curious, imploring eyes, her vulnerability melting him. Before he could measure the impact of his actions, Gage's hand slipped along Callie's chin line until it cupped the base of her neck. He kissed her, reveling in the sweetness of her lips against his and the purr elicited when their mouths met, only vaguely aware that her initial acquiescence had been replaced by a subtle rebuke.

He pulled away from her—or had she pushed him?

Callie's eyes grew wide and fierce then, her brows pulled low toward her lashes. Her lips parted sharply, tempting him to cover them again with his own. "Go" she told him, her voice like a cry. "I just want you to go. Now. Please."

CHAPTER 21

J didn't dare breathe. If I did, I knew the sound would come out rough and uneven like a wave colliding with coarse, chiseled rock. And then my presence would be discovered.

Again.

Reliving the kiss, my fingertips brushed my lips. They felt raw and cold in contrast to Gage's touch. This wasn't how it was supposed to happen. It was . . . it was unthinkable. Gage Mitchell and I were on opposing sides and even though we had taken the high road with each other and declared a truce, I had looked at it as more of a stay, a polite promise to keep out of each other's way.

Until he showed up here and turned my thinking—maybe even my heart—upside down.

He hadn't wanted to leave. His face registered a string of emotions as I pushed him away, but what made me want to turn my head was the kindness I saw in his eyes. Deep green pools of tenderness that pleaded with me to give him more of myself.

But I held my stance—I always held my stance—and in the end I was relieved that he had, however reluctantly, gone. Instead of heading for the Jamison's front door, as I had guessed, Gage stuffed his hands into his pockets and took one step backward. He paused a moment, hovering over me as if he had something else to add, his expression flickering between passion and a touch of anger, and then he pivoted in the direction of his truck out on the street.

I swallowed back something that tasted awfully like remorse, but really, he shouldn't have been here in the first place. If this house contained more than one town council member, then this so-called gathering breaks the open meeting law. Did Gage approve of this kind of sneaking around? Did he realize how brazen an act this meeting might be?

Or could it possibly be that Gage was not fully aware of what he had been invited to?

A door closing, followed by slow footsteps pricked my ears. I pressed my back against the bricks, still sitting on the ground, my bum growing colder by the second. From an awkward angle, my eyes strained to watch the figure descend to the street below. Moisture from the ground had begun to absorb through the seat of my capris, sending a chill through me. I rubbed my arms.

After the lone figure got into a car and drove off, I gently lifted myself out of the damp dirt and peered into the window. A rumble of voices from inside the house caught my attention and I crouched beneath the sill. What was I doing here? The ludicrousness of my actions began to seep into my bones much like the slow absorption of moisture through my clothing. Gage must think I'm mad. Then again, how many crazy women was he likely to kiss the way he just did?

No use. I couldn't see or hear anything going on in the house. And now that someone had left, who knew if I'd ever be able to prove my suspicion that this meeting was an underhanded attempt to defy the law and the people of this community.

Reluctantly I stood and stretched my limbs, willing away the beginning of a cold ache. With a swift glance around the corner and toward the front door, I stepped through the damp blades of grass, intent on forgetting all about my sad attempt at espionage. Gravel crackled from somewhere behind the drive and I halted. Had I been too preoccupied with my own swirl of thoughts to notice that someone else had arrived?

My eyes darted for somewhere to hide, but how would that look? I stood still, thinking quickly, but coming up with nothing that would look less than suspicious. Another slide of gravel alerted my ears, but still, I saw nothing. Maybe the noise came from a raccoon in search of a stray morsel for a late night snack. My shoulders relaxed. I was hiding from a raccoon.

Shaking off my initial skittishness, I moved quickly across the lawn and toward the street where my car waited at the bottom of the hill. A bright flash blinded me both with its intensity and suddenness and I lurched sideways.

A familiar male voice sliced through the night. "Ms. Duflay?"

I shielded my eyes. "Yes."

He stepped out from behind a BMW parked in the driveway. "It's Eliot, Ms. Duflay. From the newspaper?"

I lowered my hand, hoping the action would slow the rapid beat of my heart, its second vigorous workout of the night. "What are you—"

"I was wondering what you were doing behind those bushes, Ms. Duflay?"

The boy with the notepad and camera had aged. Who was this man with the searing stare and pointed questions? I swallowed to wash away the dryness in my throat. "I think you must be mistaken." I forced myself to breathe. How much, exactly, had Eliot seen? "Is there a reason that you, Eliot, are standing outside here in the dark instead of joining the party?"

"So that's a party in there. Hmm." He glanced toward the closed front door. "Word was there was some big meeting going on tonight." His unwavering eyes taunted me. "Know anything about it?"

I shrugged and forced one foot in front of the other. "Can't say that I do. Nice meeting up with you, Eliot. Different, but nice." I moved past him, hoping he wasn't about to point that camera at me again, and dreading what might happen to the picture he had already snapped. "Night, now."

"Wait."

I glanced back at him, the cold night air beginning to give me shivers. "Uh-huh?"

"Do you need a ride home?" His voice sounded husky and almost man-like, until it cracked on the word "home."

Bless that young boy's heart. Who wouldn't appreciate someone of the male species who did not see anything wrong with a relationship between a man and a *slightly* older woman? "Thank you for the offer, but I will be fine. I've got my car nearby."

"Glad to hear that because if you were *my* mom, I wouldn't be happy to know you were out here on this ridge after dark."

I jerked to a stop, and this is where I made my mistake. I should have kept moving. *Just one foot in front of the other, Callie.* But no. For some reason, Eliot's *my mom* remark irked me such that I spun around, my face registering exactly the emotion his words had caused.

And that's when a second, blinding flash of light went off in my face.

Eliot glanced down at his camera screen and chuckled. "Perfect. This picture's way better than that other one."

CHAPTER 22

*G*age's head ached almost as much as his eyes burned. While sitting at the breakfast table, he hung his head forward and stretched the muscles in his neck. The action, however, reminded him too much of Callie and the way she made a similar move while seated across from him at the diner. He lifted his head and the throbbing continued.

Suz set a cup of coffee in front him. "Here. Drink this." She leaned through the doorway. "Jeremiah, stop that racket. Your Uncle Gage has a headache!"

Should he mention that shouting didn't help? He chugged the coffee, thankful he hadn't had to grind the beans and brew the pot himself.

"You seen the paper today?" Suz glanced at him over her shoulder, pursed her lips, and looked away. "Suppose not. You must've had a hard night, because your eyes are more red than the apples I picked up at the store. You want a slice, by the way?" She held out a crescent slice of apple to him.

He waved her away. "Not hungry. Thanks."

"I wasn't going to say anything, but here." She dropped the paper onto the table in front of him. "Thought you might be interested in this article mentioning my boss. Not a very good likeness, unfortunately. Sounds like she might be getting herself into some trouble."

Gage's forehead shifted forward. "What kind of trouble?"

Suz gestured toward the paper. "See for yourself."

He adjusted his glasses, blinked a couple of times to get his eyes to focus, and realized how old the prescription must be. His contacts had outworn their welcome last night, and he'd had no choice but to put on an old pair of specs. "Where?"

Suz sighed. "You are worse than Jeremiah today, you know that?" A slight smile flexed his mouth as Suz reached over him and turned to page A2. "There, see?"

He did see, and unfortunately Callie's scowl in the picture was all too familiar. She'd looked the same way at him when he'd found her last night, spying in that cleft of trees.

"Says there she might have been doing something suspicious." Suz ran a wet paper towel over Jer's mouth as he clamored into the chair next to Gage. "I really like working for Callie but didn't get to see her all that much yesterday, so I have no idea what that girl was up to. She's so funny. Did you know she has little verses tacked on her walls?"

Gage squinted at Suz.

"She really does. Psalms and proverbs—all kinds of inspirational sayings—hand printed on cards and tacked in weird spots. I spent most of yesterday patching the walls." His sister sighed. "Anyway, you think she was spying or something, like that reporter suggests?"

Gage's cheek twitched. She was doing something all right. With him. As for the spying, he'd have to take the Fifth. "Who knows."

Suz flopped down next to him. "Says there she was caught walking out of some bushes up at the Jamison's house late at night. Doesn't that strike you as strange?"

He forced his face into a bland expression. "If it's true. Did it say what she might be looking for . . . if she were actually spying?"

Suz eyed him. "Says here she told the reporter there was a party going on in the house, but see how he uses the words 'according to Ms. Duflay' and 'Ms. Duflay claimed he was mistaken'? You'd think we were reading the tabloids or something right here at the breakfast table."

"You say that like it's a sin."

"Maybe it's not as bad as all that, but it sure isn't healthy, reading about things that might not be true. It's called gossip and from someone who's been on the other side of all that ugliness, well, it's not good. I can attest."

For the most part Suz held in the pain that had brought her all the way across the country to live with him. Occasionally, though, a wound would surface the way a change in weather might arouse an old injury. Something in Gage's chest twisted at the thought of all his young sister and nephew had been through.

He closed the paper. "Then I think we should just let it be." Guilt flicked him. "Suz? I should mention that I, uh, was invited to a gathering up at the Jamison's last night."

She sat down. "Really? Did you go?"

He hesitated. If he told her yes and she asked follow-up questions, he might end up telling her about things that he had not fully vetted himself. Plus, Callie's presence on the property would certainly substantiate the reporter's claims—and how would that make her look to Suz?

He shook his head. "Should have, but didn't make it after all."

Suz nodded. "Well, it's a good thing. You've been working too late as it is. Just look at those eyes beaming like brake lights at me. Besides, if you weren't careful, you might've had your mug plastered all over the newspaper just like Callie."

Now there was a disastrous thought. He saw the title inked across his mind: "Architect Sleeping with the Enemy." He'd certainly have plenty of explaining to do—on all fronts.

Gage downed the last sip of coffee as Suz left the kitchen to get Jer ready for preschool. He winced as it trickled down his throat cold and thick. In the silence he had no control over his mind, which flickered over the memory of Callie and last night: her soft skin against his face as he kissed her so brazenly.

Awfully forward of you, Mitchell.

Yeah, but she didn't resist. At least, not at first.

No doubt about it. As the fight for the Kitteridge property dragged on, Gage felt certain that the tabloid-esque nature of the debate would become worse.

CHAPTER 23

"*W*ell. You didn't waste any time. Did you?" Sheila's voice provided my first human connection of the morning. I tried to think of what might have been worse, but nope, couldn't think of a thing.

I yawned as Moondoggy clicked down the hall toward my bedroom. "Not sure what you are referring to, sis."

"First you go on television, without telling your sister, and now I see your face in the morning newspaper. A less than becoming photograph too."

I sat up and shook away my early morning disorientation. "The newspaper?" Pulling on my robe, I slid into a pair of ratty slippers and padded to the front door, craning my neck to see where the paper delivery guy had tossed it.

"Page A2. Quite the story too. You weren't really sneaking around in someone's bushes, were you?"

Where is that paper? I spotted it near the front walk, *of course*, and padded out to get it. None of me had seen a mirror yet, like I cared, but in case Eliot lurked nearby with that camera of his, I'd rather not be discovered in my robe and slippers.

While pulling the rubber band and an attached envelope from

the folded paper, I slipped back inside. "Where is it again? Oh. Wait. I've found it."

"Kind of hard to miss."

My heart sank deep into my core. My skin prickled as if chilled. Not only was the picture hideous, but as I scanned the article it became obvious that Eliot had planted the piece with speculation and conjecture, having forgotten everything he'd learned in Journalism 101. Who cares if it was the truth? This ruined *everything.*

"Jim's concerned about you, Callie."

I slapped the paper onto the table. "Jim? I can hardly believe that."

"What a thing to say. He's your brother and he's concerned that you might find yourself with charges of trespassing leveled at you. I know your causes mean the most to you, but this is serious, little sister. Pay attention."

I sank into the couch, wishing I could crawl back into bed and revisit the dream I'd been having about finding a treasure map and sailing away on calm seas to seek my fortune.

"Are you even listening?"

"Yes, Sheila, I heard you. I doubt seriously that any *charges* could ever be filed against me because it would be my word against that reporter's."

"But he has a picture!"

I glanced again at the unflattering shot and winced. My wretched, scowling face filled the whole frame. "That picture proves nothing. Well, other than my mood. He could've taken that at the RAG or in church, for all we know. You can tell big brother not to worry his legal mind over me. I'm not."

My sister sighed and paused, most probably to give me time to think about all I'd done. She sighed again. "For someone who's created such a stir and raised a lot of money in a short time, you've become downright surly. Look at that picture of yourself

—you would think you had just fought off the enemy with that glare in your eye."

Sheila was right about that and her words gave me pause as I thought back on the night and all that had transpired. Although Eliot surprised me by showing up with his notebook and camera, Gage's sudden appearance startled me most. And not in a bad way, exactly. I barely had time to digest the emotions that had shown up with him, uninvited. Frustration, anger, and longing had all traced their way through me leading to that awkward, surprising, savory kiss.

I felt my body blush at the memory. "Probably had something else on my mind." I forced a laugh. "Like that time Brenna ran around with your camera on Thanksgiving, shoving it in everybody's faces. A lot of those pictures, as I recall, were less than attractive."

"Speaking of my darling daughter, you owe me seven dollars."

"Really? Why?"

"For ice cream. You didn't show up and the children were crestfallen. Don't worry. I covered for you *as usual.*"

I covered my face with my hand. "Oh no, no, no." How could I forget the promise I had made to Brenna and Blakey? "I am so sorry, Sheila."

"It's no biggie, but you will have to tell them that."

"I will. How about later today? Could I pick them up in the afternoon and—"

"Not today. Brenna has gymnastics and, well, I would rather Blake not eat ice cream two days in a row. It will have to be sometime next week because our activity calendar is quite full already."

"Fine. See you Sunday?"

"I hope so."

"What's that supposed to mean?"

"Nothing. Never mind. Hopefully Jim's concerns will not come to fruition."

"You think I'll be in *jail?*"

"Let's not dwell on the negative, all right, Callie? I have got to get going on my errands." She paused again, her voice weary, almost fearful. "You be careful out there, little sister."

"Yeah. Thanks." I hung up the phone, fully awake now and equally aware of my new menacing ways. Much as I'd like to think otherwise, my sister, not to mention my niece and nephew, all had the right to be upset with me. If I could bend that way, I'd deliver a swift kick to my own behind.

And did I really hide out in bushes last night, hoping to catch townspeople violating the law? What if I had? It occurred to me that in a small town like ours, the story of my tactics just might trump the council's crime.

No matter how much I'd like to hide away the memory of last night's spy mission, that annoyingly clear black and white photo of me in the paper wouldn't allow it. One thing I could be thankful for was that there was no mention in the article of the friendly combat I entered into with Gage. *Really missed a scoop there, Mr. Eliot Hawl.*

I put a hand to my face, both eyes closed, my thoughts wandering back to Gage. He'd made me so angry, showing up like that. I had wanted to believe that despite his work with the land developer, Gage was above taking part in questionable government activities.

Niggles of doubt wormed their way through me. Gage *had* been quick to change course the minute he spotted me. He could have taunted me awhile before leaving, but instead he didn't hesitate to join me in my grimy hideaway on the side of the Jamison's house. I groaned. Maybe that was honesty talking when he said he'd rather be playing in the dirt with me than be inside that house.

Didn't he understand, though, that I was not the type of woman to give up a cause over a guy? He could never change me, so why would he try?

The thought lingered along with a thousand others as I curled on my couch with Moondoggy in the crook of my lap. It would take strength of will to push me forward this morning. My eyes caught again on the picture in the paper, but no matter how I tried to snarl the image away, it stayed static, its ridicule aimed straight at me. If I hadn't forced myself to glance away, I might not have noticed the envelope that had fluttered to the floor when I had first opened the paper.

I snatched it up, the turn in my abdomen oddly familiar. When I unfolded the paper within, I became aware that my secret admirer had, unbeknownst to me, struck again:

You can hide, but you can't win, lady.

"SO YOU DECIDED TO give us the ol' heave-ho last night, Mr. Mitchell?" Rick Knutson's voice on the other end of Gage's phone was almost too much to take so early in the morning. "That's all right, I know how it is. Probably got yourself a curvy little number to get home to. Don't sweat it."

He knew it was immature for an educated man in his late thirties to roll his eyes, but Gage couldn't help himself. "I had intended to be there, Rick, but had a last-minute change of plans. Couldn't be helped." That was stretching it, but whenever he thought back on the two choices he had last evening once he spotted Callie in those trees, well? He doubted he could have forced himself to make any other choice.

And what a choice it turned out to be.

"No matter. Word on the street is that the press scared away most of the council members anyway. Only Jamison was there, so Redmond had to put all his eggs in one basket with him. Know what I mean?"

"I'll give Redmond a call with my regrets." Gage jabbed the eraser end of his pencil into his desk. "Wait. Are you telling me this party was actually a front for a meeting with the town council? Behind closed doors?"

Rick's laughter soared through the phone. "As if you didn't know? Right. Good one!" His laughter reduced to a silly whine. "Keep up that holier than thou front—that's solid PR."

Steam rose within him, heat passing through his veins. "I don't think you understand the severity of the penalty for violating an open meeting law. Especially in light of the project's current opposition."

Rick spewed contempt. "Don't get me started on the so-called SOS group. Those people are laughable. Ineffectual—"

"And receiving lots of press—" As soon as the words flew from his mouth, Gage wished he could retract them. Despite the whuppin' he hoped to inflict on the cocky realtor, he had no intention of exposing Callie in the process. He held his breath, hoping Rick hadn't seen the paper. Then again, if he had, wouldn't he have mentioned that news by now?

"That is exactly why we're able to fly under the radar so easily. Don't you see? SOS is so busy calling attention to their merry band of nitwits that nobody notices the swift plans we are making on this deal. Could not have planned this better myself."

Gage squeezed his eyes shut, forcing the burn from them. He tapped the tip of his pencil on his desk like it was sending out an SOS of its own. "Was there another reason for this call?"

"The plans. Where are you on the plans for the prop?"

Gage held his breath for fear of the barrage of sentiments that threatened to erupt. He'd been cordial to Rick to this point, but the guy was a realtor for crying out loud. He had no business sticking his nose into the design end of this business. "You'll have to take that up with Redmond. Now if you will excuse me, I've got a deadline to meet."

"Okay. All right. We can play that game, if you want. I don't have to tell you, though, Mr. Mitchell, that time is money. The longer you take to handle your end of this deal, the more money it's going to cost your client. That could affect you."

Did he really want to get into this with Rick Knutson,

annoying real estate broker? Besides, he didn't see how this project would cost any more money if he got the plans to Redmond this week or next. Once his client approved them, he would have to meet with his engineering consultants to bring the drawings to the final level. Might set him back another week or so, but even though construction costs continued to climb, they would not do so *that* quickly. He wanted to call the realtor on his claims, but that would only prolong this conversation. "I'll bear that in mind."

"Good. Glad you see it my way. Talk soon."

Gage listened to the dial tone buzzing in his ear. *That guy's got to be kidding.* Disruptions like that made it much more difficult for him to go back to the drawing board, so to speak. He shook his head. Actually, much more than an unwelcome phone call distracted Gage this morning. This thing with Callie wasn't going away; rather, it was growing bigger and faster than the project he so diligently worked on for the Kitteridge property each day.

He glanced at his computer screen, which lay open, ready for more inputs. Soon he'd be meeting with Redmond for his sign-off, then plotting out the construction documents, then presenting the whole exhaustive design to the city. Although he respected Callie's drive to thwart something she felt so strongly about, like Rick and the others, he doubted that this community effort would win out over Redmond's longtime plans and seemingly endless supply of cash.

So what was he going to do about Callie Duflay?

His office line rang again, keeping him from coming up with the answer to his question. Did he dare answer the phone again? It could be that reporter snooping around, digging for more manure to spread across the paper.

"Gage here."

"Gage. It's Redmond." He didn't have to identify himself. His gravel-laced voice did that for him. "You didn't answer my e-mail."

Gage squinted. E-mail? He clicked over to his account but even before he did, he remembered. Rick had phoned him last night with an invitation to the "party" at Jamison's house, but Redmond had e-mailed him too. Thankfully he hadn't answered that. "Sorry, Redmond. Had a long night last night."

"As well you should have. Those designs ready?"

He breathed easier. "As a matter of fact, I was going to give you a call myself. If all goes well, I should have them ready for you to take a look at by Friday morning. If you like what you see, I will be able to move onto the next phase, which will ultimately mean bringing the finished designs to the planning department."

"Good. Let's meet at your office Friday, 9:00 a.m. sharp."

"Great. You're on my calendar."

A thick pause filled the air between them. "Want to talk to you about something that's come up."

Gage's chest stilled, like his lungs had quit functioning. Had Redmond gotten wind of Gage's romance with Callie outside the alleged party on the hill last night? "All right, Redmond. Shoot."

"Know anything about this Callie Duflay?" Redmond's garbled voice spat out Callie's name in a way that turned his stomach.

"I've seen her around town."

He huffed and it sounded like a seal's bark. "She's a piece of work. Seen the paper this morning?"

Gage swallowed. "Skimmed it over my morning coffee." He decided to take the proverbial bull by its pointy horns. "Wasn't impressed with the rag-like quality of the reporting, however. That picture of Ms. Duflay looked like something out of a tabloid. Quite a bit of speculation on the part of that reporter, in my opinion."

"Really. So you think the allegations are suspect, then?"

"If I remember correctly, Cal . . . Ms. Duflay did not confirm the reporter's accusation. And by the look on her face, I suspect she didn't pose for that picture either."

His laughter came through like a shout. "A hideous depiction, all right."

"Yes. Well." The only picture in Gage's mind was of the beauty who received his kiss in the dark of night. He shook it away. "I wouldn't let it bother you."

"Me? I'm not bothered. Jamison and I already had a discussion about the trollop and have decided to make her day and not investigate. Because if it were proven that the little minx was hiding in those bushes, trespassing charges could be made." He lowered his heavy voice until he resembled a stalker. "Let's just say that we would rather not draw attention to our soiree last evening. You with me?"

Yeah, he was with him all right, wishing he wasn't so privy to the obviously questionable aspects of this project. It wasn't lost on him that Redmond's admission to his and Jamison's discussion over why they weren't inclined to investigate the allegation against Callie made him both disturbed and relieved at the same time, the mixture unsettling.

CHAPTER 24

*N*ever had I been happier about the prospect of going to work. I slipped into the RAG early this morning, hungry for one of Holly's creations but hoping not to be noticed by those who read the paper. It was Friday, though, and shouldn't folks who read Tuesday's edition have moved on by now?

Here was hoping.

"Mornin' Callie." Holly greeted me with her usual big smile.

I took a seat along the side wall. "I'll have—"

"A peanut butter smoothie?" Holly finished my order. "And how about a rum muffin to go with that?"

"Sounds lethal."

"Oh, it is. It'll light a fire under you for the entire day, mark my words."

I shrugged. "Okay. Why not?"

A squeal of voices entered the diner and Holly's face lit up. "There's my girls." She glanced at me. "I'll be right back with your breakfast, hon."

I watched, awed, as Holly threw herself into the group of three women near the counter. The women were all fairly new in this town, but word was they were Holly's kin. What would it be like to squeal with abandon every time my family and I got together? The thought made my heart drop a little.

One of the women caught my eye and broke free from the group. I glanced away, believing I'd been mistaken, but sure enough, she approached my table. "Excuse me? Are you Callie Duflay?"

The woman's blonde waves framed her smiling face. She wouldn't smile like that if she had a complaint to file with me, now would she? "Yes. What can I do for you?"

She snapped open her bag and retrieved an envelope. "My sisters and I wanted to give you this, for your cause." She handed it to me. "We admire your tenacity."

Speechless, I reached for it. This week had started off well with donations pouring in as I made our case on the local television station. But after my mug appeared in the newspaper the next morning with Eliot's claims attached, the tide began to reverse its course.

While pledges and support continued their steady stream, an upswing of opposition had also begun to surface. Angry letters made the op-ed page, some from people outside of Otter Bay who we'd surmised wanted to purchase a condo in the new development, but missiles from locals also appeared, many of them questioning our treatment of the Kitteridges. And I still wondered about the author of the "love notes" I had received. Rather than draw undue attention to ourselves, the SOS team had gathered by phone conference this week.

She continued. "I'm Tara Sweet, by the way." A bright diamond on her finger flashed when she pulled her left hand back after I'd taken the donation from her.

"Tara, thank you so much for this."

She tilted her head to one side, one shoulder slightly raised. "It's not a huge amount, but we hope it will help. That property's been open since I was a kid." She glanced out a far side window, her eyes wistful. "Have a lot of memories to hold onto over there."

I nodded. "Me too."

She gave her head a slight shake as Holly approached with my breakfast. "Well. I'll let you get back to your breakfast . . . hey! Peanut butter smoothie. That's my favorite."

Holly laughed. "And I talked her into a rum muffin too."

Tara smiled and winked at me. "You live dangerously, don't you?"

No kidding. I waved at her as she strolled toward her sisters who sat at a window-side table. Maybe I should take this as a sign that the blip in our campaign this week had only a momentary effect and that the generosity of these women with ties to Otter Bay would light a spark beneath the rest of the community.

Trying not to appear overly eager, I slipped a glance down at the envelope, noticing that its seal had been left open. I pulled the check up slightly and bit back a smile. We were another three thousand dollars closer to meeting our goal.

I enjoyed my breakfast more than anticipated and Holly was right—not sure if it was the rum muffin or not, but a fiery charge had lit into me and I couldn't wait to get to camp. I paid the bill then drove straight to work.

While hikers enjoyed a needle-softened path to get from the sea and back to camp, the drive was longer and windier. I didn't mind. Emerging from the bending road that tunneled through a canopy of Monterey pine gave an aerial-like view of the vast ocean the horizon muted by light fog. Up here, it seemed, cares were but a memory.

I pulled into a spot next to Squid's, surprised to see him here so early. *Must be working on some new activities.* To the left of the Adventure Room marked the beginning of a narrow pathway lined by plantings of eucalyptus that led to a circle of stones set around a wood cross. The outdoor chapel was one of Squid's ideas, a brilliant one, and another reason he was so good at what he did. Getting excited children to march single file could test the patience of Mother Teresa, however, so I created the path only one person wide with the "mysterious" stone circle at the other end.

The breeze carried the minty scent of eucalyptus, and I couldn't resist ducking down the path. On occasion, before or after particularly busy weekends, I liked to meditate or pray in that chapel beneath the forest where I was headed now. The air hung cooler along the shady path, and I took my time, inhaling the fresh scent and letting the stresses of this week filter out of my worry zones and into the brush at my feet.

A rapid flapping of wings caused me to flinch, then laugh, as a hummingbird whizzed overhead. All the money in the world couldn't replace this heady feeling of stepping through a natural wonderland. This is what my ex-boyfriend Justin never understood. Or it's what he had forgotten along the way. For him, the business had become the means to an end—his wealth. Well, *our* wealth until Tish and her father's money showed up.

If Justin's bus bench ads and truck fleet were any indication, he may have found a measure of success with Oasis Designs, but did he still have that spark that drew me to him like a moth to a candle? He used to drag me into the greenhouses at school and give me endless rundowns on the propagation of new plantings. The glee in his face over learning more about how plants grew and prospered reminded me of Blakey's the day he finally learned to tie his shoes. All out, abandoned joy.

Justin had lost that and though I had to fight the bitterness of his betrayal at times, I had begun to understand that had we stayed together, I too would have lost something meaningful to my life.

As I rounded a sweeping curve along the pathway, my breath caught. It always caught at this point because the children became so mesmerized. They anticipated what they would find at the other end when light flooded their eyes and curiosity had overtaken them. I slowed my pace, lingering in the quiet rustling surrounding me, knowing that something pleasing awaited on the other side, yet somehow wanting to slow its arrival. A crisp twig cracked beneath my heel. Water flowed through a nearby stream that had dug a meandering swath through the hill on its way to the ocean. I inhaled another deep breath and stepped into the morning's sunlight, refreshed and hopeful.

I opened my eyes expecting to see the grand cross rising alongside the pines. Instead, my gaze landed on two people wound so closely together that not a crack of light could pass between them. "Squid?"

A high-pitched gasp disrupted the breezy quiet and I recognized her as the woman Squid had introduced me to at the diner. Peyton.

Squid yanked his arms from where they'd been adhered to Peyton's body. I let my eyes flit away. "Callie, what are you doing here so early?"

I pulled my gaze back to him in time to observe Squid shoving both hands into the front pockets of his jeans. Peyton fumed at me, while smoothing her hands along the short length of her tankini dress. I shrugged, raising both palms. "Came to, uh, pray, but didn't realize anyone was here."

Squid's face reminded me of a hairy tomato as we stood there the three of us, no one quite sure how to ease the awkwardness that bound us.

Peyton rolled her eyes and huffed. "I need a latte."

Squid slid a compliant glance her way, his shoulders bowed. "It's all yours," he said with a nod of his head toward the stone circle at the base of the cross. He slowed as he passed and spoke with a low voice. "Saw the paper. I'll send Luz for you if you want to stay here and pray for awhile."

They left, Peyton marching ahead of Squid as he followed dutifully behind. I exhaled a full breath and looked upon the outdoor chapel. Lowering myself onto a cold rock, I realized that the wondrous moment of finding this place at the end of that twisting, shaded path had ebbed.

I blew another sigh, like a balloon that had been untied. Squid had this annoying way of using doublespeak. Hadn't really noticed that trait until now. It might work when trying to help children dissect real meaning behind a person's words, but when he used it on me, I vacillated between offering him my gratitude and suggesting he jump off the nearest cliff.

And what about him? What was it with men who found tiny, impatient—and *young*—women so attractive? Peyton had nearly stomped her petite and pedicured little toes when I'd appeared, messing up her early morning romance. *Like Tish.* Justin's girl-toy made a similar maneuver once when I showed up at Oasis Designs to clean out my desk. Instead of toe stomping, she tapped them continuously as if hoping I'd grow tired of her petulance and leave in a hurry. Didn't she realize behavior like that only slowed me down?

The cross stood unmoved before me, urging me to focus my mind on something other than the confusion that men and their quest for toys and prominence could cause. *Have I got it all wrong, Lord?*

After contemplating awhile, I picked myself up, no longer as enthused as when I'd wandered over here, but ready to take on whatever God had planned for the body of campers eagerly anticipating their weekend ahead. Somehow I hoped he had plans for me as well.

REDMOND TOOK A SEAT in the plush, black armchair Suz had picked up at the dollar store one town north of Otter Bay. When he did, a dusting of stale smoke floated through the office. "Let's get this started."

Redmond Dane and Gage had spoken face-to-face only one time before. That rainy night the formidable developer stumbled into a coffee bar in Westwood after having a monstrous argument with his ex-business partner. Unknown to Redmond, Gage had just been laid off after having negotiated two high-end design projects, including one for a reality star in the Hollywood Hills. He discovered that his boss had planned to use non-licensed contractors and pocket the extra profit. What should have been a celebration was instead a caffeine-bender for Gage before heading home to his apartment over-looking The Getty Center. He planned to sit and stare at the museum's outer walls until he figured out what to do next.

Opportunity showed up before he left his counter stool.

As Gage walked around his desk, ready to lay out the Kitteridge project design for Redmond's approval, he hoped to live up to the expectations of the man who had hired him on the spot for this project. Although they had never worked together before this, they were both aware of each other's reputations. Destiny brought a tipsy Redmond and a discouraged Gage together that night in the coffee bar. They also both knew that Redmond's former business partner waited on the sidelines, hoping for failure, which meant that Gage's client had much to lose. As did he himself.

Suz stepped into the office with a stocked coffee tray. She bowed out of painting at Callie's house this morning, insisting instead on stepping in as Gage's assistant during his important meeting with his lone client. Gage waited as she set a large mug before Redmond on the side of the desk. "Coffee?"

The older man, his skin blotched and uneven, furrowed his brow. "Thought you'd never ask." Despite the steam rising from the top of his mug, Redmond guzzled down half the coffee, then cleared his garbled throat.

Suz refilled his mug. "I'll be in my office if you need me."

Gage thanked her, watched her leave, then turned to address his client. "I think you'll appreciate the project's cohesive transition from man-made to natural surroundings." He used a fat pencil to guide Redmond's eye through the design set spread across his desk. "I've woven in the natural elements you requested, offering organic styling while keeping with the quintessential beach town design."

Redmond stroked his chin. "Hmm."

Gage pointed out the shape of the buildings that flowed with the natural curve of the land, the cantilevered decks that provided views of the borrowed landscape, the plans for radiant heat in the floors and solar for everywhere else. Intact within the multi-use complex were places of refuge where dwellers could wander outside the confines of their condos and offices and sit among the pines and sustainable landscape—which included a wildlife pond to attract native and migratory birds and a rain garden added after Gage had stumbled across the miniature one near Callie's home.

Gage knew better than to talk too much, so he paused, giving Redmond a chance to collect his thoughts and formulate his comments and questions. Much like he did the night they met, when Redmond, slightly inebriated and wholly angry, offered Gage the chance of a lifetime—to design this property. He had been sitting at that counter that night, drinking a frothy latte in a tall glass, assessing his future, when in blew Redmond and his plans for Otter Bay.

Gage couldn't give his landlord two weeks' notice fast enough.

Gage stood by, waiting for Redmond to review the design he had been toiling over for weeks. He figured there would be many questions. More often, there would be inappropriate suggestions, the classless kind that made a designer's skin freeze and cause a chill deep in the bones.

Gage had already determined to answer all of Redmond's comments without cringing—at least visibly—at suggestions that would undoubtedly run counter to his design. This was the part of the project that could try an architect's confidence, when clients might look beyond the skill and vision of a particular design and be offended by what they see, mainly Gage believed, because they could not picture what the architect had drawn. Cockiness had ended his career once before, however, and that piece of history was never far from his mind.

Ultimately Gage knew he must walk that line between fighting to keep the design as he saw it and giving Redmond enough of what he wanted to secure the project's ultimate construction.

He held his breath, wondering if Redmond's silence indicated that they were about to head into battle.

But all Redmond did was peer up at him, a silver Cross pen poised between his thumb and fingers, a question in his high brows. "Sign at the top?"

No questions? Not even a rogue comment or scoff? Gage hesitated, knowing he should be leaping with relief. Redmond's reaction was highly unusual. Gage was momentarily stunned, like when handing a cashier a five-dollar bill for a cup of coffee and receiving eighteen dollars in change.

Gage mentally righted himself. "Yes. At the top." Gage understood that a verbal acceptance was more typical at this stage of the design process, but wariness had settled over him and he chose instead to allow Redmond to sign the set on his desk, thereby creating a paper trail.

After scrawling a large RD in the designated space, Redmond stood and handed Gage an orange business card with a woman's name and phone number printed in fancy script.

"Thanks," Gage said, still perplexed over the brevity of their meeting. "Who is this?"

"Call her." Redmond shuffled toward the door. "She'll be doing an artist's rendering of the design for a full page ad my staff will be placing in the local papers over the next several weeks. We'll also be posting an oversized sign on the property. She'll make your sketches so attractive the town'll be begging us to develop that land." He gave Gage a pointed stare. "You'll want to put those construction documents on the fast track. The council wants to see them within a week."

A week?

Gage stood, ready to balk, but Redmond put up a hand. "I'll see myself out."

Gage lowered himself into his desk chair, exhausted. Rocking back and forward, wincing at the squeak, he attempted to sift through an onslaught of varied emotions. *I knew it was too easy.* Redmond hadn't even mentioned SOS or the picture of Callie in the paper, almost as if neither existed. By signing off on the Design Development and hiring an artist renderer, Redmond seemed to imply that everything was moving forward as planned.

Except that he only gave Gage a week to draft a complete set of drawings for both permit and construction. Impossible.

Suz appeared in the doorway and leaned against the frame. "That was fast. Did he sign off on the project?"

Gage nodded.

"And? This is good news. Right?"

"Right." Regardless of the worries that hammered him, Gage gave his sister a thumbs-up and watched as she slipped away, beaming.

He tucked his elbows into his ribs and leaned on steepled fingers. If he had a drafting staff, plenty of time, and not a doubt in the world, then Gage would have no trouble admitting that this meeting had gone wildly beyond his expectations. Without all of that? It felt more like he stood on a precarious, rickety swinging bridge over a churning and unreliable current. And what worried him most was that a young mother and her little boy clung to that bridge with him.

CHAPTER 25

*T*he campers arrived in rambunctious spurts, dragging sleeping bags and over-stuffed suitcases off their buses and into tight-fitting cabin quarters. Giggles and shouts whizzed around camp, and the few times I ran into Squid, he was doing his big brotherly camp director thing—tossing footballs to the kids, proclaiming his favorite sports teams, asking campers if they were here to have F.U.N.—that sort of thing. Otherwise, he ignored me.

My work was fairly light that first night. No overbookings to worry about or ill children—although one first-time camper had to fight off a wave of homesickness. One hour and two ice cream sandwiches later (hers and mine), she blended back in with her group, which had begun to play the night's game: "Rock? or Sand?"

Maybe *ignore* wasn't quite the word for Squid's non-acknowledgment of me. He wasn't rude or surly. He didn't look me up and down, then purposely snub me (as far as I noticed). But the playfulness we often shared—the teasing winks and eye rolls, the private guffaws over a camper's dance moves—were all missing. If he needed me to do something, say, make sure the sound guy knew which songs were on the night's play list, he'd ask. Only his communication with me had turned sparse and robotic.

I wasn't sure if this had something to do with my surprise upending of his quiet moment this morning with Peyton, or if mentioning that he'd seen the newspaper on Monday was his way of letting me know that, as my boss, he was not amused.

The man was a mystery.

But today was a new day. The sun, and a nest of chattering wild finches near my open window, woke me early. Being up here, even though it was just a short drive from home, isolated me from the daily news and hometown gossip. I rolled my shoulders, luxuriating in the gentle pull of taut muscles as they stretched and relaxed.

Luz approached me. "Whee. Beautiful here today, isn't it?"

I let out a sigh. "Sure is."

The kids had assembled on the lawn at the base of the hill, the counselors corralling them with megaphones and toughness that was merely an act. The campers knew that.

Luz touched the cuff of my shoulder. "It's quiet in the office. You should go and watch the game today."

"You sure?"

"Yeah. Go on. It's fun."

As assistant camp director you'd think I would have more time with the kids as a whole, but I didn't. So watching more of the camp theme unfold during this sunny morning drew me like a butterfly to wild lupine. Besides, after a week like this one, I needed the distraction.

The rock wall had been erected two years ago near a hilly area so that kids could cheer on their friends from the sidelines. This year, though, the hill had been layered with a ton of sand. Instead of kids sitting on the hill to watch their friends, they lined up at the bottom, with their eyes on climbing their way to the top through nearly knee-deep sand. Squid said he got the idea for this activity after driving along Pacific Coast Highway near

Malibu and spotting a similar sand hill that drew kids to its challenge.

I curled up on the lawn amid one of the groups waiting for their turn. Those at the front of the rock climbing wall strapped on helmets and pads and waited for instructions. At the base of the sand hill, counselors had to keep calling boys back down, telling them to wait for the whistle.

Squid's voice boomed through his megaphone. "Hello, my friends! Everyone will have the chance to climb both the rock hill." He pointed toward the towering setup. "And the sand hill."

The kids cheered.

"Settle down, settle down." The campers squealed and hollered but Squid would not budge. Little girls pointed and whispered, their ponytails swishing in each other's faces as they assessed each activity. Several boys had to be reminded to sit. Squid held up the sign of respect and, slowly, the voices quieted.

He put the megaphone up to his mouth. "Now. I want you to think about a couple of things when you're doing your climbs. First, ask yourself, 'which one of these climbs is easier?'"

Shouts came from the peanut gallery.

"The sand, of course!"

"No way, the rock wall's much harder!"

Squid waited for the kids to quiet. He raised the sign of respect. "And which one of these hills do you think is stronger? Don't answer that now. Just think about it."

The girl next to me grabbed her friend's arm. "I think that was a trick question."

Her friend's eyes widened. "You do?"

The girl nodded vigorously. "Yeah. Adults are always asking stuff that's too easy."

Her friend nodded in agreement, her eyes and mouth stuck open.

I bit back a smile, although, really, the girl's proclamation carried some truth. Sometimes the answers to our questions seem so simple, yet it was not always the easy way that worked best. It would have been easier for me to say yes to Justin's desires for our business. Once while I watered a braided ficus tree inside a bank branch, a woman asked me a question. When I didn't respond right away—I hadn't actually realized that her question was directed to me—she jabbed an arched finger in my face and said, "What? No hablas Ingles?" Even after all this time, her condescending tone still flattened my smile.

It would have been easier to walk away from that kind of treatment, to give away ownership rights to the business, hire staff to handle the daily service to clients and marry Justin. Easier but not necessarily the right thing to do. After turning down that investor's offer, it didn't take much for Justin's eye to be drawn to the next tempting scenario. Only this one had long and shapely legs and the hip action to match. Not to mention a wealthy father.

If I had married Justin, who's to say he would not have strayed eventually anyway?

Squid raised the whistle to his mouth and blew, charging up the campers in the audience and those at the start of each hill. On my knees now, I clapped and shouted my support for the climbers along with the rest of the campers, my voice becoming one of the chorus. I'm not sure why I let my eyes wander from the frenetic activity at that moment, but when I did, Squid's gaze locked with mine and he sent me a wink. A deliberate, happy-eyed wink.

Not long ago a look like that from Squid would have turned my legs to boiled noodles. I would have interpreted it one way, when clearly, that wasn't how he meant it at all. My mind switched to Gage's kiss, that surprising, sultry, shocking kiss, and all at once I lost my balance and collapsed backward, landing on my backside in the dirt. Could I be wrong again?

I glanced back at Squid. This time all that moved within me was the sense that, although he may have read the paper, it did not appear that my boss was holding my indiscretion against me.

GAGE NEEDED TO GET out more. Although this convenient office with its proximity to town had caught his eye the moment he first drove into Otter Bay, he'd begun to tire of the arduous days spent splitting his time between the complicated design in front of him and staring at that dreary wall beyond his window.

Although he awoke to sunshine this fine Saturday, duty called and he had slid behind his desk with only a cup of coffee and one of Holly's muffins for company.

He wondered what Callie was up to today.

He reassigned that thought to somewhere in his mind's recesses, but strings of curiosity dangled in front of him, willing to be pulled, threatening to unravel him. She worked for a camp —that he knew. She also fearlessly spoke her mind and radiated beauty doing it. Callie had so much going for her that he wondered if something else kept her from realizing it. There was so much he didn't know about her, so much he wanted to learn. Gage battled the urge to call her, wanting, if nothing else, to hear the smooth purr of her voice in his ears.

As if in a trance, Gage picked up the receiver, only to slam it down when the dial tone jarred the air, breaking into his meanderings.

The wind he created fluttered papers across his desk. Why would he consider calling a woman who had let him know she wasn't interested? He'd probably stunned her with that kiss. Maybe if she'd known it was coming, she would have darted for the first break in those trees. *Smooth, Gage, real smooth.*

His eyes noted the hot orange card Redmond left with him. "Call her," his client had commanded. Gage twisted his lips and sighed. Somehow thinking of Callie and his design for the Kitteridge property all at once did little except remind him of the searing divide that—no matter how this played out—would always be between them.

He turned his thoughts to the number on the card, reading the name aloud, something he always did to make sure that he had the pronunciation correct. "Amelia Rosa Carr." Even her name had an artist's hum to it.

He dialed, his eyes flitting impatiently about the room as he waited for someone to pick up.

"Hello."

The bubbly pitch of her voice threw him. "Hello. I'm . . . calling for Amelia Rosa Carr."

"You've reached her."

Really? He figured the person attached to the youthful voice would excuse herself and fetch her mother. "This is Gage Mitchell calling. I'm looking for the artist who will be doing the rendering of the Kitteridge property for Redmond Dane."

"Like I said—you've reached her." Her singsong voice kept him off-guard. "I'm about to go to yoga, Mr. Mitchell, but I could stop by your office afterward to pick up a copy of the DD. Would that work for you?"

He straightened. Young or not, the woman knew her stuff. "That'll work. And call me Gage. Do you know where I'm located?"

"Sure do, Gage. My yoga class is a block from there. See you."

Over the next hour Gage cleaned up as many stray notes as possible and copied the design documents for Amelia. He also left messages for the structural engineer on the project as well as the contractor, Gus, who'd been chomping to get started for the past month—even though escrow had yet to close. Gage planned to spend the next forty-eight hours working on the next phase of the project and wanted to be sure all the players would be ready to consult with him Monday morning.

A woman with a brisk step and carrying a rolled up mat appeared in his office. He gave her a blank glance.

"Gage Mitchell?"

Perky . . . yoga mat . . . casual wear . . . "Amelia?" He stood and offered her his hand. "Come in. Have a seat." He pulled out her chair then moved to the side of his desk where he had laid the DD set for the artist to see. His ears had not betrayed him. Amelia was about Suz's age, with long, straight hair the color of wheat parted in the middle. She folded herself softly into the chair like a dancer and eased into it, her ballet slippers crossed at the ankles.

She peered at him, then at the pages on his desk. "I want you to know, Gage, that I will take good care of your baby."

He felt his mouth crook as he glanced at her. "Come again?"

"Your baby." She gestured at the DDs. "Trust me. As an artist, I understand how much of yourself you have put into this project. Art is always a personal investment whether we are talking about paintings on canvas or buildings along the coast." She blinked at him, as if waiting for him to comment, then must have decided he had not understood her meaning. "My interpretation of your design must not veer from your intent. I take that very seriously."

He considered her words. "Thanks." First Suz had impressed him with her creative spirit, and now Amelia was making a promise that sounded lyrical to this architect's ears. He wondered if he should take up art collecting.

Amelia leaned back. "I have a proposition for you."

Funny how she was doing all the talking.

She blinked her eyes again. Or maybe that was batting the eyelashes. Yes, she was definitely batting. "Let's discuss the rendering over dinner tomorrow night. Say Chez Rafe at six o'clock?"

Now it was his turn to blink. Marc would have a field day with this. Was the sunny artist about the age of his baby sister asking him out? His eyes flickered over her face and then back to his comprehensive drawings. Maybe she really did just want to discuss the rendering of multiple buildings and surroundings that she had exactly one week to complete. Possible. Then again, maybe Redmond had put her up to it. Was his client using her to keep an eye on him?

Mighty paranoid of you, Mitchell.

Then again, he had to eat. And what was it he'd been saying about needing to get out more? "Sure. Bring along your sketch pad."

She laughed, the sound reminding him of Cindy Lou Who talking to "Santy" Claus in *The Grinch*.

CHAPTER 26

The weekend had exceeded my expectations. Not only had I gotten the chance to interact more with campers, including s'more snacking at the fireside chat and this morning's worship-a-thon during chapel, but the reverberations from my brush with Eliot "investigative reporter" Hawl had no effect on anyone here at camp. Maybe no one other than Squid even noticed the picture.

Tidal Wave bounded through the cafeteria door where I restocked the game cabinet. I tensed, knowing how much he loved to sing out at the end of a successful weekend. He spotted me, halted, swept out a thick, hairy arm, and let loose in his best operatic baritone. "Cal-lie-e-e! Oh-o-oh, Cal-al-lie-e-e!"

"Pfsst."

He splayed wide fingers across his chest, his monstrous voice filling the dining hall. "What? You no like my singing?"

I jerked my face into a "lightbulb moment" expression. "Is *that* what you were doing?"

He grabbed a just-washed frying pan from the counter. "That's it." He raised it over his head and started for me.

A squeal escaped from me as I darted for the side door.

"You dare to ridicule my pipes!"

I pushed on the open bar, but the door was locked. Tidal Wave continued to bear down on me, pan held high, ridiculous scowl zigzagging across his face.

Another squeal flew from my lungs as I pushed two chairs out of the way and lunged behind a corner table.

"Raaaarrr!"

One of the main doors rattled as it opened, slamming shut seconds later. Tidal Wave spun around, both arms—and that fry pan—stuck in the air like he was under arrest. I stretched up on my tiptoes to see who had saved my life.

"There she is! Callie the hiker? Or huntress, perhaps?" Natalia stepped into the hall in her traditional suit and heels, a teasing smile belying the accusation behind her probing questions. "What would be the proper title for someone allegedly hiding in the bushes of a town council member's home?"

Tidal Wave lowered the pan and cast me a quizzical eye. "Stalker?"

I brushed back stray hairs that had slipped down around my face, working to keep the grin on my face from fading. "Hello, Natalia."

Her red lips stretched into a smile. "Callie."

I glanced at Tidal Wave who winked in a show of solidarity before he turned toward Natalia and lifted one of his big round hands in a wave. "Nice to see you again, Ms. Medina."

He exited the way Natalia entered. The door clicked behind him. "Not used to seeing you here on Sundays, Natalia." I resumed straightening the game cabinet. Plastic Candy Land people cavorted with Monopoly symbols and it must stop.

"Well, actually, I drove up here hoping to talk with *you*." Natalia strolled across the dining hall, dodging tables and chairs. "Quite a picture of you in the paper. Have you heard much backlash?"

I frowned. "Can't say that. No."

Natalia joined me in my quest to retrieve wayward fake money. She stacked the hundreds while I, ironically, chased after ones. "Because the board sure has been chatting about it."

I froze. "Are you saying they're concerned, Natalia? Because you should reassure them that SOS is doing well. I'm doing well. The campaign is moving forward." A shrug drew my shoulders upward. "Nothing to be worried over."

"I'm glad to hear it." Her face said otherwise. "I wonder. Have you thought about how your involvement in what is . . . hmm . . . in what is becoming a heated campaign might reflect on the camp?"

Her question hung between us. Even as my back stiffened in defense, though, I could not deny that I had not thought about that until this morning as I recapped the weekend in my mind. Hadn't even considered how leading a fight for the Kitteridge property might affect anyone other than myself. At least not how anyone might be affected *negatively.*

I guess I'd always viewed my passion for this open space as altruistic in nature, something for the community at large. While I knew that those who wanted to wrest the property from the Kitteridges would be none too happy about this fight, I never thought this campaign could cast a negative glow on anybody. *Including my family.*

But that's not the point. I hadn't considered the affect of negative press, and as a board member she certainly had. And although I had successfully dodged answering direct questions about the night Eliot snapped that hideous picture of me, my heart knew the truth. No matter how often I justified my actions with suspicions over who attended that meeting, the truth remains that I had trespassed on private property.

A shudder chilled me. I'd been caught not just by a reporter, but also by Gage. Being away from home and the frenzy over the campaign, that reality of my brazenness weighed down my shoulders like an iron cape.

"I didn't know what to expect going into this, Natalia. The people of this town love the Kitteridge property and, I don't know, it seemed like a slam-dunk idea at the time."

Natalia wore a look of deep contemplation. "Have the donations come in to support that?"

"Well, there have been many. The problem is there's a deadline and—I don't even want to think about this—but if money doesn't flow in faster, we will have failed."

"I see. And then what?"

"I move far, far away." Natalia's mouth popped open and I laughed. "I'm kidding, of course. I haven't really let my mind go there, Natalia. I can't. Not yet."

"May I make an observation, Callie?"

Here it comes. Would it be acceptable to tell the camp's board chair no? "Sure."

"You are a gutsy woman. I've been impressed with how you defy convention and follow that beat of your heart. Thomas paid you an enormous compliment recently when he told me how tirelessly you work for this camp, and how much the children love you. He said it was a shame you did not get more time with them."

Thomas told Natalia that? About me?

"As someone who I've observed to be quite remarkable about thinking outside the box, I would encourage you to do the same thing about this quest you are leading up. As you reluctantly noted, the money necessary to purchase the property may be too little too late. It's a shame really, but a possible reality as well."

I swallowed back creeping disappointment even while fighting off the possibility that we could lose.

Natalia took hold of my free hand with both of hers. I'd never seen her be so . . . so . . . motherly. I struggled with a sense that she had something to say but was not being forthright about it. "Be open to what God has in store, Callie. It may or may not be as you hope, and yes, I absolutely believe in the power of prayer, but what will be, will be. It's God's will we should all be praying for. Wouldn't you agree?"

It may or may not be as you hope. Starting a business fresh out of college with soaring dreams and idealistic expectations made me understand the truth of Natalia's words. I had let go of all the disappointment that came with losing those hopes to Justin, though, hadn't I? Or maybe not. Maybe the memory of dashed dreams had lingered.

Natalia watched, waiting for me to say something so I nodded in agreement, still nursing the suspicion that she had more to say —but wouldn't. The idea continued to niggle at me. Were her admonitions really all for me? Or maybe I was being too obstinate to recognize God staring me down. If he wanted to do so by way of a woman with a not-a-hair-out-of-place updo who wore nothing but wool blend suits, he could. He was God. He could do whatever he wanted to make his point.

AMELIA STROLLED INTO CHEZ Rafe fifteen minutes late wrapped in a gypsy skirt, her rubber slippers flapping across the restaurant's burnished pavers. "Sorry to have kept you waiting, Gage." She slipped into her seat and plopped a sketch pad, some files, and a case of pencils on the table.

"Do you eat here often?" As soon as he said the words, Gage had to stifle the gasp that caught in his throat. The bar scene had never been his thing, but there he was offering a variation of a standard pickup line, to a woman who reminded him of his little sister, no less.

To her credit, Amelia didn't blanch. "Actually, yes, I do." She looked at an approaching waiter. "Good evening, Terrance."

He kissed her on both cheeks like they were in France. "Amelia! How are you, darling?"

"I'm doing well, love." She gestured to Gage. "I'd like you to meet Gage Mitchell, architect extraordinaire."

With all the drama of a beginning acting student, Terrance

pressed his fingertips into his chest. "An architect! How *fabulous*. Working on any projects around here?"

Gage ignored the waiter's appraising stare. "I am." He took a sip of water. "Transforming the Kitteridge property. Know it?"

The exaggerated smile on the man's face shrunk considerably. He glanced at Amelia and then back at Gage. "I'm afraid I do." He pursed his lips and paused, glancing around the restaurant as if to reformulate what he might say next. He took in a quick breath through his nose, his eyes continuing to focus anywhere but on them. "What can I get you both?"

Amelia smiled at him, unaffected by their waiter's countenance change. "You mustn't react that way, Terrance." She tsked-tsked. "Gage here has put together a sustainable design that, eventually, the community will love."

Terrance stood stick straight, unable to make eye contact with Gage. "Perhaps. Now if there's nothing I can get you from the bar, I will return in a moment to take your orders." He spun away, his shoulders more tense than a new wooden fence.

Amelia turned to Gage. "I see you're quite the popular guy around here." She laughed lightly as if attempting to lessen the sting.

He shrugged. "Saw the welcome wagon riding down my street the other day, but all the driver did was spit on my lawn."

Amelia nearly choked on ice. She laughed so loud that several nearby diners glanced uneasily at their table. "You almost made me get my files wet!" She laughed with abandon, apparently unworried about the attention she garnered. She and Suz could be good friends.

"Speaking of files, I'm here to answer your questions." He paused. "Would you like to take a look at the menu first?"

She waved him off. "Nope. Already know what I'm having."

Gage smiled. "All right. I do too."

She held up her hand and Terrance came running. His stance had softened slightly, but he still appeared to have trouble making eye contact. They gave him their orders and he darted into the kitchen.

Amelia opened a file, pulled a pencil from her case, and looked at Gage. "Now, I've looked over the DD set carefully, Gage, and I definitely have some questions for you."

Gage nodded, knowing rendering consultants often flashed their claws at this point in the process. Less of this happens when renderers were working from construction documents—but he hadn't gotten to those yet and Redmond was hot to get this rendering completed for the upcoming ad campaign.

He nodded. "Shoot."

"Love the condo design, so free-flowing and all, but what especially intrigued me was the way you have structural support going through the middle of several floors of showers."

Gage kept his face neutral. "Like that, do you?"

"Oh, yes. Nice design, but where are you going to place those drains, I wonder?"

He leaned forward and clasped his hands on the table. "The ceiling?"

She laughed. "I take it you'll be fixing that."

He unclasped his hands. "I'm sure you are aware that you are working from the early schematics. The roofs haven't been worked out, windows still need detailing, haven't met with the engineer yet to coordinate all the mechanical, structural—"

"I get it. Okay. Still more to do."

Terrance arrived with their salads. "Pepper?" Just how did the waiter manage to so evenly grind pepper onto Gage's salad without looking?

Amelia tasted her salad. "I'd be remiss not to mention that in Plan A's elevation, you're missing a chimney. Is your client going to just have to deal with the bellowing smoke or—"

"Tell you what. Why don't you just draw one in and we'll go with that."

She closed one eye and assessed him like he was one of her paintings. "You're kidding, aren't you?"

He shrugged. "Not really, like I said there are still many details to work out. Guess you're going to have to improvise."

She tipped her glass. "You're on, but we most definitely will have to stay in touch. If you don't watch out, Gage-man, I might have to put you in my speed dial."

She threw a smile at him, and he could see a glimpse of her tongue resting on the underside of her top lip. Queasiness turned his stomach. He wanted to kick himself under the table, hoping she hadn't mistaken his banter for something romantic. Reading a woman's signals never did come easy for him stretching all the way back to Franny Holmes in sixth grade. He'd taken her frequent phone calls asking for help with math to mean she wanted to go out with him, when all she really wanted was—help with math.

And Callie. She bristled when he came near, but when he'd kissed her underneath that ledge at Jamison's place, there was no mistake in the soft way she responded. Her faint groan still reverberated in his ears and the confusion in her eyes continued to melt him. One day soon he wanted to find out what was behind all that fight she had in her.

Amelia the artist sat across from him, a smoky smile lounging across her face. "That all right with you?"

He answered her with the professionalism she deserved. "Call me during office hours, and I'll be glad to answer your questions."

By the way her grin reduced, he figured he had not given her the answer she was after.

CHAPTER 27

atalia's admonishment to seek God's will replayed in my head as I scooted across the Kitteridge property on my way to Sheila's house. The waters below had taken on a blue-green cast in the afternoon sun, making me think of the sea glass I'd collected over the years. Something touched me about the way an ordinary bottle came away beautiful after churning through chilly, salty waters. I'd felt tossed around lately too, or to be honest, more like the past few years.

The gentle music of the waves drew me, making me want to linger awhile on the great cliff overlooking the sea. Natalia had told me to be open to what God had in store and she was right. That's really what I should be seeking in everything I did, and yet, the thought scared me. Maybe God had no intention of blessing this campaign. Maybe he didn't care about such trivial things, not with so much human suffering to handle.

Or worse, maybe God would punish me for not seeking his will first before opening my big mouth to Ruth. If only I had been patient and prayed and sought his advice, this whole thing could have turned out much differently. I knew that the moment June Kitteridge came to see me with her sad tale. Guilt over having already set a campaign in motion gnawed at my heart.

For once, I remembered to bring my cell phone with me. Checking the time, I tore myself away from the cliff's edge and hustled toward Sheila's home determined to put more effort into these weekly gatherings.

Once there, Brenna answered the door, a stern furrow across her brow. "Hello, Aunt Callie."

I dropped to my knees and smiled right in her face. "Hello to you, dear niece Brenna."

A smirk turned the end of Brenna's petite mouth upward. "I'm trying to stay mad at you, Auntie."

I whisked her into my arms, one hand tickling her. "No way. You can't do it. I just know you can't!"

Brenna squealed and giggled. "Yes, I can. I'm really, really mad at you, Aunt Callie."

Blakey appeared, tugging at my pants. "I'm mad at you too!" Fat chance of that. All of his baby teeth showed when he smiled.

The three of us huddled on the floor, wrestling and laughing until my lungs were spent and both sides ached. I pulled Blakey onto my lap. "Listen, little man. You too, Brenna. I am so, so, so sorry that I forgot to take you to ice cream last week."

Brenna crossed her arms. "You broke your promise. You should never break promises."

I swallowed down but couldn't hide my regret. "That's right and I need you to forgive me. Can you do that?"

Brenna pouted. "I . . . don't . . . know . . ."

Blakey laid a pudgy hand on one of his sister's crossed arms. "C'mon. She said she was sor-ry!" He rose on his knees, placing his face inches from mine. "I forgive you, Auntie Callie. We gonna go to ice cream tomorrow?"

His earnest expression moved me and I wanted to cry. I'm going to buy this kid the biggest—

Two arms flew around my neck and squeezed. Any more

strength in them and I might have had to be resuscitated. "All right, I forgive you too." Brenna's voice tickled my ear. "I can't stay mad at my auntie."

I grabbed their hands and tucked them into my sides. "You both have to promise me something, okay?"

They nodded, both waiting, eyes wide.

"You eat everything on your plates tonight with no squawking."

Blake wrinkled his nose. "Even the broc-lee?"

"Yes, even the broccoli. Promise me now because I'm going to talk to your mama about letting you both come out with me for . . . are you ready for this?"

Brenna's voice came out hushed like a whisper. "Yeah? Yeah?"

"Hot fudge sundaes with nuts and a big red cherry on top!"

Both kids squealed and tumbled over me. Somehow I landed on my stomach and the two kidlets climbed onto my back, bouncing like I was some kind of wild pony. An *oomph* escaped from my windpipe, but it was the approaching *click-click* of Sheila's heels across the laminate flooring that made me wince. I drew up on my elbows.

"Hey, Sheila."

"When I heard the children screaming, I should have known that Aunt Callie had arrived." She placed a hand on her waist. "You're early. This is a first."

"Glad to see me?"

Something flickered in her eyes. She paused. Sheila never paused. "Of course I am."

I didn't expect that.

"Come help me set the table."

Okay, now *that* I expected.

Vince offered me a hug in the kitchen as I grabbed the silverware drawer and headed for the dining room. He opened the fridge and hovered there. "Something to drink?"

"Mineral water, if you have it."

He followed me to the dining area where Sheila arranged giant hollyhocks and a spray of honeysuckle in a clear glass vase. I stopped, holding the large drawer on my hip. "Wow, Sheila. I would never have thought of that combination. Pretty."

A smile lifted her cheekbones. "Just thought I would give it a try."

Vince entered the room and handed me a tall glass of mineral water. "How's the campaign coming?"

"Lots of donations and questions. I keep my phone turned off, otherwise the ringing drives me crazy."

"You never seemed to keep your phone on anyway," Sheila said.

I sipped my drink and shrugged. "This is true."

Vince's gaze pointed toward the west. "That sure is a beautiful piece of property. If I had the money—"

Sheila looked up, sharply. "Don't think about that, Vince. As it is, you already work too much."

A rueful expression fell on Vince. He lowered his eyes to his glass. "Guess so."

Sheila set down her shears and grabbed Vince around the shoulder. She planted a swift kiss on his cheek. "Don't go worrying about what we can't buy. I have all I need right here." She patted his rump. "Now please get my large blue platter down from the top shelf."

Vince snuck me a smile as he left. The doorbell rang.

I stopped wrapping silverware. "I'll grab it."

Greta pushed her way through the front door like a mother racing after her chick. "Oh, honey, get me a chair. I need to put these tree trunks up!"

Bobby ushered her in, his arm around her waist, a grim set to his mouth. He glanced at me and I wished I could wash away the worry I saw there.

My heart picked up speed at seeing my dear friend and sister-in-law in such a state. "Are you hurting? Can I get you a drink? A pillow?"

Bobby helped her lower into a chair and she seemed breathless. "I . . . just . . . want . . . a baby!"

Vince stepped into the room with a glass of water and Sheila on his heels. "Drink this." He thrust the glass into her hands as Sheila shoved a pillow beneath Greta's swelling calves.

Greta eyed him. "What is it?"

I scrunched my forehead. "Greta, it's just water. What's wrong with you?" I grabbed Bobby's arm. "What's wrong with her?"

He threw up both hands, using one of them to rake through his messy brown hair. "She wanted to walk, you know, to see if labor could start so I took her out to the Kitteridge property and we, uh, walked."

I felt my eyes widen. "*All* of it?"

He nodded vigorously, biting his lower lip. "Pretty much."

We turned to see Greta downing the water like a woman lost in the desert. I swung my gaze to Bobby. "That's miles of shoreline. Did you do the interior hikes too?" The wince on his face gave it away.

"Oh, Bobby!"

He pressed his palm to his cheek. "Not all of them, of course. She had all this energy this morning. Kept cleaning the house, even though it didn't need it. She washed all of the baby's new bedding—"

Sheila nodded. "Well, it's always a good idea—"

Bobby faced us, his expression bewildered. "But she'd already washed them and put them in the new cradle!"

Sheila's hand found Bobby's arm. "You're describing nesting. It's perfectly normal for a woman who's about to give birth to experience sudden bursts of energy. The trick is to know how to use that energy wisely."

Bobby blew out a long breath. "In other words, no long hikes." He glanced at his wife then back to us.

Sheila shrugged. "A nice brisk walk around the block would have been just fine."

I knelt next to Greta and stroked her belly, hiding the climbing panic within me. The thought of childbirth made my forehead perspire. "How's my little Clementine or Norwich today, huh?"

Greta's head lolled against the back of the recliner. "Giving me all sorts of trouble. He or she has been kicking me in some awful places."

The color had returned to Greta's cheeks as well as her sense of humor. Sheila was consoling Bobby over his regrets, and Vince was running around refilling everyone's drinks. Blakey rolled around on the floor with his toy diesel truck, while Brenna padded around behind her father, pretending to tend to everyone's needs.

Bliss like a fluffy cotton blanket wrapped comforting wings around me. It felt good to be part of this family. Flaws and all, when it came down to caring for one another, we were there. All of us. I leaned my head on Greta's shoulder and relaxed, noticing how her hands, clenched when she and Bobby arrived, now draped along the sides of the chair. She let go a ripple of a sigh.

I barely heard the door open and more family trail in. From somewhere beyond the living room wall, Jim's booming voice made it to my ears first.

"This may not be over yet. Callie has some serious explaining to do and without counsel she may find herself in a deeper pit."

Sheila shushed him. "Now, Jim, this is neither the time nor the place."

"Are you a lawyer, Sheila? Because last time I checked, I was the one who attended three hard years of law school. Trust me when I say that girl has made terrible choices and they may not only bury her, but this family as well!"

A frown replaced Bobby's panicked expression. He offered me a hand, pulling me up, and together we made our way out of the living room and into the dining room where Sheila stood toe-to-toe with Jim.

She spoke between gritted teeth, as Vince held her shaking shoulders. "I'm telling you that I'm tired of the way you treat this family."

Jim trivialized her with a sarcastic smirk. "You're tired of *me*? Spare me."

Sheila wouldn't let up. "We have been over this a thousand times and I already told you that Callie has it under control. Jim, I'm beginning to realize that you are nothing but a bully, always seeking your way, always bellowing about something."

Jim caught eyes with Vince. "What's wrong with her—that time of the month or something?"

One of Vince's brows stretched into his forehead. "Cool it, man."

This only served to make Sheila rise more. "This is the way you've been for as long as I remember, Jim. But let me remind you how it really went when we were kids. While you were off hanging with your friends in high school, *I* was the one keeping things running around our house. Mom and Dad left *you* in charge when they traveled, but you were never around. *I* cooked, *I* cleaned up after everyone, and *I* tucked Bob and Callie into bed at night." Her face flamed red, her breathing loud. "Frankly, I'm surprised that all that pot you smoked didn't fry your brain. That was one thing *I* couldn't help you with!"

She threw a rag at his feet and spun around only to be stopped by Vince who hugged her in the tightest hug I'd ever seen. Like a mood ring, the skin on Jim's face evolved into pink followed by purple and ultimately deep, dark red. Neither Bobby nor I could breathe, let alone move; and although the drama between our older siblings shocked us beyond belief, I found comfort in solidarity with Bobby. Like old times.

"Well." Jim pursed his lips so tightly I thought they might

disappear inside his big mouth. "The truth finally comes out. Sheila here thinks—"

"Bobby! Callie! Oh! Oh . . ." Greta's cry broke us from the scene in the dining room.

"Greta? What is it, honey?" Bobby said as we flanked Greta, each kneeling at her side.

"My water. I think it broke."

A gasp flew from my mouth and an instant sheen of moisture covered my cheeks and forehead, my body's attempt to cool me down. Bobby looked equally stressed. Greta's gaze whipped from him to me. "I'm the one about to push a baby out of me. C'mon. Get it together."

Bobby smacked a swift kiss on her forehead. "There's my girl. Always keeping me in line." He pulled her up while I dashed into the dining room to get the others.

Apparently Sheila had already figured what was happening. Flushed with worry, I met her at the bottom of the stairs where she landed with an oversized beach bag. At my raised brow, she said, "Things to help Greta during labor."

As much as I'd anticipated the birth of Bobby and Greta's sweet baby, I had also feared this moment. Sheila's presence, though, offered comfort in the midst of swirling confusion. Of all of us, she seemed to know exactly what to do. After helping Greta to the bathroom, Sheila put Vince in charge of the children, told Bobby to get the car ready, and asked me to wet down a washcloth, for what reason, I had no idea.

Sheila supported Greta back to the living room and flicked her chin toward the door. "Jim, open it up. Come on, Callie." She turned her gaze to me. "We need to get to the hospital ASAP."

My normally blustering eldest brother did what he was told, as did I. Cool water from the washcloth soaked into my skin as I followed Greta and Sheila out the door and to the waiting car, unsure how big a help I could actually be.

GUS STONESBY, FROM STONESBY and Sons Construction, jingled spare change in his pocket for ten excruciating minutes, long enough for him to get the gist of the project's newest additions—and to drive Gage nuts in the process. He'd heard of guys that needed to be on their feet or squeezing a stress ball or drumming their fingers just to think, but Gage had never been one of those people. God had given him the gift of focus, meaning he could sit for hours and concentrate fully on one project. Of course, it might be said that the gift had its downsides, especially when it came to being able to free the mind enough to figure out something equally important—like women.

Specifically, like Callie.

It was Sunday and although he had planned to meet with Gus first thing Monday morning, the contractor pressed him to meet this afternoon instead. He'd been preoccupied, though, thinking about Callie, wondering how camp went, when they would speak again and how that might go. Allowing too much time to pass might backfire. Would she think that he had gotten what he'd come for? That the fire inside him had fizzled?

Dude, get it together—you don't even know if she's into you.

He shook away his thoughts, trying to concentrate as Gus started up the coin jangling again while taking another look at the schematics for the Kitteridge property. Learning that his client had crossed the line with the town council didn't make his job easier, as some might think. He had no desire to circumvent the law in any way to get his job done. Standing up to his former boss had gotten him fired, and he'd taken that as a sign that God had something new for him, something better.

But doubt had turned over inside of him. Was looking the other way as bad as participating in questionable activities?

Suz leaned into the office. "Gage, you have a call on the line."

He raised both brows and she answered by mouthing, "Redmond." With a nod, he moved to his desk and took the call. "Gage here."

Redmond's voice crackled, as usual. "You with the contractor?"

"Yes, we're meeting now."

"Make sure you tell 'im this is no free-for-all. Don't let him make unnecessary changes that are going to cost me more money."

Surely Redmond knew Gage had little control over that.

"And you listen to the guy. He's been throwing up buildings all over the state. If he tells you something's not right, fix it."

"Of course." Why was he wasting his time? Gage would be working with the structural engineer to make sure that all aspects of the design were drawn up properly. Having Gus's input as the contractor should add another keen-eyed voice into the mix. When this project finally got off the ground, nothing within Gage's power to fix would be left to chance.

He cleared his throat, the sound of Redmond's phlegm was more than Gage wanted to hear first thing in the morning. "I'll be out at the golf course tomorrow morning with Rick and a couple of key players in this project. We have some things to iron out, and I'll be tellin 'em to expect those construction docs real soon. Nose to the grindstone, know what I mean?"

Key players? As in council members? Gage considered the consequences. "Those things you need to iron out . . . anything I can answer for you?"

"Not unless you're a legal whiz. Any experience in drafting proposed amendments?"

"Well, I—"

"That's what I thought," Redmond spat out. "You take care of your end of things—and don't delay. And I'll handle securing this property once and for all. Capiche?"

He clicked off without a goodbye and all Gage could think was that his client had spent too much time with his fast-talking realtor Rick Knutson.

$\mathcal{I}$t didn't take Sheila much time to transform Greta's plain hospital room into a soothing day spa. Tranquil ocean sounds emanated from iTunes, flameless candles flickered on every open surface—she even rubbed lotion into Greta's feet and ankles before tucking them into a pair of fuzzy socks. As for me, I kept the washcloth saturated by running back and forth between the bathroom sink and our patient.

Sheila kept the room buzzing along. "Callie, hurry with that compress."

Doing as told, I approached the side of Greta's bed. Worry lines marked her forehead making me both want to comfort her —and run away. Shame heated my cheeks. *Pull it together! Greta needs you.*

Greta touched my clenched fist. "Where's Bobby?"

"He's filling out your paperwork, honey. They said you were too far along to sit in the hall."

"Right. I knew that. Oh!" She fixated on Sheila. "What . . . do . . . I . . . do?"

Unlike me who shrunk back into the corner, fear causing all

my muscles to contract, Sheila hovered like a mother hen, cooing into Greta's face. Her voice came through like a whisper. "Breathe slowly. Keep breathing. It's all good. You and Bobby are going to have a precious baby to hold real soon. That's nice. You're doing very well."

As quickly as the etched pain on Greta's face had appeared, it drifted away. Sheila massaged Greta's temples and cheeks with her fingers, and every bit of lingering stress seemed to leave her. I marveled.

A nurse arrived with a harried Bobby following on her heels. The petite woman with brown shoulder-length hair talked to Greta from the end of the bed while stroking one of her ankles. "I see you've been having some nice contractions already. Good for you!"

Nice contractions? How can anything that painful be considered *nice?*

Sheila kept her eyes on Greta but spoke to the nurse. "I take it you have her monitor hooked up to screens at the nurse's station?"

The nurse bobbed her head. "Absolutely. Nothing gets past us. I'll just do a blood pressure check, then I'll call the doctor." She glanced at Bobby, then at me. "Looks like you have your own pit crew here to help out. Terrific."

I lunged toward her. "Oh, but you're not leaving, are you?"

Bobby ran a hand through his disheveled head of hair, looking from me to Sheila, who scowled. Her voice belied that look, in an effort, I'd guessed, to keep Greta calm. "Thanks, Nurse. We're a great team and we're all going to help our Greta through her labor."

Greta's eyes locked with mine. "Will you really stay, Callie? I'd love it if you would." Her face took on an odd mixture of fear and hope. "Please?"

I stepped forward and held her hand. "Of course I'll stay."

"What about me?" A lopsided grin lolled on Bobby's face. "Isn't anyone going to beg me to stick around?"

"Oh, Bobby!" Greta's face crumbled into a wet mass of tears, and I lifted her hand, my eyes suggesting he get his booty over there. Fast like a spark, he moved to her side as I stepped out of the way.

After that, time zipped through space faster than a catapult shot spun through air. Greta's labor, from what I gathered by the quick succession of strong contractions and sudden entrance of a doctor and nurse, was atypical. At least, how I understood the drawn out process of labor.

Rarely had I attended a gathering of former high school friends when a glowing mom did not treat the guest list to a blow-by-painful-blow of their labor and delivery. I smiled sympathetically during those memory-charged conversations, but how easy could it be to enjoy noshing on crisp bread smeared with olive tapenade while someone described in agonizing detail their delivery of the afterbirth?

Difficult as being hemmed in between clicks of new mothers had always been, my own mom was the one to provide enough detail to solidify my desire to never ever become pregnant.

Children, I loved. Pregnancy? Not at all.

"They damage you forever!" Mom had said, in my watery memory of long ago. "Men, Oh men! They get to enjoy the process of creation while we women—yes, we *women!*—are forever altered by the audacity of childbirth. I will never forget the ripping, the tearing, the excruciation of needle and thread as it sought to repair what pregnancy had wrought."

I fought the very real urge to slip into the restroom and vomit out every inch of that speech she gave.

Greta's animal-like growl snapped me into the present. More nurses arrived with gloves and metal tools and serious expressions. Bobby had taken over labor coaching, but Sheila stayed close enough to offer support for both of them. My friend and sister-in-law looked more like a woman in the deep throes of disease rather than one about to give life. Several minutes passed along with another torturous cry from Greta before I noticed how I'd been twisting my fist into the center of my own chest.

Fat drops sprung forth over Greta's face and head, her body straining against the pressure of another contraction. Sheila's steady hand stood by, mopping. Helplessness wove its way through me, and I spun around, hiding myself from the drama.

Pray for her. The admonishment came quickly and without doubt, as sure as Greta's labored breaths. I recalled my late night chat with the young girls in my cabin and how they grappled to understand what it meant to hear God. Sometimes I did too, but I knew in this moment that *this* is what it meant.

The doctor moved into a crouched position at the end of Greta's bed, and her cries grew louder and more intense. I too moved into position, only to the far corner of the oddly shaped room, in a space just large enough to drop my head in prayer. What began as a muddle of requests slowly became more assured and specific. Bobby cheered Greta on from the sidelines. Sheila continued to give measured direction, unwavering in her encouragement. Peace began to flow through me, its warmth oozing through those places that had lain cold and barren.

The doctor's reassuring voice cut through the chaos like a beam of light in a dark room. "Almost there . . . almost . . . almost . . ."

Greta's hoarse cry turned mournful and I stepped up my prayers. Electric energy filled the room, however, peace never left.

"We're almost there, Greta." His voice so laced with both serenity and a spark of anticipation, the doctor could have been coaxing a cake to rise.

And then, as if the entire room had taken one collective

breath, a pause fell over us, the kind that anticipated good news. Or in this case, great news. I held my breath, still praying, until hearing Greta's lungs gasp in one heavy sigh of relief followed by the unmistakable bleating wail of a newborn babe.

THE MYRIAD SUGGESTIONS DROVE Gage nuts, mainly because he knew the unwillingness of his client to accept changes that might incur more costs. Surely Redmond knew the inevitability of rising prices in this business.

But the day had dawned anew. Gage hunkered down in his chair, poring over the list of updates the structural engineer had left him. Now *this* he could handle. Taking the engineer's notes and applying them to his own ideas brought his drawings closer to completion. At this point he could work out kinks and amp up the accuracy, like what an editor did for a book.

He might have stayed in that position all day had it not been for the growl that roared through his stomach. Gage glanced at the clock and blinked unbelieving eyes: 11:30 a.m. Where was Suz?

She'd said last night that Callie had not called her back all day. Her plans were to work with him in the morning until she heard from Callie. Maybe she had.

He rubbed his eyes and the phone rang. He shook off a welling sigh. "Gage Mitchell."

"Hey, dork."

"Same to you. What are you doing, Marc?"

"Sick of working and thought I'd see what trouble my old buddy has gotten himself into lately. Seeing as you never call or write or send me a Twitter." Marc pretended to sniffle.

"Oh, man. It's crazy. This development has taken over my life. I'm sitting here right now with the schematics and engineering notes side by side."

"So that's a good thing, right? You've always wanted to head up some big project and now you are. Unfortunately we little people must suffer in your absence."

"Right. Last time I heard you and Lizzy were traveling the globe in search of Egyptian earrings or something."

"Hey, don't knock it. Egyptian collectibles are big business, my friend. Did I tell you the one about the camel and the jockey who got confused? Heh-heh. Okay, forget about all that. What's going on with the girl? Made progress there?"

"You make it sound like she's one of my drawings."

Marc laughed. "Well, I *hope* you didn't make her up." He paused. "You didn't, did you?"

Gage pressed a hand to his face and dragged it down his cheek. "No, she's as real as you and I." He sighed. "Long story."

"I got all the time in the world, man. Lizzy's out on a spa day with the girls. Hit me with it."

Gage proceeded to tell Marc about finding her dog running loose on the Kitteridge property and then Callie's ultimatum at the diner and their ultimate truce. He filled him in about the SOS team's progress, providing details about her television interview and how mesmerized he found himself while watching her on the small screen.

Marc laughed. "Welcome to small town USA. I hope she's into you because Otter Bay sounds like the shrimplike town I grew up in. Couldn't walk out the door in your undies to get the paper or the whole town'd see you."

One of Gage's eyebrows darted upward. "You step outside in your underwear?"

"Well, maybe not every day, but c'mon, sometimes it's hot."

Gage laughed, the feeling washing over him like clean water. "You never fail to crack me up."

"Hey, it's a gift. So what else? You saw her on TV and then . . . where? The Five & Dime? Laundromat? Pig Slop Café?"

Gage hauled in a deep breath. He glanced at the door, still wondering about Suz. Did he want to get into this story now?

Marc's voice dropped to a lower-pitch. "I'm waiting."

"Fine. Well, here's what happened." Gage couldn't seem to find the words, or know where to start, the whole thing sounded ludicrous even before he told the story. "I was on my way to a meeting and I discovered her hiding in the bushes outside the home where it was being held and, well, I skipped the meeting."

Marc roared. "What? Oh, man, this is priceless stuff. Price. Less." He gave way to more laughter before getting hold of himself. Gage knew it could be awhile. "Okay, so you and she were hiding in the bushes and, hey, what was she doing there anyway?"

Gage tried to corral the thoughts that collided like free floating stars in his head. What was he saying earlier about his God-given gift to focus? Callie, it seemed, had a new effect on him. "Actually, I was invited to a gathering at a town council member's home. I was exhausted that night—didn't want to go. This is between us, but Callie was, uh, spying."

"Spying? Why did she have to . . . oh. So was this a secret meeting, then?"

Gage swallowed. "Guess you could say that. Man, you're quicker than I am. I didn't suspect a thing, but like I said, I was tired and ready to leave my office for home when the invite came in."

Marc's grunt sounded grim. "This is beginning to have a familiar sound to it. Man, what are you gonna do?"

"That's just it. Nothing. I'm keeping my nose clean, staying out of whatever it is my client is doing. I'm not even sure this is anything but a bunch of rich guys all trying to one-up each other. Could be innocent as that." He paused. "No matter what, though, unlike my former employer, *my* firm will not participate in anything shady."

Marc snorted. "Yeah, that's obvious. Sounds to me like you owe Callie a favor. She kept you clean. If you had gone into that meeting, you'd have given the impression that you were cool with whatever was going on."

So much of Gage's energy had been focused on finding Callie there, teasing her, kissing her . . . well, he hadn't quite thought of it like that. Marc was right. Callie had kept him from that meeting and only now did he wonder what he would have said should he have discovered more than one council member at that meeting. Would he have walked out on the biggest paycheck he'd seen in years? Or look the other way?

Was he doing that now?

Marc broke in. "So what's going on with you and Callie now? She warm to you out there under the moon, in the bushes, with only the—"

"Quit it."

"Ooh. Testy."

"We haven't spoken since then. We . . . I sort of kissed her and she asked me to leave her alone. So I did."

Marc whistled. "Lizzy would be loving this. Our Gage Mitchell kissing a local rabble-rouser underneath pine branches in the dark of night. What else happens in the story? You gonna run into each other around town, acting like it never happened? Or are you gonna call that girl and hash things through?" He paused. "Take it from a married guy—chicks dig hashing things out."

"Thanks a lot for the advice. I don't know whether to follow it or burn it."

"Hey!"

Gage laughed. "I'll take it under advisement for next week. This week I'm too buried to be able to *hash out* anything with any kind of skill." His other line lit up. "Marc, hang on a second. My other line is ringing."

He punched the blinking button. "Gage—"

"Gage?"

"Yes?"

The voice on the line sounded distressed and warmly familiar. "It's Callie. Moondoggy's gone and . . . would you help me find him?"

He told her to hang on and clicked on over to Marc. "Gotta go, friend. Callie's on the other line and she needs me."

"Oh, man. Bringing you good luck from across the miles. You can thank me later. Bye."

He clicked back to the other line. "Callie? I'm on my way."

CHAPTER 29

My feet had worn a path through the dust, driven by worry over Moondoggy's disappearance and the person responsible for it.

After such a beautiful night, one I will never forget for as long as I breathe, I stumbled into bed at around 5:00 a.m. When I awoke, Moondoggy was gone.

Had I not been so distraught and confused by lingering fatigue, I might have looked into a mirror before picking up the phone and calling Gage. The circles, the wild hair, the tear-stained cheeks all made for quite the picture of distress. The rest of my beleaguered family members would probably still be lost in slumber.

I heard the porch steps creak. I shook my hair as if it would matter, cinched my hoodie tighter, and opened the door. I hadn't seen Gage since the night at Jamison's and while the memory had stayed fairly tucked away within my mind, seeing him here at my home made them flood my memory again.

What had I done?

His eyes tipped at the corners, displaying his sympathy. "Would you like me to come in?"

Startled, I nodded. "Yes. Sorry. Please." I shut the door and faced him. "I'm sorry to bother you. It's just that I've been at the hospital most of the night."

"That doesn't sound good. Everything all right?"

A pin-light of peace shone in my mind. "Actually, it was amazing. My niece was born this morning. I watched her."

One of his brows rose and he tilted his head.

"Being born." My voice broke, surprising me. "Most magical thing I've ever witnessed." I cleared my throat. "When I came home I fell asleep. I finally woke up and Moondoggy was gone. I called the neighbor boy, J.D., thinking he might have come for him—"

"He didn't?"

"No. I've been everywhere: down by the water, up the hill toward camp, through town, and I can't find him."

"Was he here when you got home?"

"I figured he was asleep so I fell into bed." Tears sprang to my eyes as the reality of this situation settled deeper into my core. I dropped my gaze to my feet, shaking my head. "I'm such a terrible mother."

Gage's hand found my shoulder, giving it an awkward rub. "Not true."

"It gets worse." I held out a worn piece of paper. "When I first noticed Moondoggy was missing, I searched around the house for him. I found this in the birdbath in my front yard." The note had dried to a dirt-colored patina, crisp to the touch.

Gage reached for it, watching me. "What's this?"

I nodded for him to read it, too choked up to reply.

I warned you to leave the land alone.

Even your dog is sick of you.

Gage shot me a look. "Someone's been *threatening* you?" He pressed his fist into his bottom lip and began to pace, his gaze focused on the sparsely worded note before finding my eyes again. "How long has this been going on, Callie? Are there more notes like this?"

I retrieved the other two from my bookcase and handed them to him.

"Outrageous. Have you reported these?"

"No. I haven't. I figured it was just someone from the developer's office trying to scare me off. I never thought they would actually do anything like this—lure my dog away. They wouldn't hurt him, would they?"

Tension clouded Gage's features. Either he was annoyed with me for not reporting the two previous threats or just worried, like I was, about Moondoggy. I watched him work out his thoughts. The silence nearly shouted between us. And then he did what, instinctively, I knew he would. He wrapped both arms around me and pulled me into him, crushing me with comfort.

In this moment we weren't enemies fighting a bitter battle over property, but friends.

I had ridden endless waves of emotion lately, including the crescendo of my niece's birth last night, and the abrupt crash of this morning's events. In the silence Gage embraced me, rubbing my back and inviting some of that emotion to spill over. My tears flowed unencumbered, saturating the soft fabric of Gage's shirt and releasing those pent-up things that have a way of building forts within the soul.

One of Gage's hands dug into my hair, massaging my head. I flashed on the pain that wretched across Greta's face and coursed through her body last night and the way she later held that sweet child with the barest of available strength. She'd said, "Some things are just worth the pain, Callie." I knew she meant every word of that.

So many tears came, I could barely see. I didn't need to, though, because Gage's steady arms held me up. I hadn't experienced the support of a man for a very long time and I wondered if I ever really had. I was beginning to understand what Greta meant.

SURREAL. THE WORD SPRANG to Gage's mind as he stood in Callie's paint-cloth draped home, cradling the distraught woman in his arms. She needed someone and she called him. *Him.* On any other day this would have rocketed his heart, but instead, agitation stirred within starting with a piercing sting of anger at the thought of the threatening notes she had received. Had Redmond done this? Or Rick? Neither seemed the type, but then again, they were hot to get this project going.

And with Moondoggy mysteriously missing, Gage didn't know what to think, but he did know this: He would canvass the entire town until he found her beloved pet.

He waited, though, and held her, sopping fresh tears with the front of his shirt. Something was different about Callie this morning. The stiff resistance that seemed to come easy for her had not made an appearance since he arrived. Morning sunlight streaming through the window fell across her hair, the moment like a snapshot. She melded into him and though a flame had fired him up to be her knight and solve the problems at her feet, Gage wanted to ride this feeling for its entirety.

Gently she pulled back and peered up at him. Despite her tear-stained skin and sad eyes, Callie was beautiful.

"I know things haven't been very good between us, Gage. Thanks for coming anyway . . ." Her words trailed off into a new spattering of sniffles and sobs until she sucked in a breath and raised her head again. "I'm not usually like this." She forced a sad laugh. "Always kind of prided myself on that."

Gage lifted her chin with his thumb. "I'm glad you called." *I dreamed you would.* He fanned his hand on her cheek, flicking tears away with his fingers. "You and I . . . there's something going on here, and I think we should shove aside our differences and face it."

She stared at him, rubbing her lips, sad eyes threatening to fill again. She nodded once and her lips parted as if to say something.

It took all his strength to hold back. He wanted to cover her mouth with his own, but a caution sign flashed in his mind. *Halt. Don't take advantage of the situation.* He leaned toward her, his voice a whisper. "But first, I want to help you, Callie. Let's go find your pup."

She pulled away abruptly, one hand covering her face. "You're right. What was I thinking letting myself get so emotional." She tucked wayward hair behind her ears. "I'll just go splash some water on my face and be right back." She turned toward the bedroom and stopped to look back. "You really don't mind, Gage?"

"Stop being a lone ranger, Callie."

Her eyes and forehead frozen in fear and sadness, she just nodded.

An hour later they left the police station with a written report and the realization that the SOS campaign was about to make the news again. Just how far would opposition to the campaign go to see this project—the one he should be in the office finalizing—built? If anyone connected with the proposed development of the Kitteridge property were the perpetrators of the threatening notes, they'd be guilty, of at the very least, harassment, and at the other end of the criminal spectrum: terrorist threats. Might also be suspected of dognapping, i.e., dog-stealing, to be precise.

Next priority—finding Moondoggy. Gage had to twist Callie's arm, so to speak, to get her into his truck. If given the choice, Gage would walk too, but they had much ground to cover and not a lot of time.

They rolled through town again, just like earlier before stopping at the police station. It didn't take long since the entire village of Otter Bay consisted of just two winding blocks with a few side streets thrown in for local color. Callie held on through the often bumpy ride, her jaw set and eyes focused on every measure of space around them. She didn't look surprised when he detoured from the village and pulled alongside the Kitteridge property.

Before he could unbuckle his seat belt, Callie had opened the door and landed on the ground holding onto the leash they'd brought with them. She jogged ahead of him, lean legs carrying her up the incline, loose hair bouncing behind her.

"Moondoggy!" She shouted through cupped hands. Without glancing at him, she spoke. "He's here. I can feel it. Let's spread out, okay?"

Doubt nudged him, but he couldn't refuse her. "Sure. I'll take the hills—" She had already begun jogging up a trail. He shrugged. "—or I could wind along the cliffs."

He set out, moving along the edge of the cliff walking close enough to view the beach below. *Wish I'd worn something with tread.* He had thrown on deck shoes this morning, for comfort, fully aware that they'd long since outlived their usefulness for grabbing unsmooth surfaces.

The land curved at this spot, providing a deep inlet to long, frothy-whipped waves. He'd passed the stairs already and knew the only way down to the beach from here came compliments of God. Rocks and wild bushes provided uneven support that only a four-legged animal could safely traverse. He glanced down. *No way.*

Callie continued to jog the upper trails, the outline of her body rigid against the threat of losing her dog. A part of Gage half-expected to leave this place dog-less and to find a ransom note back at the house. He didn't like the thought, but it had crossed his mind more than once.

A breeze from the west stirred, rustling wild poppy and sea grasses intertwined on the ledge. Sea lions and elephant seals began to bark in the distance. In his study of the area, he learned about the fragility of seal rookeries. One gross disturbance could scare the animals away forever.

He swallowed the thought. Sea lions, or otters for that matter, could live anywhere along this vast California coast. Was it up to him to worry over whether construction equipment and workers would disturb the creatures enough to make them leave?

Another bark made it to his ears and he scowled. He knew it wasn't his responsibility, but it bothered him just the same. He shielded his eyes against the flowing rays from the overhead sun, hoping to catch sight of a raft of slithery creatures lounging on the water. Instead, he saw something he had not expected.

Moondoggy.

He threw a wave into the air, catching Callie's attention until she began to run full force down the hill in his direction. On the beach Moondoggy's nose noticed the swelling excitement, and he lifted his pointed face from where it hovered over the sand, sniffing the air. Fearing the animal would run, Gage crouched down, placing one foot on a scrubby patch of sea grass that grew out from a crevice in the earth. Slowly he climbed down the face of the cliff, using his hands for balance while his feet found less-than-desirable places to land. At about halfway down, with one foot on the tip of a sharp rock and the other balanced against crumbling wall, he looked up to find Callie peering at him.

"You're crazy," she hissed. "I'm afraid to call him. He might see you hanging off that cliff and run like mad."

In one swift action he held a finger to his lips.

She frowned, still whispering. "I'll go north, in case he runs. You going to be okay?"

He nodded. If he could make it past the sheer face of the middle section of this rock, he will have made it to safety. The last quarter way down consisted of mostly plant-supported ledges and rocks. Moondoggy, for his part, had resumed his stance, sniffing the sand beneath him.

Despite the sheerness of the rock's face and the flatness of the bottom of Gage's shoes, he took a chance and ran toward the first ledge near the bottom. Actually, he slid, tried to catch his balance, and fell backward, hard, landing on his rear. If it weren't for the toughness of his jeans and the wallet in his back pocket, he'd be more sore than ever tomorrow.

Recovering, he sneaked down the rocks and sunk into the sand, thankful for minimal damage. Moondoggy lifted his head again, sniffed the air, probably catching wind of the cavalry's eminent arrival. Gage slowed and glanced into the distance, not wanting to scare the animal away. He could see Callie up on the cliff, looking for a safe way down.

He needn't have doubted, for when he caught sight of Gage watching him, Moondoggy, mouth wide open and tongue hanging free, launched into a sprint and nearly knocked him over.

CHAPTER 30

I didn't think a dog could make me cry this hard or this much. By the time I reached Gage and Moondoggy, a jet skier could have skimmed my face. Heart racing, I dropped into the sand where Moondoggy had snuggled next to Gage.

I crooked my arm around Moondoggy's neck. "Come here, you." He licked my face mixing my drying tears with slobbery spit. "Where have you been? Oh I missed you—you scared me to death. Don't ever do that again? Okay? You hear me?"

Gage watched us intently.

I froze. "What? You don't think he understands?"

He shook his head, laughing. "Nah. Just thinking what a lucky dog he is."

"Oh." I measured a breath. "Some rock, uh, climbing you did over there. Impressive."

"Huh. You were going to say falling, weren't you?" He pointed at me, a teasing smile on his face. "You were going to accuse me of rock *falling*."

I shrugged, biting back a smile of my own. "But you did it so well."

He shook his head and looked out to sea, that smile still on his face. "What can I say—it seemed like the fastest way down at the time."

"I'll say." I made a swooshing sound. "Skidding's like that."

"Fine. Be that way." We both laughed as I continued to pet Moondoggy as the lapping waves inched closer to us. "I haven't done this in awhile."

My hand froze, tucked into Moondoggy's fur. "Done what? Rescued a crazy woman and her dog?"

"Never actually did that before. But I was talking about sitting on the beach. Reminds me of being a kid, building castles and moats and burying my father in the sand."

"So is that why you became an architect?" I asked, tongue in cheek. "Because you liked building things so much?"

He paused, considering. "Hmm, well, that's when I learned to site the castle so that the tide would just barely hit it when it rose to fill the moat, thus supplying the castle with enough water to use but not enough to destroy it in a high tide." He laughed. "So in answer to your question, yes, I'd have to say that my interest in architecture—green building in particular—did start then."

"And you mustn't forget about those lost-in-thought beach-combers," I said. "Or worse, big kids with heavy feet."

"Ah, yes. The ones who stomp on castles just to be mean. Then as in now, I work by simple, common sense principles."

"Which are?"

"Avoid those people at all costs."

Laughter bubbled up from some deep place within me, forcing out the stress and worry of the morning. "Gage, thank you, from the bottom of my heart. I mean it. When I woke up this morning, I knew that no one in my family could help—not after the night we all had." Fingers of relief wended their way through my body. "You may find this hard to believe, but you were the first one that came to mind. Suz always sings your praises, so somehow I knew you would come."

His eyes knit toward each other, a faint upside down V formed above the bridge of his nose. "I'm honored."

I lowered my chin. "Honored? You make me sound like the Queen of England."

His cheeks widened in a smile and those liquid-pool eyes captured me. "More like a princess."

Goose bumps danced up my arm. *Princess?* Four little words and I softened, like butter. Faint sprays from the tide landed on my skin. What could I say to that? He hadn't laughed nor scoffed after uttering those words, instead Gage Mitchell kept a never-wavering gaze on me. I'd resisted him so far (except for that one lapse in the dark in Jamison's bushes), and at this moment I didn't have an idea why.

"I feel like you and I need to start again—again. Know what I mean?"

"You mean you think we should forget about all our previous, uh, meetings."

He shook his head. "No. That's not at all what I meant. All of those times—the confrontations out at Kitteridge, the impromptu dinner—the kiss that took us both by surprise—they're all part of our history together."

My heart caught on the word *together.*

"But some of that history, especially with my work and your cause, keeps a wedge between us." He glanced out toward the horizon. "I hate it."

My lips rubbed together before I managed to eke out a response. "I hate it too."

Gage swung his gaze back to me, but I looked away. When I did, he moved closer. I knew by the way the sand shifted and Moondoggy's tail started slapping against my thigh.

Gage's fingers reached for my chin and turned me toward him, his touch sending a spark down my neck. His gaze caressed my eyes, my cheeks, my mouth, and I felt steady as a kite in a light wind. Gage kissed me then, lightly at first then more hungrily. I pulled him toward me, letting him know what I was discovering too—that I didn't want to send him away again.

A wave crashed and rolled until cold water slipped beneath us, but neither of us shied away from it. If it were not for Moondoggy's insistent pull on the leash wrapped around my forearm, we might have sat there in each other's arms past sunset.

GAGE DROVE THE TWO miles home after dropping off Callie and Moondoggy, bouncing along as if sitting plopped in the middle of Cloud Nine. How stupid was that for a guy to say? Then again, he could hear Marc in his head now, egging him on, telling him how much chicks dig a guy's softer side.

Until recently, he wasn't aware that he had a side that was quite so . . . so . . . pliable.

This should not have surprised him, however. His and Suz's parents had the ultimate love story until their mother's sudden passing at fifty. Their father didn't live much longer after that. The doctors called it cancer, but he had always surmised that his father's heart had been too broken to beat. Gut-wrenching as losing their parents was, they'd always found a foothold of comfort knowing how intertwined their lives had been.

He pulled into the drive, aware that a grin had become embedded in his cheeks. Suz's car sat at the curb as he strolled up the path alongside his clipped lawn and bounded toward the door.

"Suz? Hello?" He stepped into the living room, only silence to greet him. He wandered into the kitchen and opened the refrigerator. In all the chaos of the morning and afternoon, he had not stopped to eat, and though he'd need to get back to work soon, the grumblings of his stomach called. Spying a plate of Suz's leftover lasagna, he retrieved it, served up a slice, and waited while his plate heated in the microwave.

A pile of envelopes and advertisements on the table caught his eye. One piece of mail, an envelope ripped at the corner, lay on top. *Heinsburgh Valley Correctional Facility.* The microwave bell rang, but he ignored it.

He climbed the stairs two at a time, calling for his sister, stopping at the closed door to the bedroom she shared with Jer. "Suz?"

A weak voice answered. "Come in."

Suz lie buried in rumpled bedding, an empty box of tissues teetering at the edge of her nightstand. If it weren't for the envelope he held between two fingers, he might have thought she was ill.

"Want to tell me about it?"

"It's from Len. He found out where I was from my old landlord."

It took considerable control to keep Gage from swearing. "Let me answer it for you—"

"No!" She sat up, her face red and puffy. "Stop trying to be my knight in shining armor—I'm not a child, Gage."

He raised both hands like paddles. "Give. Sorry." Since when did his little sister not want his help? "What did the guy want anyway?"

"Men suck, you know that?"

Gage stood. "Whoa. Don't compare me to that . . . that—"

"Say it! Len is a loser. I pick *losers* real well, don't I? If I were going to be in a beauty pageant that would be my talent: How to Choose a Loser with a capital *L*!"

"Don't say that. You're a beautiful, talented woman. And I'd say that even if you weren't my sister." He sat on the bed. "I don't know what this guy has said that has upset you this much." Well, he could *guess.* "But don't shut me out. You and Jer . . . you're my life, you know that, don't you?"

Suz released a throaty sob. "He stole drugs, leaving Jer and me to fend for ourselves. You should have *heard* how catty all the neighbors got. Did you know they called Jeremiah a criminal's spawn?"

Gage flinched.

"I never told you this but they said that Len had a girlfriend, someone he brought into our home while I worked. I denied it to everyone who spread that nasty little rumor, always tried to protect Len's reputation." She winced. "But it was all true."

Gage's heart sank lower than it had already gone since finding his sister in this state. "He never deserved you."

Suz gave a sarcastic laugh. "Yeah, well, seems you're the only one who thinks that." She shook her head and threw the covers off of her. "I don't care anymore. Forget it all—forget him."

"What did the letter say, Suz?"

"He wants a divorce." She choked back another sob. "Yeah, apparently his girlfriend wants to marry him. *In the prison.*"

He crushed the envelope in one hand and pitched it into the trash. "Let him. You don't need that guy and you know it. Now he's guaranteed to stay far away from you and from Jeremiah. Isn't that what you wanted all along?"

"What I wanted?" Suz stared like he had ordered her to jump off a bridge. "No, Gage, what I *wanted* was for the man I loved to love me back. What I wanted was for my son to have a father."

"I don't get it. The man committed a felony, he cheated on you, he's not worthy of either one of you."

Suz sank onto the edge of the bed, her head hanging low. "I guess I had this small hope that one day he'd listen to me. He'd find God and surrender his life to him, and then he'd realize what he'd lost."

He slid an arm around her. "And want you back."

She nodded, her voice dull with sorrow. "Yeah."

"You're right that anyone can be reformed." Gage shrugged and pulled her close. "Hopefully that will happen someday for Len. But your life is now. Your life, Jer's life, they're both gifts from God. Don't waste these years waiting for someone who's not ready to accept the grace of God in his life."

"I'll never stop praying for him, you know."

Something twisted inside Gage. His sister had been praying all along for her loser of a husband. There was something so right about that simple, merciful act, and yet it had never occurred to Gage—not even once—to do the same. He caught eyes with his little sister, seeing the woman she had become. "I know, Suz. I believe that you never will."

Later, after she'd gone to pick up Jeremiah from an afterschool care program, Gage sat in his kitchen, finally finding time in this hectic and emotionally whipped day to nourish his body. If Marc were here, he'd be on his case, urging him to nourish his soul too. He knew he should be in the office, head down, pencil to paper, yet he couldn't get Suz—nor Callie—out of his head. Both women, in different ways, were being threatened. He understood now some of what Suz had been experiencing, that despite her husband's abandonment—among other things—her heart had been broken by a man she had trusted.

What about Callie? A charge ran through him that first time they met, when she chastised the surveyor for flicking a cigarette into the ocean. She had glared at the other men, but when she looked at him, the sharp lines around her eyes softened. He knew he had not imagined that. Her soft gaze hardened once she learned he would be designing the Kitteridge project, though. But now that she knew him, and how similar they really were—except for the position on the project, that is—was that the only reason that, until today, she chafed at his presence?

Contentment rose to the surface as he thought about how they reconnected today, and yet a sickly niggle kept him from over celebrating. Someone had been leaving threatening notes at Callie's door. They may have even lured her dog away. He set down his fork, unable to take another bite, firm in his resolve that it was time to ask his client some serious, direct questions.

CHAPTER 31

*M*usky, hearty breathing awakened me, my eyes adjusting to the slow absence of light from the dimming sky. Moondoggy slept beside me, his slobbery snores making me question my sanity. I turned over to avoid his breath, my heart revving back up as my thoughts rolled over the past twenty-four hours. First a squabble at Sheila's, then the beautiful baby, followed by Moondoggy's disappearance and, finally, Gage. I pictured him, my knight, showing up at my first call, never giving up on finding Moondoggy . . . stumbling down that mountain.

I bit my bottom lip as it stretched into a smile. *Exactly why had I been fighting this man so long?* My smile faded as the answer quickened within me. Justin, had been attentive too—in the beginning anyway. At what point should a woman begin to believe that the prince won't abandon the castle?

I rolled onto my back, my eyes becoming lost in the textures on the ceiling altered by low light. My phone buzzed, again, and I knew that I'd have to face the messages eventually. Ruth had called three times so far, saying she had tough issues to discuss with me and *when will you be getting back to me already?*

I retrieved the phone, dialed, and pressed the phone to my ear. I waited as it rang several times.

"Hello?" Bobby's voice floated through the phone.

My own voice slipped out softly. "Hello, new papa. How's our new baby?"

"She's . . . she's the most wonderful, beautiful creature I've ever known. She already turns her head when I speak."

I laughed. "*Toward* you, I hope."

"Unlike you."

"Ha! And my sis-in-law?"

He sighed. "Greta's perfect. Okay, she's exhausted, but to me . . ." He paused. "She's perfect. I'd let you talk to her but she's asleep right now."

"I just wanted to check on you all. I would be there but . . ." I hesitated, not wanting to cloud Bobby's blissful day. "I'm still in bed, exhausted—what's my excuse?"

"Callie? Thanks so much for being here last night. Greta's so grateful. I am too."

"My pleasure. And I can't wait to hold the little sunshine again. You doing okay?"

"Better than okay. I've been holding her here for more than an hour—and yeah, my arm's asleep—but I've had an epiphany about my business."

"The storage center?"

"Yes. It's like I've been afraid of going forth at full speed, Callie. Jim's always been the smart one in the family, you know, the one with all the education. It occurred to me that I've never thought myself smart enough to be trusted with running a full-fledged business."

"You're kidding? But you've been doing that, and expanding, and—"

"And leaning on Henry as my crutch. You know what Greta said this morning? She said she can't wait to have another baby."

Part of me cringed, but another part of me grasped what she

said. We all watched her go through some horrendous moments, but in the end she held a tiny, precious life, and I'd be lying if I didn't admit that envy had risen like cream to the surface. "That's beautiful, Bobby."

"Yeah, it is. I remember her saying that some things were worth the pain, but when she said that, I wasn't sure if she meant that enough to do it all over again." He chuckled.

I couldn't not smile at that.

"So my new baby girl has given me a gift. She's helping me drop the fear and offering me hope that I can make wise decisions on my own—without the obsessive need for Henry's advice. If the guy decides not to offer more financing for the expansion, so be it. I may even let him loose myself."

"Really?"

"Yeah, really. I'm sorry I gave you such a hard time, Callie. You're driven by your passions, and I respect that. I know you're busy, but it meant a lot to us that you were here last night. We hope you know that."

Moondoggy stirred beside me, so I lowered my voice. "I wouldn't have missed out on little Heliotrope or Sumner's birth for anything."

Bobby's voice garbled into laughter, as if trying to constrain the decibel level in the hospital room.

"What have you decided to name my baby girl, anyway?"

"I forgot you hadn't heard. We've named her Callie, um, Callie." He chuckled again.

My breath held and with it a torrent of tears backed up against my eyes. I swallowed, trying to wash them back where they came from, but they only grew in number.

"You okay?"

I nodded, knowing full well Bobby could not see my response. "Yes." My voice cracked. "Are you serious about that?"

"Already told the nurse who's having it put on the birth

certificate. Can't imagine what it will be like with *two* Callies in my life."

"Trouble, maybe?"

"Wouldn't have it any other way."

Buoyed by Bobby's news, I hung up the phone and pulled myself out of bed. Baby Callie? Had they really named her after me? Astonished, I shook my head, still unbelieving.

And my brother's about-face regarding his investor also stirred me, bringing out my own kind of resolve. Gage Mitchell had been nothing but kind from the day I met him. We disagreed on the Kitteridge property, but he wasn't from here. He couldn't know what a sad loss that would be to this community. I thought about what Greta had said about pain, and how some things were worth it. Maybe it was time to let my heart take a chance again.

The phone buzzed, causing Moondoggy to snuffle and yelp. Ruth. What could she possibly say that could sully my near perfect mood?

A VIRTUAL CHAIN-LAYERED cloak lay across Gage's shoulders. He should be at work. He had much to do and much to talk over with his client, but his heart had disconnected from the project. Instead, Marc's insistence that he get his rear end into church drove him to this stranger's home on a Monday night. It wasn't church, but it'd do.

Slowly he wove his way up to the front door of the redwood-clad house and knocked. A tan-darkened man of about fifty with a quick smile opened the door. He remembered his name was Kevin. "Good to see you, Gage. C'mon in. The guys are in the back."

He drew in a breath, hidden behind a smile that felt anything but natural, and followed Kevin to a family room in the back of the house. A flat screen TV hung from the wall playing ESPN sport's highlights as several guys looked on from a leather couch.

At the other end of the room, three guys hovered over a table filled with chips and drinks, talking about whatever.

Kevin switched off the TV to a throng of groans. "All right, looks like everyone's here. Let's get started, okay?" He stopped and pointed his Bible at Gage. "By the way, that's Gage Mitchell. Gage? This is everyone."

Gage raised a hand in a wave and found a chair in the back. Even though he barely knew the men in this room, having only seen them the one time he stepped into church after moving to Otter Bay, a strange sense of belonging moved through him. He only wished Marc were here too. Marc had a way of shining a light on Scripture while entertaining him with witty and insightful questions of his own.

"Okay, so Gage, we've been working our way through Mark," Kevin said. "Just follow along and don't feel obligated to add anything unless you want to."

Gage nodded, forcing his mind to pay attention. How appropriate that they were studying the book of Mark. His friend would take that as God's way of not allowing Gage to forget his buddy. Like he ever could.

A man on the couch spoke, but Gage missed it. Another guy spoke up. "But don't forget, when Peter tried to correct Jesus—by suggesting that his prediction of his own imminent death was wrong—Jesus rebuked him."

"That's right," Kevin said. "Jesus told him flat out that he did not have in his mind the things of God, but only the things of men."

Another guy he remembered as Barry called out, "Yeah. What Jesus was telling them was so opposite of what seemed right for the Messiah. But it was all about doing the right thing, the work that Jesus had come to earth to do. And by suggesting he do otherwise, Peter was sinning against God."

Kevin took the floor again. "We do that whenever we do the

opposite of what God wants, even if we're only trying to save our own butts."

"The moral of the story is God's way is hard," one guy said. "Study over."

Kevin continued. "Not so fast. It's not that his way is hard, but purposeful. Listen to this, from Mark 8:37: 'What good is it for a man to gain the whole world, yet forfeit his soul?'"

The words pounded in his brain, like a needling headache, just like the same verse had done six months earlier when he'd walked off his job—actually, he'd confronted his boss and then been *thrown out* the door. His coworkers had shaken their heads. "Let it go, man." They'd said. "Look the other way. It's not your problem."

But that's not how he was raised.

The men in the room had stopped on this one passage, the debate among them growing louder and more animated. Gage couldn't keep up and longed to dart back down the hallway and out the front door. If he were to ask the tough questions, and discover answers he could not live with, would he have the courage to walk again? Even though his sister and nephew relied on his support so much?

Or would he risk his own soul for good intentions?

A brown-haired woman with glasses and a sweet smile caught his eye as she stepped shyly into the room carrying a white-frosted cake. Quietly, she deposited the dessert on the back table, followed by a miniature replica of herself, a young girl of about ten, carrying plates and silverware. The woman left and returned with a pot of coffee and tray of mugs.

She must have given Kevin the signal because he closed his Bible. "Let's take a break and get some dessert. We'll pick up with Mark 8:38 in a few minutes." The men clamored to the back table while Gage picked up his Bible.

Kevin approached him. "Hope we didn't scare you away."

"Not at all. I just need to head back to my office tonight."

Kevin squinted at the clock on the wall. "Tonight?" He shrugged. "Well, glad you could stop by, if only for a while."

Gage nodded. "Appreciate you having me—more than you know."

CHAPTER 32

I'd been living in la-la land. That was it. A fantasyland of possibilities with absolutely no grounding in reality. Funny how one call could swing the emotions from one end of the jungle to the other and cause a person to realize just how much they were beginning to resemble a monkey.

My conversation with Ruth was brief.

"Pledges have halted."

"What do you mean *halted*? Maybe they've just slowed or have come in a bit lower than others."

"No, they've stopped. Altogether. The team thinks it was your mug in the paper last week that did us in."

I breathed in and back out. "I see. How short are we?"

"Well, that's just it. Not only have the pledges stopped, but of those that had already come in, half of 'em have not been paid."

"Okay."

"That's it? *Okay?* Because if you ask me, this is not okay. Time is running out and if a miracle doesn't happen, we will have failed. Do you want that on your head?"

I should have stayed on top of things. Should have been checking my phone and answering calls and updating Stephanie with prayer requests. But I'd gotten complacent. I figured that SOS had been set in motion like a giant millhouse wheel that drew water continuously from a pond.

"Don't forget, I've got that radio interview at noon tomorrow, and hopefully I'll be able to make one last-ditch effort to save our cause."

"You mean *shores*. Save our *shores*."

"Right." We hung up, and I placed a call to June Kitteridge.

"Hello?"

"June, this is Callie Duflay. How are you and Timothy doing?"

"Oh, not good. Not good at all. Timothy's been more agitated than a washing machine on the spin cycle. Says everyone's out to get us. Are you calling to give us good news?"

I shut my eyes, trying to draw courage from some invisible place. "June, we're in trouble. The money's not coming in and without a miracle, I . . . I don't want to say what might happen."

"We'll be forced to sell our property, won't we?" Her voice sounded so small. "It is very difficult to think about, Callie. But it is not your fault, dear. I have seen your efforts and you have tried so hard for us."

"June, please don't give up on me now. I'm not giving up. In fact, I wanted to tell you that I'm going to be on the radio tomorrow at noon. Tell everyone you know, okay?" I paused, wanting desperately to ask her one more time if I could have permission to tell the public the truth about their predicament. "Will you do that?"

"I would, dear, but so many of my friends are either dead or not speaking to me these days. They say we've sold out to developers."

Then tell them the truth—that you are being strong-armed into selling your property! I opened my mouth, willing myself to make one more plea when June's sweet voice filled the phone line again. "But I would rather hear them say that than for them to know how foolish we've been with our money. Besides, as I have said many times before, Timothy would never forgive me otherwise. Never!"

My mouth slapped shut, but not before releasing one harsh sigh.

The next day I sat across from Ham, the DJ of our local radio station, KOTR, trying to curtail a yawn. I had slept fitfully through the night, often waking from overactive dreams that pitted me against angry mobs of all types. Sometimes the opposition contained faces I recognized like Eliot, the reporter, and Jamison, the council member on the hill. Other times, they were faceless beings, some children, even, moving toward me with purpose, yet never quite able to reach me. When I awoke at seven, my mind already felt restless yet tired at the same time.

After walking Moondoggy then securing him back inside the house—too afraid to let him stay outside, I showered and stopped in to see Bobby, Greta, and baby Callie before they were released from the hospital. Finally I arrived at the station ready as could be under the circumstances. A familiar voice poured from overhead speakers, the same man I heard during the noon hour on those days I chose to drive. Only instead of hearing his voice wafting through my car speakers, he sat in this tech-infused, glassed-in room, beyond the lobby's painted walls.

He motioned for me to join him in the studio where I slipped on the earphones as I'd been instructed and waited for Ham to introduce me to his listeners. We talked briefly about the campaign and then he invited listeners to call in with questions. A string of buttons lit up.

"Caller, you're on the air."

"Hi. This is Donna Marie, and I'm wondering, will the community be building a playground for children on the property?"

Ham nodded for me to respond.

"Great question, Donna Marie. As you know, the urgency of our cause has prevented us from outlining every detail of the property's use once it's back in the hands of the community." *Good. Sound positive, like this thing was likely to happen.* "However, once we receive enough funds to make the purchase, I'm proposing that a committee be formed to look at things like adding a playground or maybe even some soccer fields."

"Next caller."

"Hello. I heard your answer to that last caller and you don't mean to say that the property is going to be sliced and diced though, do you?"

"Not at all. Remember, there are several hundred acres of land and while most of it will stay preserved as open space, there's no reason not to consider using parts of it for more dedicated community use."

Ham announced a commercial break and I reached for a tissue, using it to wipe the sheen of moisture from my forehead. I watched as Ham pushed buttons and wiped away sweat droplets of his own with the back of one hand until strands of wet hair stuck to his forehead. Until today I hadn't realized the energy output necessary to participate in a radio program. Ham smiled at me briefly, before leaning into the microphone to give a plug for Holly's smoothie concoctions at the Red Abalone Grill. "Something smooth and cold for those up-and-coming hot summer days!"

He flashed his pudgy fingers at me . . . 3 . . . 2 . . . 1. Some callers had questions; others had opinions. I did my best to present a positive and knowledgeable response. The hour passed quickly and I felt good about the interview. We came to the last few minutes of the show. Ham led us out of the break.

"We're back with Callie Duflay of the Save Our Shores campaign. If you don't mind, Callie, we have another caller begging to speak with you."

"I don't mind at all."

"Hello. Is this Callie?" A male voice.

"Hello. Yes, it is."

"I saw you interviewed on television last week. Very impressive campaign you're running."

"Thank you very much."

"Your hard work is reminiscent of a 'hometown girl does good' story. Really, it is."

"Thank you very much."

"The Kitteridges must be thrilled with the prospect of selling their property to the community."

I hesitated. Saying they were thrilled by the forced sale of their property would be pushing it. Still, June was grateful to have found a way to stay in their home. "Hmm, well, yes."

"Now I read somewhere that prior to the SOS campaign, the Kitteridges had made a deal with another buyer. Is that true?"

"They had been talking with someone, yes."

"Okay, okay. Um, let me clarify something then: would the community be offering the Kitteridges more money for the property, then?"

I swallowed. While it was true that the developer had forced the sale, their buyer had agreed to a larger sum than the SOS team could possibly raise in such a short time. "The Kitteridges have agreed on the price offered by SOS and we are grateful."

"I see. So the Kitteridges, an elderly couple, were talked into selling prime oceanfront property at a fraction of their previous offer."

"No. Like you said, they are thrilled to know that the community will have access to the property forever."

"Even if that means that their golden years will be spent living on meager funds? Is that what you're saying?"

"No—"

"My understanding is that Tim Kitteridge is uninsured and showing signs of dementia, and that June needs money to pay for her husband's care." He paused. "I wonder how much this SOS campaign will end up costing these longtime pillars of the community."

I opened my mouth to speak—even though I wasn't sure what to say to that—but Ham took over the microphone. "That's all the time we have here, folks. I'd like to take the time to thank our guest, Ms. Callie Duflay of SOS . . ."

As he rattled on, wrapping up the show, the low throb that had started in my temple grew to encompass my head until it felt as if a vise was tightening its grip. Somehow I knew it would take more than a couple of aspirins to wipe away the effects of this interview.

"YOU COULDN'T PAY ME to be that woman." Amelia's silver arm bracelets jangled as she tossed her shiny black hair back over one shoulder. "Cheating an old couple for her selfish cause—that's rich."

Gage turned off his office radio. The caller had baited then buried Callie with his questions about the SOS campaign. The program host announced that the barrage of calls received after the segment ran two-to-one against Callie's cause. He fought off a wince at the thought of how her voice began to shake on air.

Amelia poked his shoulder with one sharp fingernail. "Wouldn't you agree?"

He looked down one shoulder at the artist who had sidled up to him as he stood in front of his drafting table. "Excuse me?"

"The woman on the radio you were just listening to. Don't you think her cause is over with now?"

He crinkled up his forehead, trying to remember why she was here in the first place. Right. The flirty artist had some questions. "I stay out of all that." He directed her attention back to the CD on the drawing table. "I don't have much time today, so let me show you what you need to know. Here." He tapped his pencil on the document. "This is where the roof line will be drawn out. Make sense?"

When she didn't respond, he glanced at her only to discover

her eyes fixed on his face, a teasing smile playing on her lips. "How about lunch?"

He set his pencil down and stepped away from the table and over to his desk. "Sorry. No can do."

She followed him, undeterred. When he sat, Amelia leaned over his desk, apparently defying gravity with her low-slung blouse. He was neither blind nor stupid, but certainly uninterested. "You have to eat, Gage. You'll waste away if you don't."

His phone rang and he grabbed the receiver, grateful for the interruption. "Gage here."

"Well, well, Mr. Mitchell. How are we doing this fine weekday morning?"

Great. More of Redmond's minions to give him grief today. "You're chipper today, Rick."

"We-hel-el, why not? Just cleared the way for my client to finally close the deal of the century."

"You did." He wanted to know but didn't want to ask.

Rick clucked his tongue. "Did you happen to catch Ham on KOTR just now? The SOS queen was on and, let's just say . . ." He paused for dramatic effect, a habit that clawed on Gage's last nerve. ". . . she didn't make her case."

Gage stopped tapping his pencil. Amelia stared at him like a hungry cat and he glanced away. "And you were somehow involved with making that happen?"

"Let's not get into semantics, now, brothah. Just wanted to give you a call, you know, to check on how the plans are shakin' down. Won't be long now."

Gage bit the inside of his cheek, willing himself to keep his mouth shut. Rick must have had someone call Callie on that radio program. Really boxed her into a corner. Made it sound like she had strong-armed the Kitteridges. He squeezed a fist. She wouldn't do that, so why didn't she defend herself?

"You there, Gage?"

Gage blinked. "Rick, I've got someone in my office right now, so if you don't mind, I'll have to get back to you. When I have something to report."

"Fine. Good. You do that. Remember—we're counting on you, man."

Gage couldn't hide the sarcastic roll to his eyes. "Yeah." *Whatever.*

Amelia leaned forward again. "Glad you got rid of him on my account. Now, about that lunch . . ."

Gage stood. "Sorry, Amelia. But I've got another meeting to run to." He picked up her sketch pad and pens and advanced around his desk, holding them out to her. "Call me if you have more questions."

Her expression dimmed in light of his dismissal, but Gage didn't care. He had a long overdue call to make—to Redmond.

CHAPTER 33

*F*or once, I wished I had driven. The way the townspeople avoided my eyes as I edged through town after my radio interview, you would have thought we were in the middle of Manhattan. No eye contact whatsoever.

A hundred retorts battled in my head as I made that walk, heart heavy over not being able to think of even one of them while being pummeled by that caller. Who was that man anyway? The developer? The person who's been threatening me? Someone who wanted to purchase an office condo with attached garage on the Kitteridge property?

Steph swung around the corner, moving toward me, her body bent but purposeful. Until she spotted me. I watched her pull up short, as if the toe of her shoe was about to connect with a mouse. Her gaze landed in several places, but never on me, and she turned to go the other way.

I raised my hand. "Steph!"

She slowed, her head bowed.

I caught up to her, dread slithering around my extremities at the flat line of her mouth. "So you heard the interview too."

She nodded. "Had it playing in the library."

I winced. "He caught me off-guard, but you know things aren't how he made it sound. The Kitteridges are good about all of this. I've spoken to June . . ."

Stephanie's leg shook and her gaze darted around. "I've been praying, Callie, but I think you should know something." Her mouth pressed into a grim line and she raised her head, looking at me with guarded eyes. "The Otter Bay Banking Association has decided to pull out."

I reached for her with both hands. "No."

She nodded over and over again. "Steve said there's nothing he can do. They were on the fence until a few minutes ago. Callie, it's become a PR nightmare for them. I'm so sorry."

"But—"

She wagged her head again. "I have to go."

She left me standing there, with nothing but embarrassment and shame to keep me company. If the association was pulling out, then the other corporate sponsors would follow. This campaign was, essentially, over.

The chill of disappointment filled my veins, making it hard to breathe, difficult to walk, but I made myself move one leg in front of the other. A knot pressed into the base of my throat, until my neck ached. Cars passed by, their occupants oblivious to the world that crumbled all around them. My world and theirs would soon be given over to those who didn't care one whit about the land or its current owners.

And I couldn't do a thing about it.

The ocean churned as if catching wind of the destruction that lay ahead. I'd made it to the Kitteridge property, drawn evermore by the smells of native brush burned into the wind by the day's sun. Few traversed the land today, and for once I was glad. I roamed along the winding path that hugged the cliff, not far from where Gage spotted Moondoggy moseying down on the beach, my mind far too overcome to caress all the good memories made that day.

Instead I sat on the ground, unconcerned that my eggshell-colored capris might never be spotless again. Another memory replaced the one from a day ago on this land. Justin and I had just agreed on a deal to release me from our business. I remember taking him in with my eyes, following the shape of his face, hoping to see some flicker of awakening. I wanted my signature on those papers to shake something up in him, to make him come to his senses. Surely he still needed me, still wanted me to work beside him, still . . . loved me. Didn't he? *Didn't* he?

I pulled in another breath, attempting to stave off the bursting of a dam that had been built, not over a couple of months, but over *years.* In an odd bit of logic, I thought signing over the business to Justin would bring him back to me. But he said goodbye as easily as if he might a business client, or one of the kids we hired during summer months. My signature on those papers failed to do anything but end the very thing I wanted to save.

And now I had failed again.

My cell phone rang in my pocket but I ignored it, switching off the ringer. It fell silent again. A formation of cormorants flew overhead toward a massive leafy tree, landing there. I'd have to find another favorite spot to sit and watch the wild birds make their nests. The cell buzzed this time, and I glanced down to find a text from Squid on the screen.

"Need to talk to you."

My eyes squeezed shut. Not now. What would I say? Six weeks ago I dabbled with the dream of dating Squid. After working with him so closely, seeing his commitment to the kids and to God, I dared to consider the possibilities. He was the first guy I'd noticed since Justin. Now those thoughts were like wisps of smoke long since dissipated.

Before I could answer, another text lit up the screen. "Can you meet at the camp first thing in the morning before the kids come?"

I shook my head and answered to the wind. "No. I can't. Leave me alone!"

My cell vibrated in my hand and would keep doing so until I acknowledged that text. Anger spiked in me. "You going to beat me up too, Squid? Going to tell me how I botched this? How I've taken down the camp along with my own reputation?"

My breathing resounded in my ears and I answered his text with a simple, "sure." Then I let the tears rip.

"WHAT DO YOU MEAN you're not buying the property from the Kitteridges?" Gage gripped the phone receiver until his hands turned red. Slivers of white ran through his fingers.

"It's of no concern to you, Gage. You're the architect. Do your job and my staff will handle the rest."

"But if you're not purchasing the property, then who is my client?"

"Gage, Gage. Relax. I will be purchasing the property in due time. These things have a course to run, which is why I've been on you to get those plans finished. We'll break that ground the minute the property is transferred to my company. If there is nothing else then—"

"Your realtor tells me he had something to do with a phone call made today during a radio show."

"Ah, yes. The bimbo on the radio. Shut her down fast, didn't we?"

Gage gritted his teeth. "We?"

"That SOS group was getting a little too close to their goal for comfort. Had to expose them to the community, and my sources tell me it worked."

Gage's heart sank. Poor Callie. "You don't happen to know anything about some letters Callie Duflay has received?"

"Letters? From who?"

"Anonymous letters. I heard she has received several and they were threatening in nature."

Redmond chuckled. Then he swore. "Sounds like we got ourselves an ally. Just when you think the whole world is rotten, something good happens."

"I wouldn't consider threats to be a good thing."

"Well, you got me, kid. I hadn't heard about it, but can't say that I'm sorry for her."

A muscle in his jaw twitched more than once. "Getting back to the Kitteridges. If you don't know them . . . if you're not purchasing the property from them, how did you discover Tim's dementia?"

"Let me give you a bit of advice, Gage. Don't burn bridges. I get my information from people who know that I can be trusted with it. Now that information about Tim Kitteridge, that's well-known to anyone who's paying attention, but most people aren't. Most people just think he's just some doddering old crank who owns the best piece of land for miles."

"Wait a minute. If he has dementia, maybe he wasn't able to . . . Redmond, if Tim Kitteridge was forced into signing away his property while mentally unstable, that would never stand—"

"You are on the wrong track with this. Everything that Mr. Kitteridge signed occurred long before dementia settled in. His current state just makes everything simpler."

Gage shook his head, trying to get the numbers to add up. They didn't and he smelled something foul. "Redmond, I can't in good conscience go forward on this project unless you assure me that everything is being done by the book." He took a determined breath, knowing the last time he faced off with the boss, he found himself unemployed. "I need assurances that the property is being obtained legally."

Redmond's voice turned gruff. "Be careful or you might find yourself alone in a coffeehouse, wishing you had a decent job." He exhaled a garbled laugh. The sound turned Gage's stomach. "I'm pulling your leg, Gage. Relax. Everything's legal, I can assure you."

He hung up with Redmond, feeling anything but assured. His client promised him the legality of the project, but why hadn't he asked about the ethics? The more he studied what he knew, the more he turned over the facts in his head, the more perplexed he became.

Someone from his client's camp had worked awfully hard to throw Callie off her game today and they succeeded. What he could not understand was why Callie had not defended herself better. If they had never met, he might have wondered if the allegations were true—that she had twisted the old couples' arms to sell their property to her group instead. Just why hadn't she blasted that caller out of the water?

CHAPTER 34

*B*y the time I reached camp the next day, all signs of tears had stopped. The SOS team held an emergency conference call, but little transpired other than the begrudging acknowledgement that the group wanted to disband. I'd signed off with a dull heart and a pledge of my own: to believe in a miracle.

Instead of driving, I'd chosen to hike off some of the burden that weighed on my shoulders. I tugged at the cotton fabric that clung to my skin and stepped into the office.

Squid sat behind his desk, head in his hands.

"Squid?"

He lifted his head, displaying saucer-sized dark circles.

"You look exhausted." I pulled up a chair. "What's wrong?"

He sucked in a harsh breath and spit it out in one sentence: "Callie, I'm leaving camp."

I jerked up straight. He never called me by my real name. "No. Why? I don't understand."

His face took on a mixture of fear and anger. "Remember when I was telling you all that something was missing with the kids? That I didn't want the kids to have a mountaintop experience then go home and not be able to live it each day? Remember that?"

"I do."

"I figured out what was wrong. I've had problems with this series because I haven't been living it. I'm a failure, Callie."

"Squid—"

He waved me off. "Don't. I'm not finished."

I searched his face, trying to figure out what had happened with my old friend, the one who always seemed so self-assured and full of faith. He caught me watching him and his eyes turned sad. "What is it, Squid?"

He held my gaze. "My girlfriend is pregnant."

I blinked, my mind not accepting the information. A jolt ran through me. "She's pregnant? With your—"

He nodded. "Yes, the baby is mine." Squid flashed his brows at me, his mouth screwed into frown. "I'm a big disappointment to you right now, aren't I?"

New life isn't a booby prize, but I'd be lying if I did not admit the size of this blow. I stumbled to find the right words. "This isn't about me, Squid. What are you going to do?"

His hairline rose. "What do you mean? There's only one choice, of course. I'll be marrying Peyton ASAP."

I nodded. "Of course. I-I didn't mean . . . I guess I was just wondering about the logistics."

"And like I said, I'm leaving camp."

"Oh, Squid."

He held up a hand. "Might as well fire myself so the board doesn't have to, right?" His laugh sounded rueful, melancholy. "Even if they wanted me to stay, I couldn't do so in good conscience. I messed up."

"But you're doing the right thing. Facing your situation directly, not weaseling around it, or hiding it. I applaud you."

"Don't expect me to be taking any bows for this. I'm always telling the kids to build their lives on the rock, to not allow themselves to make choices that will have them sinking into sin, but I haven't been living that life. I leave here on Sunday afternoons with all the good intentions in the world and by Friday, I've pretty much turned my back on all of them."

"I see. So you're human."

"Don't you get it? I've failed those kids and this camp . . . and you."

I tilted my head to one side, watching our illustrious leader melt from the pressure. "Do you love her?"

"I think so." He scratched his beard, then shrugged. "Not sure."

I broke eye contact with him. My mind swirled. I didn't envy either one of them.

He cleared his voice. "You and I, we were a good team. I'm gonna miss that."

I nodded, my mind still a whir. We needed to find a new leader quickly, and until then I'd have to refine my understanding of the camp theme, that is if the board will still have me after the Kitteridge debacle. Squid's probably correct—the board won't be thrilled with what he has to tell them. Will they ask for my resignation too?

I exhaled one long breath. "No matter what you have done, God loves you, Squid. He wants to see you—and Peyton—restored. He's going to bless that sweet baby of yours no matter what."

"Well, that's not going to happen until I get my act together."

"What's that supposed to mean?" I stood over him, hands on my hips, reminding myself of Sheila. Yet I couldn't seem to stop myself. "Do you tell those kids that they can't go to God when they're broken? That's exactly when they need him the most."

He dropped his hands onto the desk with a slap. "I don't know. I'm just mad at myself. Feeling pretty stupid right now."

"Don't wait for your own perfection, my friend—that won't happen until heaven. You need God in all of this, so don't abandon ship now. He's not about to leave you, you know."

"This wasn't how it was supposed to be."

"When is it ever? I've got a proverb tacked up on my wall that says, 'In his heart a man plans his course, but the Lord determines his steps.' We never know our path to perfection—only that on our own, we'll screw it up. Let the Lord decide how to use this for his glory. You just have to stay on the path, my friend."

"Wow. Never knew you had the preacher in you."

I laughed. "Me neither." The proverb I'd quoted wove through my head. I'd made many plans that had not turned out like I had laid them out. Was I willing to let go of my plans too?

"Thanks for your understanding about all this." He raised his chin a little higher. "I meant it when I said I'd miss working with you."

"I know you did."

"Better get to it, right? Kids'll be here soon." He handed me a clipboard. "You might want to take a look at my notes, so you can help whoever takes over next week."

I nodded, as Squid headed out of the office, soon to be lost in new plans of his own. The office walls seem to sag from sorrow.

THE VIEW FROM THE camp's perch at the crest of a winding hill stunned him. Miles of placid ocean shimmered as if sprinkled with sugar in the morning sun. He pulled into a parking spot at quarter till noon, hoping he'd find her here.

At the top of the steps, he leaned in through the office doorway. A woman with short brown hair and large glasses raised her head. "May I help you?"

"Looking for Callie Duflay?"

She narrowed her eyes at him. "She's had enough of reporters."

"Good thing I'm not a reporter."

The woman didn't laugh.

"Actually, we're friends." He stepped into the office. "I'm Gage."

"Gage? Haven't heard of a Gage."

"Gage Mitchell. Architect on the Kitteridge project." He cleared his throat. "Would you know where I could find her?"

Clearly this woman considered herself Callie's protector for she scrutinized him in silence for several awkward seconds. "Leave your keys on the desk and I'll tell you."

"My keys?"

"So if it turns out you're one of those paparazzis, you won't be able to get away."

He dropped his keys on her desk. "And now?"

She flicked her head toward the door. "Follow the path to the chapel. There's a sign outside."

Gage tapped his forehead with his index finger in a salute and headed outside. The sign pointed to a flowing, planted trail. He made his way along the dirt, unable to miss the sweet smell of jasmine hanging in the air, intrigued by the artistry and unique-ness of the undulating path, and surprised by its length and "secret garden" feel. Before long, he noticed a figure, crouched behind an L-shaped bend in the path, hiding behind thick vines.

He slowed his approach, noticing the man had a camera. A reporter. Doubling his pace, Gage strode up behind him, taking a fast look through a break in the foliage at a horseshoe-shaped chapel in the woods. Callie sat alone on a stump, oblivious to her stalker. The man spun around, but not before Gage snagged him at the collar.

"What are you doing here?"

The bespeckled kid gasped. "My job."

Gage squinted at the kid, holding him at arm's length like a shirt on a hanger. "Your job is to spy on praying women?"

"I'm a reporter."

Gage shook him free. "What for? A tabloid?"

"N-no!"

"Then tell you what—stop acting like it. You want to be taken seriously, then you need to learn to be upfront with people." Gage nodded at the pile of leaves and stems that littered the ground. "You tear that hole in the vines?"

Terrified, the kid nodded more than necessary.

"You'd better pray your newspaper's willing to pay for the restoration. That's someone's work you messed with." Gage had a feeling he knew whose work that was. "Now what do you want? You're Eliot Hawl, I presume."

"Yes, sir. I wanted to find out Ms. Duflay's reaction to news that Tim Kitteridge has been hospitalized."

"Hospitalized? Why?"

"Don't know exactly—that's someone else's beat. It's news 'cuz he and his wife are at the center of the SOS campaign."

Gage's mind turned that one over. Callie had just been accused of orchestrating a campaign against the elderly couple, of taking advantage of them. This news wouldn't make her life any easier, and he wanted to be there to catch her should she fall.

Gage kept a steely gaze on the kid. "You the one who's been leaving those threatening letters at Callie's home?"

"N-no." He glanced through the man-made peephole. "Someone's been *threatening* her?"

"That's what I said. You're the only one I can think of who's been following her around. What do you know about her dog?"

Eliot's eyes popped open till they matched the size of his wire-rimmed glasses. "Nothing!"

Gage searched the kid's face for some sign of lying but found none. Yet something like recognition seemed to move across his face. Eliot looked away.

"You suddenly remember something?"

Eliot's eyes slid back toward Gage. "Maybe. I'll need to investigate—"

Gage grabbed Eliot's collar again and the kid flinched. "Hold on. Forget about any more investigation. Callie's a friend of mine, and I'm tired of seeing your byline next to her name. You just go ahead and tell me what you've thought of."

Eliot swallowed and swayed under Gage's unyielding grip. "Nothing really, just that I saw Tim Kitteridge a couple of times hanging out at Ms. Duflay's place."

Gage shifted and dropped the kid's collar. "What do you mean 'hanging out'? As in visiting her?"

Eliot straightened and threw a daggered look back at him. "She was never home when I saw him there. No, he was just walking around her garden, sniffing stuff. I think he might have brought her some mail."

"Where were you hiding during all that?"

He hesitated until Gage narrowed his eyes. "Behind her shed on the side of the house, mostly. Sometimes behind a truck on the street. Wherever I could get a good look."

Gage stepped backward, snapping a twig. A thought tore through his mind. *I think he might have brought her some mail.* Could Tim Kitteridge have been the one who had been threatening Callie? He glanced at Eliot, hoping the kid hadn't settled on the same thought.

Too late. Eliot smiled. "Poor Tim Kitteridge."

Gage quirked up his chin. "What do you mean by that?"

The kid's smile grew into a nasty grin. "Thanks a lot for the tip, Mr. Friend of Callie's. I think I just figured why old Tim Kitteridge had been hanging around her place." He looped his camera around his neck. "Guess I'll be leaving now."

"Hold on. You've got some explaining to do about the hole you've left."

Eliot had already begun to back away. "Send the paper the bill. They'll handle it."

Gage swung back toward the spray of light at the end of the path. Callie, who still sat in contemplation at the foot of that cross, had no idea how far the kid might go to win a gold star from his editor. He entered the clearing and pulled up beside her. "Callie?"

She spun around from her perch on a stump. The sober look on her face relaxed into a smile and she stood. "Gage. What are you—"

He hadn't planned to kiss her, but he did, closing her mouth with his before she could finish the question. She didn't resist and he reveled in her arms. For the moment Gage let all the questions that filled his mind fall away.

CHAPTER 35

Finally I pushed him away from me, surprised by my sudden lightness of heart. "You haven't answered my question, Gage. What are you doing here?"

He smiled, but something faltered in his expression. He caressed my face with one hand. "I missed you. Been working 'round the clock but didn't want to wait another day to see you."

He wasn't exactly my boyfriend—do thirty-year-old women still use that term? What was he to me? Our hands intermingled and my fingers played with his as I stood wondering where we would go from here.

Abruptly he dropped his hand from my face and pulled me toward two tree stump seats. "Let's sit a minute, okay? I wanted to talk to you about something."

"Sure." I took my seat again. As I did, the reality of my morning whooshed through my head. The last time I stepped into this chapel, I discovered Squid and Peyton locked in an embrace of their own. Now, she's pregnant. Sobering thought.

Gage glanced at me. "You okay?"

I forced myself to brighten, which wasn't terribly difficult considering he sat next to me. "Yeah."

Gage huffed out a sigh. "I heard you on the radio the other day."

What could I say to that? If he heard the entire thing, then he heard a disaster. He probably figured I had given up, and that I would merrily take his hand and let him show me the plans for Otter Bay. Could he handle knowing I wasn't ready to compromise?

I squeezed his hand. "Sorry you had to hear that. Admittedly, not one of my best moments. Okay, actually, one of the worst."

"You were boxed into a corner. It was obvious."

I searched his eyes. "Thanks. You're right about that."

He opened his mouth, took a breath, then closed it again and pressed his lips together as if not sure of how he wanted to phrase something. His eyes were penetrating, his brows furrowed.

I cocked my chin. "What's bothering you, Gage?"

He shifted. "Just wondering why you didn't defend yourself better. I don't know, Callie. You don't seem like the type of woman who would take advantage of a little old couple."

I withdrew my hand. "Of course not!"

"Then why not say so? Why let that caller cast you in such a dark way?"

I couldn't look at him, couldn't tell him June's secret. I had promised her. I shrugged. "I don't know. Let's leave it at that, all right?"

He didn't look all right. Gage's eyes appeared cloudy and his jaw had a firm set to it. If I had more confidence about how he felt about me, I might grab that jaw of his and turn it until his mouth found mine again. As it was, I figured that he had doubts about me now and that I couldn't say anything that would make them go away.

He stood and I expected him to leave. "I need to tell you something else, Callie." He pulled me up and placed his hands on my shoulders. "I just ran that reporter out of here."

"Eliot?" I looked around. "He was here?"

Gage nodded. "Spying on you. Nearly scared the kid out of his loafers when I grabbed him by the collar."

Argh. "What did he want? Did he tell you?"

Gage paused, his face sober. "That's just it. He wanted to know your reaction to the news that Tim Kitteridge has been hospitalized."

A gasp flew out and my hands found my chest. "No. I've got to go call June. She must be beside herself."

I turned and Gage caught me by the elbow. "You and she are close, then?"

I shielded my eyes from the sunlight dripping through the canopy of pine. My voice broke. "She's become a dear friend. I really need to go check on her . . . and the camp's going through something difficult right now. I'm sorry, but I've got to go—"

He slid his hand from my elbow to my hand. "There's more, Callie."

"Is he . . . is Tim going to make it?"

"That I don't know, but I think I may have made things harder for you."

A spike of tension shot through my shoulder. "How so?"

"I questioned the kid about why he's been following you, even suggesting that he may know something about the threatening letters you have received."

"And did he? Has he been the one leaving them?"

"No, but he said something about noticing Tim Kitteridge hanging around your place and he put two and two together."

"Tim? At my home? I don't remember . . ." My voice faded. June had spoken often about Tim's agitated state and how he didn't really seem to understand how quickly he was about to lose his property. "Oh, no. It was probably him. Poor Tim's confused, the dementia makes him think that I'm somehow after them."

"This is my fault. I'm sorry, Callie, but the community may be after you once they read about his hospitalization in the paper. That reporter's going to write about those letters, solidifying the accusation that you were pressuring the Kitteridges."

The realization crashed into my mind. Gage was right. This would not look good and any chance of SOS regaining ground might be lost. I peeked into his eyes again, heavy with concern, and reached up to touch his face. "He would have found out eventually—the letters became public record when I reported them to the police. I don't blame you."

He captured my hand and held it there against his face. "If I could fix this for you, Callie, I would. You know that, don't you?"

Words caught in my throat as I nodded. Somehow, I knew he would. If he could.

HE HAD MADE THINGS worse for Callie. It didn't matter now that he knew Redmond had nothing to do with the threats made against her. The fact remained that Gage had helped point the way toward a story that just might drive the final nail into the SOS coffin.

He gripped the steering wheel while driving slowly down the winding hill from camp, ignoring the buzz of his phone. He knew it was Rick calling because he'd attached a special ring tone to the man's calls to warn himself. The pit of his gut felt hollow. What would it be like to draw up a "normal" project for people who found as much joy in the creative process as he did?

His boss at his last firm was crazy, had him making all kinds of changes after the permitting process had been completed. Not uncommon in the building world, but in this case Gage was asked to make dangerous, structural alterations in the plans just to save a few bucks—and that brought out the fighter in him.

His cockiness had landed that assignment in the first place, his willingness to hopscotch over anyone to succeed, but when he sat back and considered the young children who would live in the eleven thousand square foot building—he wouldn't do it. It was unconscionable. And just like that, he had been cut loose.

His phone buzzed again, this time from a text. *The guy's getting smarter, if that's possible.* Gage pulled to the road side and checked his phone:

Need plans to town council. Stat.
Showdown at the OK Corral blowing in.

Rick. The guy never met a drama he didn't like. Gage glanced at the construction documents on his passenger seat. They'd be dropped off in town this afternoon, and if all goes as expected, given rubber stamp approval.

His phone buzzed again and Gage sighed. What now? He straightened, realizing this note was from Suz:

At the RAG. Big powwow going on behind me. Reporter Suz at your service.

He crinkled his mouth into a tight smile and replied:

Explain yourself.
Suz: Realtor Rick seated behind me w/Redmond & some guy named Henry. Heated conv. They don't recognize me. (Jer's w/me).

Must be the reason Rick got on him about the plans. How would it look if he were to show up at the RAG right now? Gage sighed and glanced to the sea before texting his sister again:

Anything I need to know about?
Suz: Redmond's worried about Tim K being in hospital. Wants Henry to hurry up. Henry says R keeps jumping the gun.

Gage wracked his brain but no recollection of Henry resided there.

What's Henry's role in project?
Suz: He's buying it from Mr. & Mrs. K, it sounds like. I think Rick's working deal for Henry to sell property to Redmond.

Gage's thumbs could not move quickly enough.

Anything else? I'll wait.

A breeze had kicked up, rustling through the pines. Drying needles slid across the hood of his truck.

Suz: There's some deadline. Next week. If Ks don't come up with loan payment . . .

He sat up. Loan payment? C'mon Suz, what else you got for me? He waited, tensing.

Suz: Loan payment is on their house. If can't come up w/it, they have to sell land to Henry. Sounds like he will sell it to Redmond right away.

Gage groaned, the sound startling in the confines of his truck. "I knew it." He'd seen this type of thing before. This guy Henry must be a type of investor who got the Kitteridges into a bind with some kind of loan. They can't pay, so he takes over their house. It sounds like he also has the option of buying their additional land out from under them. Legal, but putrid to the senses.

Suz: They're talking about you. Do you know Amelia?

An invisible pull, like a tight wire moving upwards, tugged on Gage's brow.

Yes.

Suz: She's supposed to distract you from all this. Gross. (Hope they don't discover me here.) Redmond's niece. Did you know that?

Gage ground his teeth.

Didn't work. Not interested.

Suz: Redmond thinks you're squeaky clean, but that you ask too many questions. Says he wants to see plans finalized soon. Wait a second.

Gage made himself breathe, otherwise the fuming anger rising in him might have made him ill.

Suz: Henry says no worries. He's made sure that all council members are on his team. Once you turn in plans, they will be okayed right away.

Gage let out a sarcastic sigh. "Of course they will." He sent a final text to Suz.

Thanks. Off to the town council to drop off plans. Will see you at home.

He set his phone onto the passenger seat and looked out to the horizon. "You've really got to be a better judge of character, Mitchell." He shook his head. "Pretty desperate of you to take on this job before investigating it thoroughly."

But what could he expect? When this job landed in his lap, he moved on it with little forethought, the same thing the mysterious Henry had accused Redmond of doing. Strangely enough, Gage had considered this job, this new company of his, as his way of setting down roots on a sure thing. He started his truck and began driving the downhill. The only thing he was sure about now was that after today, he'd have a lot of extra time on his hands.

CHAPTER 36

I made it through Day One and the campers did not appear to notice the heavy hearts in the camp staff. Squid, for his part, led by example by not letting on that this would be his last weekend of spring camp. The kids laughed and carried on during the Friday afternoon game: Are you Rock? Or are you Sand? They chose sides, sang songs, and tried not to be tricked into changing sides.

Saturday morning rolled around, and usually news of whatever happened down the hill did not make it to me until after the weekend. Usually, but not today. Luz laid the paper down in front of me, first thing this morning, *bless her heart.* My eyes swept over one of the headlines: *Tim Kitteridge Hospitalized.* The sub-head read: *Has the SOS Team Gone Too Far?*

This was not unexpected. Eliot Hawl's article went on to say that a "reputable source" confirms that Callie Duflay had been receiving unsigned, threatening notes and that Tim Kitteridge, who suffers from dementia, had been seen delivering envelopes to her home.

Good grief. Apparently the editors weren't too concerned

with their paper's transformation into a tabloid. Didn't matter anyway now. The campaign was over. I confirmed this via phone this morning. Even if all the pledges made came in, we'd still be thousands of dollars short, and with only a week to go, what hope was there?

I shook off my disappointment while standing to the side of Saturday's morning game. The kids had taken turns at both the sand hill and the rock climbing wall, and Squid was working to bring down both the noise and chaos level.

"We all have to look out for weaknesses in our foundations," he told them. "Once, I was sitting on a piano bench and it crashed right out from under me. I fell on my bottom in front of my friends." The kids snickered. "That bench was made with flimsy materials, and that's how our lives will be when we don't make sure that our foundations are strong."

Squid's eyes brushed with mine and I nodded, offering him support. As he continued with his message, before leading into instructions for lunch, Natalia sidled up to me wearing camo pants, a linen blouse, and green scarf tied around her neck. I wondered when the safari would take place. "Hello, Callie."

"Natalia."

She folded her arms at her chest and watched Squid while speaking to me. "It has certainly been a rough week."

"It has."

She turned to me, her red lipstick blazing in the sun. "And for you personally, as well as Squid."

My eyes found the ground. "Yes. Tough."

She released her arms and touched my shoulder. "The SOS campaign is over, isn't it?"

It wasn't a question. Natalia was a tough businesswoman, always had been. She probably knew for weeks what I had only hours to digest. A million thoughts darted through my mind, how I might have worked harder or been smarter, maybe this wouldn't be just another failure to add to my growing list. I closed my eyes. At least Gage will be guiding the project, making it somewhat palatable.

Tidal Wave rang the lunch bell and the kids scrambled to their feet.

She touched my shoulder again. "You did what you could, Callie, but it was a tough road from the start." She dropped her hand to her side. "I'm here to discuss camp business with the board. With Squid's sudden departure imminent, we're going to have to make some tough decisions."

I let her comments sink into my mind.

"Listen, Callie, depending on what information is tossed about at the meeting, well, I'd like to meet with you, perhaps on Monday. Can you make the time?"

I pulled it together. "Sure. No problem, Natalia." *Won't have much else to do with the campaign defunct.*

She turned to go, then stopped. "By the way, Luz mentioned you know the architect on the Kitteridge property. Friend of yours?"

Hearing reference to Gage, especially when my thoughts had sunk so low, sent a ripple through me. The one bright spot in all of this mess. "Yes, I know Gage Mitchell. He's a friend."

"Gage Mitchell," she repeated. "I think I can remember that. See you Monday."

She left me to wonder if she had a remodel in the works. For the rest of the afternoon, the kids and counselors played an elaborate game of hide and seek that pitted guys against girls, cabins against cabins. Squid had disappeared for much of that time, but I hadn't looked for him knowing he had much to contemplate. When everyone had reassembled on the lawn, he reappeared and took the stage where worship leaders had begun leading campers in rounds of "Jesus Loves Me."

Squid raised the bullhorn. "Everybody hap-py?"

The kids whistled and cheered, "Yes!"

"Everybody full from lu-unch?"

More cheers. "Yes!"

"Everybody wi-ise?"

Some of the kids cracked up, a few whistled, some shouted, "Yes."

Squid lowered the bullhorn and surveyed the crowd of children until all the noise died down. He raised the megaphone again. "You know, the wise man, he built his house on the rock. He says: 'The rain came down, the streams rose, and the winds blew and beat against that house; yet it did not fall, because it had its foundation on the *rock.*'"

He quieted, his face serious as the evening news. "I want to be like that—how about you? You gonna build your life on what you hear on TV? Or on what your best friend tells you? Or are you gonna hear the word, learn the word, and live the word. 'Cuz that's what building on the rock means. It means that if you put into practice what God says, you will be like the wise man whose house did not fall."

I knew that Squid spoke from a fractured place within himself. He believed he had veered off the course he'd planned for himself and acted unwise.

Couldn't we all relate to that at some time in our lives? I pushed around the dirt with my foot, wishing I could stay up here on this hill and never have to face the community or my failures again. Then again, hadn't I reminded Squid that it's the Lord who determines our steps? Who am I to dish out advice to others but ignore it for myself?

GAGE SAT ON HIS front porch, wind tickling his ears. He'd wanted to relax in the shade like this since the day he moved in, but until now, had not had the chance.

Suz leaned through the doorway, looking better with a few days rest and some needed perspective. Marc's wife Lizzie called and offered to fly her and Jer out to their lake house for some R&R in the summer, and just receiving the call had brightened his little sister. "I made some lemonade. Camille Sweet from down the road dropped off a box of lemons. Want a glass?"

"Sure. Sounds great." Homegrown foods might be an option worth looking into, now that he had zero income to expect. Of course, there was that phone call . . .

Suz brought two glasses onto the porch and plopped into the chair next to him. "How does it feel to be free as a bird?"

He took a sip, biting back the tartness, hoping his eyes didn't water enough for Suz to notice. "Stressful."

"Yeah, I figured."

"That's not entirely true. Initially, when I dropped off the approved designs at Redmond's office, I couldn't believe I was actually doing it. What am I saying—*he* couldn't believe I was doing it. But he confirmed what I suspected."

"Which was?"

"That the owners of the property had less than a week to make payment on a large loan or they would be forced to sell the property to a guy named Henry, who owns HMS Properties. He would then turn around and sell it to Redmond. Everybody wins —Henry makes a mint, Redmond stands to make his money off the sale of finished home and office condos, even the realtor will be raking it in."

"Everyone except the little old couple who didn't know better when they signed that loan."

Gage grimaced. "Had to endure a head full of swearing when I told Redmond, but you know what? I'm glad I left. Glad I had the guts to do it first this time."

"Yeah, well, I couldn't believe the way they were carrying on in the restaurant, pointing fingers. Don't they know the walls have ears?" She laughed at her own joke. "And did you really go out with Redmond's niece?"

He gave his sister a mock glare. "Please. It was a *business* meeting."

Suz laughed lightly. "Her uncle sounded mighty peeved that you wouldn't cross that line." She held up her glass. "Cheers to you, big brother."

He tipped his glass to her before taking another sip.

Suz looked over the neighborhood. "So what are you going to do now that you've pulled out of the Kitteridge project? Put an ad in the paper? Knock on some contractors doors? What?"

His brows dipped. "Can't say that I know yet. I've been paid for the completed construction docs, thankfully, so we'll have that to survive on for a while. It's kind of hard to run a business, though, with no clients."

She peered at him. "No plans to pick up and move the company, then?"

"Nope. None." Even to him it sounded ludicrous. Half the town probably hated him for his involvement in the Kitteridge project, so what made him think he'd be able to win them over now? No one would know his reasons for pulling out of that project. If anything at all, they'd think he had been fired.

She looked at him sideways. "Really now."

"What's that look for?"

Suz shrugged. "Don't know. Just that you and Callie seem to be pretty tight lately."

"And?"

"And nothing. It's cute and, well, I told you so."

"Told me so *what*?"

She set down her glass. "That you two were perfect for each other, only that you were both too stubborn to acknowledge it; and that if only you would set aside your petty differences, you might look into each other's eyes and find true love staring back at you."

Gage's mouth gaped, his chin dropping forward. "You're saying you told me all that?"

Suz glanced off toward the horizon. "Well, maybe not in so many words. But isn't that the real reason you're so set on staying around here? I mean, I know you like the beach and all, but there are other coastal cities you could move to—if you wanted to, I mean."

Gage set down his glass on the side table and leaned forward, elbows onto his knees, staring into the clear air. "Maybe you're right."

"Yeah, maybe I am." She paused. "Anyway, I left her a message about some executive decisions I made in her house, so if she calls back, maybe you oughta be the one to answer the phone."

"Executive decisions?"

"More like design decisions." She chewed a fingernail. "I hope she likes them, but if she doesn't I can always repaint."

"Well, if the work you've done inside my place is any indication, I'd bet she'll be wild about what you've done for her."

The lines in her forehead relaxed. "Oh, and I can't believe I haven't told you this yet. I began looking for more steady work, something that will help us both until you can get more clients, so guess what I did yesterday?"

"I'm bad at guessing."

She waved her hand at him. "Fine. I applied for a job at Hearst Castle."

He forced a smile. He hated to see her give up her painting to work in the castle's touristy gift shop or sell lattes from a coffee cart. No shame in that kind of work, just not her calling. "Great. Good for you."

"I know. They've got a ton of restoration projects going on, so I'm hoping to get a spot on the crew for that. Wouldn't that be amazing?"

He twisted his chin upward. "Restoring the rooms?"

She nodded. "Yeah. So many fine details that need repainting —enough work to last for years." Suz's face glowed. Her eyes danced as she talked about the famed castle built by William Randolph Hearst. "Art treasures are in every room!"

Gage had been questioning God a lot lately, wondering why he was brought here only to see his hopes wither with the first shady detail. But then he found Callie and he watched his sister's enthusiasm grow while describing her dream job at the castle on the hill. Despite the otherwise dreary outlook for his firm, strangely enough, Gage felt nothing but hope.

CHAPTER 37

*S*quid gave his final message to the kids, and I had to turn away to keep from crying. He'd made the right decision, stepping away from ministry for a while as he sought to build a life with Peyton and his new child. But I'd miss him. The kids would miss him too.

As he finished with the kids, I had waited at the back of the chapel, reading over the proverb I had quoted to him the other day, the one that says the Lord determines our steps. Until then, I'd never looked at the one right before: "Better a little righteousness than much gain with injustice."

It occurred to me that although I believed the developers of the Kitteridge property had been unjust, I was not completely in the clear. I had jumped the gun when I'd first heard about the property's sale. What might have happened if I had approached both Tim and June the very moment I learned about it? If only I had gone to them first.

It was now early evening. Parked in front of Sheila's house, I debated my readiness to face everyone. The article in the paper didn't mince words yesterday and with the campaign shot, I could only imagine the comments I'd have to face. Leaning my elbows onto the steering wheel, I massaged my eyes.

My cell rang and I glanced at the number. Gage. How could the thought of one man bring on such polarized emotions?

"Hi."

"Callie, hi, it's Gage." He paused. "Are you home from camp?"

I rubbed my eyes harder. "Not yet. I stopped at my sister's for dinner."

"So I guess you've seen the paper."

I looked through my windshield at the muted sky. "First thing Saturday morning."

"Not Pulitzer prize worthy, but the kid laid it all out there. Are you okay?"

I paused to think about that, picturing Gage's penetrating eyes watching me. I wanted to tell him that I'd moved on, that I'd survive this. Of course, I would. But the whole thing still sat like an indigestible lump in my abdomen. "I'll survive."

"Callie, you gave it your all. The community couldn't have asked for more, and once things settle down, they'll find that out."

I closed my eyes. "Thanks but that doesn't matter now anyway. You won, Gage."

"No one's winning this one, Callie."

A smirk tugged at my cheek. "I wouldn't say that. You came here for a purpose, and now that purpose is in the works. So, good job."

Gage let out a sigh that revealed his exasperation. "We may have started out as opponents, but surely you know you mean more to me than that."

"Do I?" That sounded harsh, but Justin told me the same thing until one day he woke up with a changed mind. Would I ever trust in what Gage, or any other man, said? Besides, what if I had been the person to win this fight? Would Gage be professing his affection for me right now?

Silence held the line. I swallowed, waiting. Finally Gage spoke. "Don't you feel the same for me, Callie?"

My heart pricked at the heaviness in his voice and I wanted to answer him. Only I couldn't find a way. "I'm sorry. Gage, I just can't, not now. Please, give me some time."

We hung up and I continued to lean my chin against the wheel, tending to the knot in my stomach. Bobby peeked out the door and smiled at me, waving me in. The spirit was willing, but the flesh—not so much.

Still, knowing that baby Callie was beyond those doors got me out of the car.

"Hey." Bobby kissed me on the cheek. "Thought I heard something out here."

"Just planning my grand entrance."

"Nothing personal but you have a tough act to follow." He winked. "Greta and Callie made quite the entrance already."

Inside, I dropped my purse and darted across the room past Jim and Nancy and Vince, and knelt next to the same chair where Greta's water broke the previous week. It smelled freshly laundered. "How's my baby-kins?" My voice had inexplicably risen to a squeak.

Greta smiled serenely, her skin more radiant than ever. Low doses of sleep apparently agreed with her. "She's an angel."

The door flew open and in strode Mom and Dad. "Well, hello, my sweet familia!" Mom pushed her way past Bobby's waiting kiss and two-stepped across the room. "There's my babes!" She reached down and plucked Callie from her mother's arms, gently cradling the newborn in her own. We all watched as Mom cooed into the tiny pink face.

I glanced at Greta, my voice hushed, although unsure why. "I can't believe you are here. After all you went through!"

Greta shrugged. "I'd do it all over again." She leaned into me. "And you would too."

I tried to hide the doubt in my expression. Mom hadn't

missed it though, and spoke up. "Yes, that is absolutely right and besides, it's really not that bad."

"Not that *bad*? Mom, you're kidding, right? You said that childbirth damages you forever!"

She shrunk back. "Me?"

"Don't you remember how you talked about all the ripping and tearing. The excruciating needles?"

Jim groaned, and Vince ducked out of the room.

Mom winced. "Darling, I don't recall any of that."

"How about this—you once said that women were forever altered by the audacity of childbirth!"

Mom gasped and looked to Dad. My normally placid father slapped his knee and laughed. I couldn't believe his callous reaction. "What could be so funny about that?"

My mother shook her head, smiling. "Callie, those were lines from a play. You must have heard me rehearsing my lines."

I froze in place and felt as if my body had shrunk to half its length. I was ten again and looking up at my mother as she paced the living room, throwing out words that had been embedded in my psyche for twenty years. Lines from a play?

Giggles filled the room as I slowly realized that some playwright wrote one of my biggest fears in life. Probably a male one. My insides overheated until I was sure the skin on my cheeks would burn right off.

Sheila placed a hand on me. "Thanks for the reminder about what I should say around the children." Even she laughed at me.

Over dinner my siblings continued to enjoy rehashing the exchange between my mother and me. Admittedly the whole thing was kind of ridiculous. It's as if my whole life I'd allowed this tiny fear to grow into a thick-rooted weed, so much that I never even considered having children of my own. And yet I adored kids.

Funny how misperceptions could alter a person forever.

Sheila passed a platter of cookies. "I hesitated to bring this up, but now seems like the right time. Callie? How are you doing now that the SOS campaign has apparently ended?"

I shrugged, as if it didn't matter more than it did. "I'm disappointed, of course, but I'll survive."

Jim spoke up. "Like I always said, it was a lost cause."

My mother frowned at him. "What has happened to you, Jim, to make you such a prune face?"

Blakey giggled. "Prune face. That's funny, Grandma."

Mom stroked my nephew's face as Jim's chest gathered steam. His fist rested on the table with his fork piercing the air. "I'd like to point out that I am the most educated one in this room and that I—"

Dad tossed a cookie at Jim, startling my older brother as it landed on the chest of his linen dress shirt and slid into his lap, leaving a dusting of crumbs behind.

Jim's mouth flew open, wider than before. "What was that for?"

Dad sat quietly, chewing his food. He took a sip of coffee and set it back down before looking around the table. "Everything in this family seems to hinge on success, rather than on doing what is right, or more importantly, godly. I don't know where you got those ideas because it surely wasn't from me."

Mom gasped and patted Dad's shoulder. "See why I love this man?" She turned to him, her gaze unyielding. "You are so wise—and sexy!"

Bobby and Vince groaned and the table, everyone except for Jim, fell into laughter. My own shoulders lifted, not completely, but as if something weighty and cumbersome had taken flight, leaving behind a few odd pieces of my parents' mismatched luggage. Something about what my father said reminded me of the night Squid told the staff and board how he had struggled with the camp theme. Of course, none of us knew the depth of Squid's struggle and yet, wasn't I the one to point out that faith meant living for God?

To his credit, Dad didn't let up. Always the calm one in our sea of chaotic personalities, he held Jim's attention. "Son, I'm very proud of you for all that you have achieved. Very proud. But I ask that you take another look at how you measure success. Callie tried her darnedest to make a difference in the community. Maybe she made some mistakes along the way—we all do, everyday—but she makes me a proud papa." He secured me with his gaze. "I hope you know that."

Another piece of baggage disappeared from my shoulders.

Later as I stood at the door readying to leave, Sheila handed me my purse and kissed me on the cheek. "What's that for?"

My sister surprised me by cupping my cheeks with her hands. "For being you. I'm sorry that things haven't worked out the way you had hoped, Callie, but I too am proud of you for trying."

I could barely stammer a thank-you.

At home Moondoggy rocketed through his doggy door and flung himself at me. I stood in the living room, holding his head as he leaned against me, and scratching behind his ears. "So good to have you to greet me, you know that?"

He plopped his front paws back down on the floor and sat, signaling dinnertime. I filled his bowls with food and water and stopped short because there painted above his bowl were the words: "Be comforted, little dog, thou too in the Resurrection shall have a tail of gold. ~ Martin Luther."

Suz. Must be what my artist friend—Gage's sister—meant in her message when she said she hoped I didn't mind the liberties she had taken. Although she mentioned using the phrases I had pinned on the wall, this one was new to me.

I padded down the hall, chuckling to myself and thinking of Moondoggy and his tail of gold. Suz's hands had worked their magic in my little home and I adored her. I hoped my precarious relationship with Gage wouldn't stand between us.

Once again, I stopped short to take in more of Suz's handiwork flowing along the hallway wall: "I have loved you with an everlasting love."

The base of my throat grew thick as I traded laughter for what prickled in that place behind my eyes. I reached out my hand and touched the painted letters with my fingers. This familiar phrase I recognized, yet how long had it been since I had read those words—and believed them?

A vortex pulled me in. Did I believe those words? Or was I like my brother Jim, who seemed to think that accomplishments earned me access to streets of gold?

I leaned against the doorframe, lost in an endless wash of thought. I had done what I could, but maybe it was finally time to let go of this fight. Even June had accepted the finality of their plight and when Tim was well enough, her daughter planned to move them in with her.

Really, not such a bad idea at all.

Fatigue twined through me. Stepping into the bathroom, I flicked on the light, and allowed my eyes to adjust to the recently painted room. A soft hue of Bright Pearl shone on the walls, but I stepped back. Suz had once again used her artistic flair to free-hand a verse onto my wall, above the mirror: "He has made everything beautiful in its time."

That last piece of baggage, the one that continued to weigh me down, disappeared, and as it did, I felt myself release the project that had ruled my waking moments for the past several months. Maybe even years.

SUZ BENT OVER HIM, a fist in her side. "You didn't tell her that you quit the project?"

"The lady couldn't have cared less."

"She would have cared. You should have told her, Gage."

Gage shrugged. "I may not have to. One of Callie's friends gave me a call yesterday. Asked me to drive up to the camp for a meeting."

"What for?"

"Don't know really, but I can design bunkhouses as good as the next guy, so it's a start."

Suz's expression continued to twist. "I'm sure you can, and they'll be sustainable cabins with radiant heating and solar panels, I'm sure."

Gage clucked his tongue. "You mock me."

Suz dropped her arm at her side with drama. "Oh, Gage. What are you going to do? Start designing with the camp as if nothing's happened? Don't you think Callie's going to be suspicious when she sees you spending more time on that hill than on that bluff?"

"She doesn't want to talk to me."

"Gage Mitchell, you don't know what a good catch you are!"

Gage cracked a smile. "If I didn't know better, I'd think you were trying to get rid of me."

"I'd like to have some nieces and nephews, and you aren't a spring chicken, you know. Gah! Men!"

"Hey, why am I the bad guy here? Callie asked for some time, so I'm giving it to her. If anyone is tough to figure out, it's you women." He winked.

Suz flopped into a chair. Jer bounded over and she pulled him onto her lap, kissing his head. "Relationships are tough things. I just think Callie's a girl seeing her dream being dashed. I bet she knows the real reason those old people were having to sell their house."

Gage leaned forward onto his elbows. "I think so too."

Suz gaped at him. "Then she's upset. Tell her everything you know and what you've done and if she spurns you then, it's her loss." His sister reached out and touched his wrist. "Don't wait, big brother."

CHAPTER 38

*A*lthough it took much longer than predicted, Ruth and I met Syd Sloan from the bank to return the pledge money that had been received for the Kitteridge property. It was the right thing to do.

At one point Syd wriggled his furry brows at me while handing me a business card with his home number scrawled on the back. The aging bank officer probably figured my prospects were as few as the dollars we had collected.

After he slouched away, Ruth cranked her head back and forth, that one eye of hers narrower than I'd ever seen it. "Be like me, honey, and forget about men. They're nothing but trouble. Now, cats—I can do cats!"

I turned to her. "Would you excuse me, Ruth? I have an important phone call to make."

Ruth stood. "Suit yourself."

When she'd gone, I pulled together what courage I had left, and dialed June Kitteridge. "Hello June? It's me, Callie."

"Hello my dear, dear friend."

I winced. "June, I have something to confess to you, something I'm, well, really quite ashamed of, and I hope you will forgive me."

"Whatever it is, consider it done."

I refused to allow myself to get off so easy. "Please, June, please hear me. When I first learned about the development of your property—" I took a breath. "Well, I'd been having a bad day. That's not a good excuse. The bottom line, June, is that from almost the minute I heard about the development, I, well I . . ."

"Yes?"

"I opened my big mouth and recruited people to fight it." There. I said it. "It didn't take long for me to realize that I should not have moved so quickly, that I should have talked with you and Tim, and helped you weigh your options. I'm ashamed of myself, June. Can you forgive me?"

Silence.

More silence.

"June?"

"Of course, Callie. You are forgiven. I'm sorry that I did not answer you right away. I was overcome by your apology. The world would be a better place if we could all start there, I believe."

Relief washed through me. "Thank you, June. You know that I would do everything possible to help you and Tim . . ."

"I know, dear. I believe you would."

With that deed done, I longed to call Gage but couldn't. Natalia expected me, so I hustled up to the camp, arriving at the same time as she.

Natalia beamed. "Ready for our meeting?"

"Hi, Natalia." I forced a smile to my face. "Sure."

Sitting across from me, Natalia looked noticeably perky. Her eyes shined, her makeup smoothed away lines. After several nights of little sleep, I felt like a garish stepsister next to her Cinderella. She exhaled a brisk breath. "I've been praying all night about this."

I tilted my head to one side. "Really?"

"And I believe with all my heart in what I am about to propose."

I eyed her, intrigued. "Go on."

Natalia clasped her hands on the table and smiled. "The camp would like to purchase the Kitteridge property."

I blinked, but in no other way could I respond.

"Let me explain, Callie. As you know, we have wanted to bring more kids to camp, specifically, different age groups. But space is tight, plus there are safety issues to consider when bringing in groups of vastly different ages. Are you with me?"

I nodded.

"I met with the board yesterday to discuss some grant dollars we have, and well, we'd like to make an offer to the Kitteridges to buy their property for the camp's use. At this time we intend to use that site for our high-school-aged campers. We can offer Mr. and Mrs. Kitteridge almost what the SOS group had proposed."

"Almost?"

"That's going to be key. We can't go a dime above our offer. I'm here to ask if you will talk to the Kitteridges for us and make our plea."

My head began to swirl with all the possibilities. My heart followed, with a dance of its own. Never would I have thought of this. The Kitteridges could make enough to keep their house, the camp wouldn't overfill the space with buildings, and I would be right there in the middle of it all.

As quickly as the ideas formed, dread set in. What would the community think of me now if I helped another entity develop the property? A traitor? And what about Gage and all the work he had done?

I licked my lips, biding time. "Natalia, you know I love this camp."

She nodded. "Oh, yes. We all know that."

"But time has almost run out. The camp would have to come up with the money today. Tomorrow at the latest."

She nodded, smiling "Uh-huh."

"And I'm not sure I'm the right person to handle this."

A familiar voice cut in. "You're the perfect woman to handle this."

I saw him stride into the room, his soulful eyes questioning me. "Gage?"

He pulled out the chair next to mine and sat, then stuck out his hand to Natalia. "Gage Mitchell."

"Very nice to meet you, Gage." She flicked her glance my way. "You weren't aware your friend would be here?"

Gage tipped his hand up. "That would be my fault. I hadn't had a chance to tell her yet."

My mind buzzed. More like I didn't give him the chance to tell me. Remorse, thick and muddy, seeped through me. I owed Gage an apology and yet I remained thoroughly confused. "I'm sorry. I don't understand."

Gage looked at Natalia. "May I?" He reached for my hand and it warmed me on contact. "I'm no longer associated with the Kitteridge property, Callie. I turned in the designs to the city, then pulled out of the project."

That warmth turned to tingles. "But why?"

"Let me ask you something. Did you know that the Kitteridges were being forced to sell their property by a lender? That they were put in a no-win situation?"

I glanced away, hoping he wouldn't see the answer there. When I glanced back, Natalia's eyes had narrowed right at me. "You're kidding. I had not heard that."

I exhaled and set my shoulders. "June swore me to secrecy. She was embarrassed that they'd been duped. I took the paperwork to a lawyer, to see if there was anything they could do about it, but it was all legal. Unethical, maybe, but legal."

Natalia snared me with her eyes. "But why wasn't this made public? Maybe then—"

"I tried, Natalia. But June begged me to keep quiet. Tim's dementia was becoming a problem, and she was horrified that they'd signed away their rights like that. This is the reason she agreed to take so much less from SOS. All they needed was enough to pay off the loan on their house, then they wouldn't be forced to sell the rest of the property."

"Callie, you took the brunt of criticism for this. My word."

Gage squeezed my hand. "I figured you knew but wasn't sure why you'd sat on this. I understand now. You amaze me."

I gazed at him, shrinking from his compliment. I'd taken out my frustrations on him, unwilling to let up. Ever since last night when Suz's handiwork on my bathroom wall startled me, I'd been thinking about all the places I'd looked for significance. Finding it in God and in his plans hadn't been one of them.

Until now.

I squeezed his hand back. "No, you're the amazing one, Gage. I've been stupid. I'm so sorry."

He touched my chin. "Don't."

I shut my eyes, allowing my heart to swell at this man's touch. For the first time, the thought of it didn't scare me. *He makes everything beautiful in its time.* Instead I longed to see where this connection might lead.

I opened my eyes to find Gage's fixed on mine. He grinned, sending a blush so strong through me that it threatened to electrify my nerve endings.

Natalia fanned herself with a camp brochure and I jerked upright. "Whooey, is it ever warm in here." *Had we just gotten moony-eyed in front of the boss?*

Gage laughed easily. "What can I say? Callie has a hold on me."

Natalia laughed and nodded. "No need to apologize—you sent me back to when my husband and I first fell in love. Beautiful memories."

When they *first fell in love?* My eyes flickered away from Gage's, but he squeezed my hand again.

"Getting back to the task at hand . . ." Natalia's smile grew wide and mischievous. "If you two don't mind, I'm concerned with the Kitteridge's deadline. Now more than ever, I see we must work fast. Callie, the camp can cut a check today. Here's what we propose . . ."

EPILOGUE

"I've heard of double weddings, but never this." Greta cradled baby Callie in her arms, a soft breeze ruffling the peach fuzz we all considered hair.

I stroked the baby's cheek as Moondoggy sat by my side. "Aw, you dressed her in the outfit I gave her."

"The only organic cotton sundress she owns!" Greta grinned. "How could I not?"

I squeezed her elbow and then, shading my eyes with my hand, searched the buzzing acreage. Familiar faces milled about the great land talking and eating and laughing. Tim, in his plaid shirt and pants hiked-up-to-there, reclined on a bench with June next to him, patting his hand. The carnival-like atmosphere quickened my heart, almost as much as the person I searched for in the throng.

Greta's mouth quirked up, teasingly. "Looking for someone?"

There. I spotted him, coming up from behind Greta. "I wouldn't say that."

My sister-in-law gasped. "Why? What's wrong?"

Laughter flowed through me. "I just meant that I'm no longer looking—already found him."

He approached, smiling, stopping only to squeeze baby Callie on her drool-smeared chin. "Hey, pretty girl."

Greta glowed. "She always starts kicking her legs when she sees you, Gage."

I laughed. "Yeah, I do that too."

Gage pulled me close, his voice a growl. "Glad to hear that." He gave me a lingering kiss.

Greta cleared her throat. "Not to be the one to douse your little reunion there, but don't look now—officials at twelve o'clock."

We turned to watch the line of men and women walking in solidarity across the Kitteridge property, parting the crowd. Council member Jamison led the way.

Bobby pulled alongside us, wrapping an arm about Greta's shoulder. "Now that's a sight I'll never forget." He shoved me with his free hand. "Good job, little sister."

I swallowed a pea-sized knot in my throat, aware of the welling going on behind my eyes. Next to me, Gage beamed. Two months had passed since the meeting with Natalia. Not only had they offered the Kitteridges enough money to make the balloon payment to HMS Properties—enabling them to keep their home—but they had decided to deed a hunk of the acquired acreage back to the town, which included a binding stipulation for community usage in perpetuity. The remainder of the land would be used to build another wing of the camp specifically for high-school-aged campers. Truly a win-win-win situation.

Bobby spoke. "So how are the new plans coming along, Gage?"

Gage continued to hold me as he addressed my brother. He'd only been gone long enough to drop Suz and Jer at the airport, but it felt like days. "Great. I already knew all aspects of this land, so this project has been a pleasure to work on. Pine Ridge is probably the best client I've ever worked with."

I hugged him, gazing up at Gage's mesmerizing face. "And you were the best man for this job. I'm so proud of you."

He smiled into my eyes. "I wouldn't be here if not for you."

Greta giggled. "My, you two are kind of sickening. But I love it." She eyed Bobby. "Don't you love these two?"

Bobby snorted as two pairs of arms wrapped around my knees. I laughed and looked down at my niece and nephew. "Hey, you two, you made it!"

Brenna wagged a finger at me. "Of course we did, Aunt Callie!"

Blakey jumped up and down while holding onto my leg as if trying to uproot me from the earth.

Sheila and Vince arrived behind them, winded, followed by our parents and, surprisingly, both Jim and Nancy. My sister hugged my neck. "Exciting day," she whispered. "Very proud of you."

I allowed her praise to filter through me, knowing that although my family seemed to have gained an appreciation for me lately, a higher authority stood at the helm of this project. I could never have come up with such a sure thing on my own.

Jamison approached me, his family in tow. After the papers reported all the backroom shenanigans involving the council and the development ring, the rest of the council resigned. Jamison, however, apologized to the community pointing out that nothing illegal actually transpired, and in typical Otter Bay fashion, the residents chose to forgive. He faced me. "Ready?"

I cast a questioning glance at Natalia. She smiled and handed me a shovel while a photographer from the local paper focused a lens in my direction.

I held it there. "I don't know what you mean."

Natalia stepped forward. "For the double groundbreaking ceremony, Callie. We would like you to break ground for the community. I will do the honors on behalf of Pine Ridge Camp."

I glanced at Jamison who surprised me with an apologetic

smile and an open hand that ushered the way to a soft section of ground. "Please."

Gage released me, offering an encouraging nod, and I handed him Moondoggy's leash, my mind still trying to wrap its way around the past several months. Together, Natalia and I stuck the pointed edge of our shovels into the ground. Tears tickled my cheeks. On the count of three we pressed our blades into the soil symbolizing the start of both projects. The crowd cheered.

Ruth approached, her old floppy hat replaced by an even larger version of the last one. "Not bad, Callie. It's a compromise, but I can live with it."

Steph pulled me into her embrace, her voice laced with thickness. "Oh, Callie. What a miracle this is!"

I nodded, unable to speak without more emotion tumbling out. After she trotted away, a warm tug on my arm spun me into Gage's embrace.

My arms found their way around him as one of his hands touched my face. "You up for another celebration?"

I tipped my chin until our lips were inches apart. I breathed him in, fighting the urge to steal a kiss. "What did you have in mind?"

He paused, his eyes searching mine. The sea danced to its own serenade behind us, but a bright spark caught the corner of my vision. I turned my head slightly to investigate only to find the prettiest diamond ring in his other hand.

I whipped a look back to Gage.

He held me with his gaze. "That fiery temper of yours was the best thing to ever happen to me. Will you . . . ?"

I smiled.

". . . marry me?"

While taking in Gage's eyes, the color of sea grass in the spring, I thought back on that day we met. Who knew that a couple of snarky surveyors and their wayward tripod could lead to this?

My grip around him tightened and I threw back my head, laughing into the wind. "Yes! Of course, I will marry you." My heart fluttered and flapped around inside my body in a way I'd never known. I reveled in it, never wanting the moment to end, and yet longing for all that came along on the journey of a life well lived with the one I loved.

Moondoggy leapt to his hind legs and slapped me on the waist. I glanced down at my beloved pet and gave his silky head a swift rub.

Make that a life well lived with the *ones* I loved.

Would you like to know what happens in Suz's future? Find out in Fade to Blue, another Otter Bay romance.

<u>Cottage Grove Mysteries</u>

The Christmas Thief (book 1)

The Christmas Killer (book 2)

The Christmas Heist (book 3)

ACKNOWLEDGMENTS

Thank you, readers, for cheering me on to write seaside stories filled with faith, flip flops, and waves of grace. I have appreciated the letters, e-mails, and Facebook friendships immensely. I'd also like to give a shout out to those who willingly offered their time to help me in various ways while writing *A Shore Thing*.

Thanks to . . .

Tami Anderson, Sherrill Waters, and my husband, Dan, for reading, critiquing, and offering honest advice along the way. Appreciation also to Gary Anderson for the broken piano bench story!

My family—Dan, Matt, Angela, Emma, and Charlie the Dog, who must survive on mac 'n' cheese or something similar during writing season, along with my inattention—love you! My parents, Dan and Elaine Navarro, who deserve my forever gratitude for cheerleading me through life and storytelling.

A special, huge thank you goes to my architect brother, Daniel Navarro. You helped bring Gage to life and taught me so much about the journey of a hard-working, creative architect. Can't thank you enough, little brother!

My Lord and Savior Jesus Christ without whom I'd be living one empty life. Thank you for filling me daily.

31659550R00175